THE GOD FARM

Reality

It's not what they told you

A. B. COLLINS

ISBN (Paperback): 978-0-9997429-6-9
ISBN (eBook): 978-0-9997429-7-6

TheGodFarm.com

CHAPTER

1

"Being a god ain't no ordinary job. Yeah, there's all the perks you've heard about, but you still gotta work your farm, and god farming is a whole other thing." I paused to make sure they were getting it.

Someone yells out, "Tell us the story of how you became a god."

The crowd nods their heads as another one follows up, "Yeah! And, how long will it take for us to get there?"

They're a spirited group, but what could one expect, they'd all been a bunch of wizards, circus performers, world leaders and the like before they ended up here. "You guys. We're supposed to be going over moving back and forth through time today."

"We know, but we wanna hear the good stuff."

Knowing we'd end up here, from hearing their thoughts before class started, I pretended to be pressured into their request, "Oh... allll... right."

"Yessss!"

A fiery journal shaped like a cube pops into my hand and I hold it up, "You want me to start at the beginning?"

Different voices, "Yeah! Don't leave anything out! Smokin'!"

"OK, OK. Then let's pop over to the lake and we'll go from there."

We all disappear and reappear along the shore of my lake. They spread out all along the golden sand, some even sitting in the sparkling, blue water as it sloshes up on the beach.

"Make your stuff and we'll get started."

Snacks and drinks of various kinds form in their hands, as they settle in. They'd learned that lesson well, which quite frankly, was one of the first abilities I also mastered when I started out.

When I flip open the journal, a multi-dimensional scene pops up and expands all around us. We're now *in* the journal of my life, which holds sights, sounds, smells, thoughts and emotions that can be seen from every angle and from within numerous chosen dimensions. With directions from my thoughts, the class can experience it in total or in sections such as in fast forward, reverse, stop scenes and slow motion, and doing it all while they're sitting or we can even walk around through it. Journals from the Room of Records are the real deal; we're actually there as it happens.

It's a very cool journal.

"OK, strap in everyone, here we go." I push the start button.

I can see quite a way ahead now. Just more of the same. The road's full of sloppy mud with deep ruts as far as I can see. The fields all around me are full of scrubby weeds and more stinkin' mud. Farm country I guess they call it.

They can have it.

I've been coughing for a while, my heart's pounding in my head, I'm sweating bullets and my neck's killing me from constantly looking behind to make sure they haven't found me. I'm beat.

Pretty isolated around here so I guess I can slow down a bit now to catch my breath. I wish I'd grabbed some water when I took off. Running all night made me thirsty. Maybe there's a stream or pond or something around here in one of these dumpy fields that'll fix me up.

Stumbling along at half speed I still don't see anything except more empty fields, a few purple flowers here and there and some old-looking trees. Don't know what kind of trees these are but they're pretty cool with their leaves flapping around in the breeze. Kinda sounds like they're talking to me. Weird.

Man, this mud sucks. The laces on my trips are gone, making me drop my right shoe again and I don't know where my stupid sock went to.

Hopping over to one of the trees, I leaned against it to banged the mud off and outta the shoe, which probably won't accomplish much but it's better than going barefoot. While I was doing this, the breeze kicked up a bit blowing some dirt in my face. Turning my head away, I saw a rusty, old, pipe sticking out of the ground in the field behind me. Well, that looks promising.

I slapped my shoe back on and stared at my new find. Tilting my head at it to think better... that thing's gotta have water, right. Pipes usually do.

The explorer in me wanted me to go check it out, but my instincts told me I should move on. I stood on my toes to take a hard look back down the road. Nope, don't see anyone coming, so, heh, I smile, looks like the explorer gets to win this round.

I crept over, took another quick scan around, hopped the rickety, wooden, fence and hit the dirt. Peering over the weeds all I can see and hear are the dancing leaves in the trees and some bird singing in the distance. It's kinda calming.

Welp, the water won't come to me, so I scrambled up the hill in a crouch and dropped down with a thud under some branches of a bent-over tree just before the pipe. Rotten apples are on the ground all around me, covered in bees. My stomach growls in excitement to this awesome discovery. Food!

The awesomeness didn't last long, as everything here is all rotten, except for one dinky, yellow and brown apple still hanging on a branch. I snapped it off and bit in. I should have examined it more closely.

"Bleh, this is awful," spitting it out and throwing the apple in anger on the ground to join its rotten friends. The bees ignore my criticism and waste no time in attacking what I'd tossed. Guess they aren't so fussy.

Now I really am thirsty.

That pipe better fork over some water or someone's gonna get hurt. I stomped up and walked around examining it. How does this thing work? Can't be that hard.

I couldn't find a tap so I gave it a hard kick, "Make water, you stupid pipe."

It responded by dropping a large chunk of rust from its side.

"That's it? That's all you got," I yelled?

Angrily, I stepped up onto a broken, wooden board, grabbed a metal piece on the back and start shaking and jerking it around and up and down.

The pipe squeaked, made a goofy, sputtering sound and barfed out a big clump of mucky stuff to join the piece of rust on the ground.

"Stinkin' pipe," I shouted.

Flopping down on the ground, I laid my head on a rock and commenced to talking to myself, "Calm down. You'll be OK. You've been hungry and thirsty lotsa times before. Just need to figure stuff out. Be nice if someone came along to get me outta this mess. Yeah, if only."

The breeze kicked up again, moving the tall weeds around me in waves, while the leaves and trees were back to doing their thing again. Closing my eyes for a while took the sting away, but sleeping right now was a no go, as I had to put some more space between me and them. When I opened them back up, there's an orange and black butterfly with white dots floating over me. Don't see many of those in my neck of the woods. When I reached up with my hand towards him, he drifted down and landed on my finger.

"Whatcha doin' little dude," I asked? He flapped his wings, flicked his antennae and brushed his face with his front legs. "I don't speak butterfly. What else ya got?" After we both stared at each other for a while, I smiled and told him in a deep voice, "Take me to your leader."

He must speak 'boy', because he lifted off, fluttered down the hill and hovered over the middle of the road. I watched him as he flew back and forth towards me and then back over to the middle of the road a few times.

Is he saying, he wants me to follow him?

Well, why not, I mean, I *am* an explorer and he knows his way around this place better than I do.

I jumped up, brushed the dirt and dead weeds off, walked down the hill, hopped over the fence and stoped right in front of my new friend, "Well, Mr. Guide, now what?"

He shot away in a flash.

Keeping up to him was rough with my trips caked in mud and the right one flopping off all the time.

Up ahead, he took a sharp turn and headed off to the right. Now where's he going?

When I get up to where he turned, I twirled around and around while putting my shoe back on again, calling out, "Where'd ya go?"

I headed down the grassy laneway where he went, that looked like a tunnel, with tree branches overhead blocking out the sky. It's like being in another world in here.

Great. He's gone. Some explorer you are. Can't even track a butterfly. I gave up, grabbed a stick, walked over to a rock, sat and started flicking clumps of mud around talking to myself, "What a dork. Why did I come down here? Now I'm lost."

Some red birds were singing in the tree next to me. Don't know much about birds except for the sky-rats back in the city. The ickier stuff I came across in the dumpsters was flung over to them. Well... unless I was too hungry, then they got nada. A whole lotta squawking going on when I did that. These birds act nicer than them.

The leaves of the trees still sound like they're talking to me. "Yeah, I don't speak 'tree' either," I yelled out. My stomach gurgled. Maybe I should go back for that apple, as I glanced back down the laneway.

I flicked a big piece of mud that exploded when it bounced off one of the trees near me. Cool. I did it some more.

My mind was wandering, thinking about my escape when something interrupted my thoughts. What was that?

"Are you lost, boy?"

I snapped back to reality. Someone's here. Fear gripped me. Was I found? I jumped up and twirled around to face my attacker; pointing my stick at him, "I'm not going back. You'll have to kill me first!"

It's a geezer, leaning on a broken gate, chewing on a piece of long grass, smiling at me.

"I mean... uh. What did you say," I stammered, backing away?

"I said, are you lost?"

My experience told me not to trust anyone, especially adults, but this guy didn't look like a threat. He's got a funny hat on. Old man in a hat, I snickered to myself. My stick was still up. Trust no one.

"I'm good," I said.

"No problem. Was just headed over to the barn to get some milk and honey and saw you there. Just wondered if you were OK."

Did he say milk and honey? My stomach growled so loud he heard it.

He smiled again. Those eyes. Never saw anything like them. It feels like I know him, but I don't know why. I don't remember ever feeling this safe around anyone. Who is this guy?

He chuckled, "Sounds like your stomach's telling us you're hungry and your cracked lips are telling us you're thirsty." He opens the gate wider, "Come on in. You can have as much as you want."

My instincts aren't kicking in. They should be telling me to run away but my feet weren't moving. What should I do?

The answer came pretty fast. That missing butterfly showed up, lands on the old guy's hat and flaps its wings at me. Is this a sign? Are you waving at me to come?

Sighing to myself... ahhhh... why not? I tossed the stick into the wildflowers on the side of the road and walked towards him. Just gotta make sure I keep my guard up and if anything goes south, it should be easy enough to outrun this guy. As I enter through the gate it sounds like the leaves are clapping now.

I followed him up the path towards a barn that looks like it could barely stand, with pieces of the walls and roof missing. There's a grey, beat up house on the left with a sagging roof over the porch and windows that are either cracked or broken. This guy lives here? What a dump.

I don't care. Just get some milk and honey, grab whatever else I can get my hands on and get outta here.

When we walked into the barn, a rat ran off to the side. I'm used to those guys. The crows in the rafters are gazing down at me, dust is floating around everywhere and what's that stink? I held my nose. What am I doing here?

As we walked around and stepped over piles of junk all over the barn floor, my shoe came off again. When I knelt down to put it back on, the old man stepped out the back door and waved for me to follow him. Maybe I should just get outta here. Standing up to leave, my stomach growled again, at the same time my tongue ran itself around the inside of my parched mouth, making my feet decide to keep following this geezer. Jumping over the last pile of trash got me to the back door where I jolted to a stop. What the... I couldn't believe what I was seeing.

There's a long table set up with a white tablecloth on it. It's so bright, my eyes have to squint. What's all this? The table's full of pitchers of milk in crystal and gold jugs, along with jars of honey that glowed like fire. I carefully stepped out the door, walked over to the table and dropped my hands on it to gape at it all. Realizing my hands were dirty, I quickly pulled them away and rubbed them on my pants. I'm used to always being dirty and smelly but I suddenly noticed it here for some reason.

Good. I didn't stain the cloth.

The old man pulled a chair out for me that looked like it was made of gold with diamonds in it. As I slowly sat, I'm thinking, he must be some kind of crazy, eccentric, millionaire, keeping all this stuff out here. This stuff doesn't match up with the barn and farmhouse I just saw. My eyes squinted some more trying to understand. Maybe I should just head outta here. My stomach howled out again, overruling that thought.

He poured some milk and honey into a crystal glass and handed it to me. I gulped it down so fast it splashed all over my face and down my chest. He laughed as he poured me some more. He looked genuinely pleased that I'm so hungry, thirsty and sloppy. I don't know how many glasses I had. The pitchers never ran out though.

A burp came out of my mouth so loud I think it rattled my back-teeth. Ordinarily, I'd recognize such an accomplishment with some sorta self-applause, but here, I felt embarrassed.

His eyes twinkled as he laughed. I laugh with him. We were laughing so much my stomach hurt and my eyes were watering. I don't know if I ever laughed like this. Who is this guy? What is this place?

Finally, I said, "Who are you? Where are we?"

He says, "This is a farm. I'm the Farmer."

As I gazed around the fields full of rocks and weeds, I thought, you must be pretty lousy at it. This farm is a wreck. He smiled at me. Can he hear what I'm thinking?

"Are you retired," thinking maybe that's why this place is such a dump?

"Nope."

I guess he was just a lazy farmer then. Who cares? I'm leaving anyway. The sun was setting so I guess I'll have to sleep under some tree tonight.

"It's getting late, boy. Would you like to rest here tonight?"

Not used to being asked what I'd like. Usually I'm just told what to do and beat if I resist or don't do it fast enough. This old guy was making me think past my deep-rooted boundaries. Let's see now... they probably wouldn't find me way up in here and even if they were coming down the road, they'd probably go right past this place. Guess this would be a good hideout tonight. My spent body was telling me to say yes, too. "Can I have a spot in the barn, sir? I won't be any trouble. I'll be gone early in the morning."

He's so happy I agreed to stay, "Yes. Wonderful. Come."

I got up from the table and followed him back into the barn. My stomach was bursting. What a great feeling. When we got to the other side of a wall my eyes almost dropped out of my head. There's a bright gold bed in front of me, with a white, silk canopy, all made up, with purple sheets turned back and several, big fluffy-looking pillows. This wasn't here when we walked in. My head goes from it to him, back and forth. He's just smiling.

"This is yours," he said.

"Mine? How can it be mine? What's going on? I'm leaving in the morning," I said, thinking I should leave now.

"I know. You said that. Stay as long as you want. It's yours. Have a peaceful night," as he turned and headed out the barn door, leaving me standing there in shock.

I shouted out, "OK, thanks. And thanks for the milk and honey." He raised his hand up waving on his way to the farmhouse.

As I stared out the door getting ready to leave, my feet walked over to the bed and my hand brushed over the sheets. They flowed against my dirty hand like some kind of liquid material. The pillow melted in my hand like a warm marshmallow when I squeezed it. What is this place?

These saggy rips I'm wearing make me feel scruddy next to this bed. They're in rough shape. Yeah, but these holes and rips are legit from being beaten and whipped, not from some fancy rips deliberately made to look cool, like those little nerks I see walking down the street going to school.

Lucky slobs.

OK. I'm staying, but I'm keeping my rips on. And, I don't even care if I get these sheets dirty.

My trips are so muddy you couldn't tell that they didn't have laces anymore. I kicked them off and stretched out on the bed.

When was the last time I was this full and got to hit a bed?

The wounds on my wrists throbbed and bled as some of the scabs broke off when I rubbed them. Can't lay on my left side with that broken rib that never healed right. Nobody's doing this to me ever again.

The barn seems like it's asleep.

Must stay on guard.

I passed out in seconds.

CHAPTER 2

Ordinarily I try to sleep as long as possible as it's the only way to escape the world that I live in. As my mind slowly comes around, I realized that today is different though. Oh yeah, I'm at some dumpy farm. I escaped for real this time.

Then something else hits me, hey, I'm lying on my left side. That rib doesn't pain me anymore. I shifted around to test it really good. Yep, it's gone. Nice.

Before I ever think of getting up, habit makes me listen first to what's going on, then I crack open an eye for a quick peek because ya never know what's out there.

Wait... what was that?

I opened for a wider peek.

There's a nose about an inch from my face. It's a dog.

Where I come from, dogs are wild or mean or both.

There was no time to be startled or afraid. As soon as he sees me see him, a very large tongue shot out and slobbered all over my face. I've heard about this kind.

Giggling and pushing him away, sort of, I rubbe his sides. It's a shepherd. He has blue eyes and he's all white except his fur has a funny glow to it. Such a friendly guy. Must be the Farmer's dog.

I threw the sheets off and jumped up. What's this? My clothes are all clean. Actually, they look brand new. And, they fit.

Both of my socks are on my feet too. I stared at the socks a little stunned, fishing in my brain for a sensible explanation when my hand rested on my leg. What the? That rip isn't there anymore. My head twisted around left and right... all the holes and rips are gone. How's this possible? Maybe I got up too fast or I'm dreaming. OK... I'll just sit back on the bed, close my eyes and try again, and everything will be fine. Taking in a deep breath, open a crack... uh... nope. Wasn't dreaming. What's going on?

And I don't feel grungy all over either. It feels like I just had a shower. Even my teeth feel fresh. My head's spinning. I don't get this.

The dog barked, jumped towards me with his front paws, hit me in the chest, turned, headed to the door and looks back at me. OK. I get it. Follow you. You and the butterfly must be buds.

I'm still staring at my clothes as I reached down for my trips. Huh. They're spotless. Turning them over and over... the holes were gone and they had laces. These can't be mine. The Farmer must have thrown my old ones out and given me these. That's gotta be it. Wow, thought I was going nuts there for a second. Don't know how he did the clothes trick though. I quickly put the new rides on and ran out the door.

Where'd he go? Stopping to look down the path at the gate, my head dropped to think as I stared at my new shoes. I should leave. This is all too much for me.

A bark echoed out from behind the barn. OK, I guess I can always leave later. Running around the barn I saw him sitting by a pond that's covered in some sludgy, green gunk. I came over and petted his head, "So, big guy, what did you want to show me?" It's kind of misty further out over the water but something was there that I couldn't quite make out. Adjusting to try to get a better look, I could see a shape start to form until it became clear. It's some guy with his back to me, standing on the water in the middle of the pond. Rubbing my eyes and blinking over and over didn't fix this problem. The dog is smiling at me, like yeah, that's it.

Sitting down, my mouth wide open, straining my eyes in various ways to try and maybe blink in a different picture, didn't help at all. Yep, that dude's standing *on* the water. Must be a mirage or something. Maybe it's a ghost. This farm is making my head hurt.

The dog moved around under my arm so it goes over him as we both set about to gazing at this guy standing on the water. I've seen a lot of things, but never something like this. Then he barked. I quickly dropped back in the scruffy grass so this ghost or wizard or whatever it is didn't see me. Too late.

"Good morning, boy," he called out.

My head leaned up as I forced a weak wave. The words caught in my mouth. My head went back down. I should go.

My mind's whirling. I followed a butterfly to this wreck of a farm; got fed with never ending pitchers of milk and honey, by some old geezer in a hat; slept in a magic bed that fixed my rib and gives me new clothes and now, I follow a dog over to see some pond-surfer dude.

I look up at the dog, as he stares down at me. OK, you seem normal. I close my eyes.

"Are you alright, boy," the man asked?

I sat up, "Yep. Just trying to figure all this out." Guess I might as well go with whatever this is. Maybe I hit my head on a rock yesterday and I'm in some kind of coma. That's it. I think I heard about that somewhere.

He's younger than the Farmer. His back, chest and arms are covered in some pretty nasty scars. Brutal. Somebody must have laid into him pretty good. I've got a lotta scars too, but not like that. I'd wear a shirt if I was him.

"Whatcha doin'," I finally asked.

"Just out for a walk around the farm. Seeing what needs to be done."

I could give you a list. Everything. "How come you're standing on water?" Seemed like a good question.

He smiled and started coming over to me, firing up my survival instincts, but my feet wouldn't work. All I can seem to accomplish is sliding backwards on my bum. The dog wasn't running away so I guess maybe it isn't a bad ghost. The man or ghost or whatever he is, stepped on the ground and the dog and him began rolling around in the grass playing. OK, this is a good time to exit my way outta here. Standing up I slowly moved in the direction of the gate, hoping they wouldn't notice me leaving.

"Staying for breakfast," he asked?

My stomach liked that question. The milk and honey have had their day. "What is it", I muttered, staring at my noisy stomach?

"What would you like?"

Hey, if it's a coma, I'm gonna go with it. "Well, if I can have anything, I want pancakes, blueberry ones, with cinnamon on top and hot, maple syrup. And French toast with sliced strawberries. And sausage. The link kind and ham. No, make that bacon. And home fries, with peppers and tomatoes. And eggs. Two. Over easy. And a big glass of cold, chocolate milk and orange juice. And, and, an English muffin, with butter." I couldn't think of anything else. I snickered with a bit of a snort. Let's see this magically materialize on that fancy table, as I glanced over at the back of the barn, but the table was gone. Old Farmer must have taken it all down last night when I was asleep.

The man jumped up, put a shirt on and said, "OK, let's go," as he and the dog start went towards the front of the farmhouse. I couldn't look away from the pond. He must have been standing on a rock or some sand maybe. Ah yes, that's it. Finally, my brain figured it out, to let me feel better about following them.

The front steps were rotted and broken through, making me carefully pick my steps as I trailed them up and onto the porch, which looked just as nasty as everything else around here.

The ripped, screen door made a loud creaking noise when we got to it, which creeped me out, making want to make a break for the gate. That is, until the smell hit me. Food!

The inside of the house was in rougher shape than the outside. The walls were grey, chipped or peeling with empty picture frames hanging crooked on them above the junky furniture that's full of dust. Garbage was strewn across the floor and heaped in the corners. Needs a bulldozer in here and I'm being kind. Not my problem as I walked along and into a big kitchen. The old Farmer is here.

"Good morning, boy," he says.

"Morning, sir." I remember those eyes. It's like we see into each other. Connecting.

"Did you have a peaceful night," he asked?

"Yeah, it was great," as I looked down at my new gear, about ready to thank him for it when I saw the kitchen table covered in hot, steamy food. I drifted past them in a trance-like, mouth-watering state to do a quick check. It's all here. Everything I said I wanted outside a minute ago is right here. Nothing more. Nothing less. How is this possible and why is everyone smiling at me?

"Your food's been waiting for you."

Waiting? I shook my head. This is a great coma. I sat on the only chair here. "Aren't you eating," I asked?

"No. This is all yours." The dog rested his long nose on top of my leg and pushed up on my arm. My hand lands on the golden fork next to the crystal plate. For some reason, they spend more on their food bling than they do on anything else around here.

I couldn't shovel it all in fast enough. It went down in no particular order. Never tasted food like this. The tastes were so intense. In between were gulps of milk and juice as I looked over at them just watching me, smiling.

Maybe this is some kind of mumbo-jumbo, cult place. That's it. Some mystical cult farm and these two are its wacky leaders. Wonder where their coocoo followers are? I don't care. I'm leaving right after I shove as much of this in, as I can get in. Don't know when I'll get the chance to eat again. These kooks can find another disciple for their farm.

Taking one last bite of my English muffin and finishing off the glass of chocolate milk, I pushed away from the table and stood up. Didn't think I could do it but I do believe I shoved more in than I did yesterday.

Turning towards them, "Thanks, you guys. This was a great breakfast." When I turned back to the table, my eyes landed on the chocolate milk glass. It was full. But I just finished it. And the plates are all full of food like I hadn't touched any of it. My head snapped back to them, "Is this some kind of magic place? Are you guys like magicians or something?" That's it. They're magicians. I feel better now.

They smiled. "Would you like to find out," the old Farmer asks?

I've always loved magic and all that wizard stuff in books and movies.

"You can teach me that stuff?"

"Oh yes. And much more," they nod to each other. "Would you like to stay and learn," the old Farmer asked?

"I can stay? You'll teach me?"

"We'll hold nothing back. It's all yours. But...."

Yeah, right. Here comes the, yeah but. Must think I got money to pay into their goofy, magic cult, "Well, I can't pay you. I'm broke," turning out my pockets to show them.

"No, no, we don't want any money. Just do some work around here."

Only dynamite would fix this place. "What kind of work?"

"We'll show you as we go along."

My mind rolled around. I don't know these guys but they seem nice enough and I do want to learn magic. Then it clicked in, yeah, I can make millions doing this stuff. I could buy a mansion and when I'm old enough to drive, get a corvette. Better yet, forget the driving, cuz I'm gonna have me a chauffeur.

"OK, I'm in, where do we start?"

The dog barked and jumped on me. He must understand what I said. They both came over and hugged me. Not used to this. Must be part of some kind of initiation ritual to get their magic, juju stuff to rub off on me.

There's a weird, gooey feeling going on in my chest. What is that?

"What do I call you guys?"

"I have many names. You can call me, Farmer," the old man says.

The water-walker guy says, "You can call me, Ehyeh." Nodding with his head toward the dog, "His name is, Ruah." Ruah confirms it with a bark.

Weird names. They must be from outta town. "My name is…." They stop me before I can say it. "We'll call you, 'boy', for now."

"Hey, if you guys keep feeding me like that and teach me your magic stuff, you can call me anything you like."

I didn't like it.

CHAPTER 3

reakfast was done and I was busting.

"Can I hit your bathroom?"

"Sure," Farmer says, leading me to the broken kitchen window to point at a rundown shed with a hole in the roof standing by itself to the side of the farmhouse. "That's it over there."

"You're kidding? There isn't a bathroom in the house?"

"No, there isn't."

Gimmie a break. These guys are like some kind of cave-dudes living like this.

Crouching over and holding myself with my hand, I was in no position to argue. Out the squeaky front door, I hopped down the steps and did the penguin waddle over to the shed.

When I got there, the door was hanging by a leather strap on one side that barely hung on when I opened it. Peering inside I saw a little wooden bench with a hole on top of it. My eyes darted back to the kitchen window for a sign, like, come on back... we were just kidding.

"That's it," Farmer said. "Go on in and sit."

The gurgling in my guts was telling me to get at it, so I stepped in, got the door kinda closed and made it just in time.

Kinda nasty in here, but looking around I thought, well, all in all, I've had worse.

Didn't take me long to notice though, oh, come on, no toilet paper.

Why not. Fits with everything else around here.

All that's in here are some cruddy, paperback books covered in flies sitting on a shelf. Waving the flies away, I grabbed one of the books and flipped through it. It had a picture on the cover of some dorky-looking kid flying around on a broom.

These guys better teach me that one.

Welp, this'll have to do. I ripped out some sheets, finished taking care of business, got that funky, shed door closed up behind me, went over to the pond, washed up and headed back to the farmhouse. As I got to the door, Ruah burst through to meet me. The squeak was definitely getting worse. I thought, someone should fix that thing. Just as I said that, a weird-looking, little can, appeared on the porch next to me. I'm really likin' this magic farm.

Never saw one of these things before. While I was checking it out, I pushed a little lever on it with my thumb and some oil shot out onto my hand. Oh.

Must be for the door. I squirted some on the three hinges, and moved the door back and forth a few times. Nice, no more squeak. When I put the can down, Ruah grabbed my hand with his teeth and guided me off the porch.

Stopping part way down the stairs I wondered. Is it? Peeking back under my armpit. Yep. Oil can's gone. Cool. I'm gonna like learning this magic stuff. I hope it works outside this farm.

Ruah and I headed over to the barn and walked in. Farmer and Ehyeh were already here. Jerking to a stop, "How did you guys get here so fast?" Again, with the smiling. "OK, are you guys magicians or wizards?" Now they laugh hysterically out loud.

"Neither one. Those have weak, foolish powers," as they kept laughing at my expense.

Frowning now, "Hey, I was told those wizards and magicians were the best it gets." Now Ruah burps, as he looks up at me and sighs. Great. Even the dog's smarter than me.

"OK, so what are you guys then?"

"Patience, boy, we'll offer it all to you," as they hand me a broom.

Alright. They're going to teach me how to fly with this, like that kid from that book. Now we're talking.

Ehyeh says, "Sweep. Make sure you hit each level in the barn and get all the cobwebs and trash out too. Put it all in the dirt pile at the back of the barn."

Both of them stepped out the back, leaving me there with the broom in hand. Staring down at

Ruah kinda at a loss for words, "Guess I'm not flying anywhere today, Ruah." He sneezed in agreement.

Climbing up a wobbly ladder to get to the top level of the barn, I commenced at sweeping layers of dust and junk off the edge, down to the ground floor below. Got three levels to do. The dust is everywhere. Must have been here for years. Cleaned out old bird and rat nests too.

The crows made a lot of noise as they flew out of the barn and the rats scurried away as I swept. They better teach me a lotta magic stuff for all this work I'm doing, as the sweat started rolling down my face and the dust burned into my eyes.

Ruah was good company all day. Never saw the guys again. Wonder what hocus pocus they were up to?

It felt great when I finally shoveled up the last of it and dumped it outside on the pile. "Ruah, I'm hungry, how about you?" Definitely a "yes" bark. I put the broom and shovel in the corner of the barn, turned around and Ehyeh was there. He startled me.

"You shift around like a ninja. Are you guys some kinda ancient, mystical, martial artists? That's it. I'm right, *right*?"

He laughed again, "No, that's not it either. I came to see what you wanted for dinner, boy."

Still not liking that title.

Let's get severely intense this time, "Alrighty then. I want lobster and bar-b-que steak." Never had either one. "With a Hollandaisy sauce." Didn't know what that was. Heard it in a movie once. Must be from Holland. "And mashed, garlic potatoes, green beans and fresh baked rolls with butter. For dessert, apple and pecan pies with butterscotch ice cream on top." I snickered as I looked back and forth at Ehyeh and Ruah. Let's see you guys pull that off.

"Let's go," Ehyeh says, as he turns, headed for the farmhouse.

I don't know if I'm more excited to see them pull this off or about getting to eat all that I just said. I ran up beside them, up the stairs and through the now quiet screen door and into the kitchen. There was Farmer standing next to the table. It was all there. The ice cream still frozen on top of the pies. I really am looking forward to getting this power. An armored car full of money pulling up to my mansion flashed into my mind, as I sat down and started in on it.

Gorging my way through it all would be the correct way of putting it. This Hollandaisy sauce is awesome. Guessing these guys eat when I'm not around.

I finished up on a piece of pie, got up and quickly spun around trying to catch it all changing. Not fast enough. The table was full again. Like I hadn't eaten a thing.

Following them to the front door and out onto the porch. "So, what's the deal with you guys? I've cleaned out the barn and you didn't teach me anything yet." I'm thinking they're just using me to do their chores and plan on keeping their secrets. I do like the food though.

They kept going over to and into the barn which was a good thing because I wanted to show them that I earned that deal we made for training.

"You've cleaned the dirt, dust and trash out of the barn. Now you can see better, yes?" Farmer says.

"See better?"

"Yes, the barn is like your head. Too much trash, dirt, dust, nests, crows and rats in it. Can't see straight, yes?"

"OK," I say slowly, not really getting it. This has to be one of those mind twisters like from a fortune-cookie.

Farmer shakes his head. He definitely hears what I'm thinking? Gotta watch that.

"Open your eyes," he says.

I blink a few times. "They are open."

"No. Open them. Concentrate. Look."

Opening my eyes wider I still see nothing. Wait. There's something outside the big doors out back. What is that? Walking past the guys and out the door I see a massive foot. Then I see two of them. Scanning up to take it all in, I fall back to the ground. Standing straight up over me he must be over a hundred feet tall, all decked out in gold and leather clothes, his thick, blond hair and beard reach all the way down to his waist. A shield inlaid with large rubies in a circle covers his left arm and his right hand grips a sword, engulfed in white flames, that's as long as the entire barn. Steely, gray eyes bore down on me, adding to this queasy feeling that a field mouse must surely get right before it's squished.

My throat makes a low, gurgling sound as I clawed my way backwards into the barn until I bumped into Farmer, twirled around behind his legs and peaked through. I blinked a few times. Yep. He's still there. This is having my eyes open?

"You see now a bit," Farmer grins.

Funny guy. "A bit? That's a bit more than a bit." They laughed. Ruah rolls onto his side and licked my face. Nice. Ruah sees him too.

"What is that," I say with my hand shaking and pointing at it, like they don't know what I'm referring to?

"That's your angel. Well, one of them."

"*My* angel? Since when? Angel? Angels are real? One of them?" I was stammering. Couldn't get the questions out of my mouth fast enough.

"You said you wanted to learn, didn't you," Ehyeh says?

The angel is still standing there. He doesn't readily disappear like cans of oil apparently. "Uh, what does he want?"

"Want? He's waiting for you to learn faster."

Me? Faster? I just got here. "So, this is the secret. The angel does the magic." More money flashes in front of my mind now, as I finally stand up.

"No. No. Magic is nonsense. Thought you swept all the junk out of your barn", Farmer says with his forehead in a frown.

"You mean my head, right?"

So, what these guys do isn't magic. This strange talk and their abilities can only mean one thing.

They're aliens.

CHAPTER 4

 kept peeking out from under the covers. Nope. That angel's still out there. Too big to get in here, as I punched the wood wall with my fist to try to assure myself it's strong enough to keep him out. As if.

My mind races at all that's going on around here. Monster angel. Magical food. Appearing and disappearing oil can. Don't know what to think about Farmer and Ehyeh. Wonder where Ruah is. He seems OK. Why am I still here? Oh yeah. Get power. Make a fortune with it. And food. I look again out the door. Yep, that angel's still out there.

Not much happened after we talked about the angel. Farmer and Ehyeh told me to clear my head out like I did with the barn and they left. What does that even mean? How do I clear my head out? I do think of lots of bad stuff but that's not my fault. People did bad things to me. People are after me. Why should I forget about it? My eyes close to look at all the junk stored up in my mind, as I drift off to sleep.

After my standard wake-up morning ritual, there was no tongue here to slobber all over me this morning. Staring out one of the many holes in the side of the barn, my eyes glazed over thinking about that weird dream I had last night. So real. I was sweeping stuff out of my head. I swept it out my ears and mouth and nose. Farmer and Ehyeh were there pointing at different crows and rats that had to go. I chased them all out and put them in cages. I feel so refreshed. Nice dream. Must be the farm air. Wonder what Farmer and Ehyeh want me to do today?

I whipped the covers off and jump up. Clothes are clean and still fit perfectly. I'm liking this bed. Tip-toeing over to the door I cautiously stepped outside. I don't see that angel anywhere. Maybe he's on a break. I hope so; that dude freaks me out. Smoke is drifting out of the chimney over at the farmhouse. Smells nice, like spices. Never been anywhere before that had a real fireplace. Wonder what's for breakfast?

Hmmm... maybe it's time to take it up a notch with these aliens. Concentrating with my eyes closed, I could see the table with everything on it that I wanted... scrambled eggs, hash browns, toast with strawberry jam on it, warm blueberry muffins with butter and freshly squeezed apple juice. Let's see them pull that one off as I bounced up the stairs, onto the porch and up to the door. I knock, Ruah shoves his nose through, grabs my shirt sleeve and pulls me in.

Farmer and Ehyeh are in the kitchen.

"Morning" we all say at once. I quickly glanced over at the table. It's all there, just as I saw it or thought it or however these aliens work it. Now I'm impressed. Gotta have this power. I sit, Ruah rests his head on my lap as usual, and I eat.

Farmer says, "Pleasant dreams last night?" He knows about my dream?

"Unusual dream," I say. "Must be because of cleaning the barn out yesterday."

"Really," Ehyeh says? Ruah's snort startles me. Can he read my mind too?

When I finished, I stood and thanked them for breakfast. "How did you know what to make," I ask?

"How did you know what to want," Farmer says.

It was so fast I didn't see it, even with my eyes never leaving the table. They refilled all the plates again right under my nose. These aliens are good. Wonder what they do with the leftovers?

We all went outside with them behind me to the barn. Farmer says, "We have something for you." I turned to see Farmer holding a rat and Ehyeh holding a crow. The rat is baring its nasty yellow teeth at me, while the crow is wildly pecking towards my face.

I leaned back, "Wh..wh..wh..why would I want those things?"

"This barn was their home for a long time and you chased them out. They want to come back. Would you like them to come back?"

"No, what good are they. They just destroy stuff." These aliens should know that.

"What should we do with them," Ehyeh asks me?

"Let them go." Like come on. What else.

"We can do that, but they'll just come back or they'll go over to another barn to live in there. And they do have friends that'll join them. Would you want that to happen?"

"No." What they said made sense. "I don't know what to do with them then." Give em to that angel for target practice came to mind.

"How about, we just make them disappear," Farmer says?

Sounded like a good alien plan. "How do you do that?"

"You can do it," Ehyeh says.

"Me? How do I make them disappear? You guys are the aliens." I didn't mean to say aliens. It just blurted out. Didn't seem to startle them though.

"Do you agree they should be gone, perhaps, into a prison somewhere," Ehyeh says?

Funny, I just remembered that I put them in cages in my dream. "Sure, that sounds good," I said. They instantly disappeared out of their hands in front of my eyes.

"Woah... How did you guys do that?"

"You did it," Ehyeh says.

"How did I do it?"

"You cleaned out the barn and got them to disappear out of here didn't you," Farmer says, as he points to the barn?

"Yeah, but that's different."

"How so?"

"I physically swept them out. They just left. They didn't just disappear."

"You think one is harder to do than the other," Farmer says?

"Harder? Well, I don't know, you guys are the gurus in this appearing and disappearing ability. How does it work?" Now we're getting somewhere.

Farmer says, "How did you get rid of the junk in your head last night?" I knew that he knew what I was dreaming.

"That was just a dream."

"Really," Ehyeh says. "You had junk in your head. You got rid of it didn't you? Isn't it gone?"

Standing there trying to think about all those bad thoughts that angered and haunted me was hard to remember now. It's like those memories faded away. How'd that happen?

I answered Ehyeh, "Yeah. I don't know how that happened. But that's just head stuff, not physical things."

Farmer says, "So, you've determined that all there is to reality is physical. The rest, you say, doesn't exist?"

I stared at them and blinked. These guys must be joking. "What else is there?" Ruah groaned and laid down with his head between his paws looking up at me.

Ehyeh puts his hand on my shoulder and looks into my eyes. Never noticed before. His eyes are deep, dark blue. "Boy, how do you think everything exists. How do you think you exist?"

"That's easy. Evolution," I confidently proclaim.

Ehyeh drops his head. Farmer rubs his bearded chin as he squints at me. Ruah groans again and puts his paw over his eyes. "What? Everybody knows that," I say. "That's what people say."

"Boy," Ehyeh says, "We don't care what people have told you. What answer makes sense to you?"

"Well, I'm just a kid but everything had to be made didn't it? Everything didn't just make itself. But I don't know how or who did it. Some say God. But what does that mean?"

Ruah jumps up and down barking.

"What? What did I say?"

Farmer says, "Today boy, take that wheelbarrow behind you and go out into the fields and gather rocks and stones."

Wheelbarrow? What's a wheelbarrow? I turn around and there's this big bucket thing with a wheel leaning up against the wall.

"Take the rocks and stones and pile them along the fence by the laneway."

While I was examining the wheelbarrow thing, I turned around to ask how it worked. Everyone was gone except Ruah.

Ninja-aliens, for sure.

"Why don't they just abra kadabra the rocks over to the fence, Ruah?" Ruah's head turns sideways to look at me. "Or make them disappear? Wouldn't that be easier?" Make this whole dumpy farm disappear, putting my hands out and spinning around. Maybe it's time for me to go, as I look out the barn door at the gate by the laneway.

Ruah came over, gripped my hand with his teeth and pulled me over to the wheelbarrow. OK, I smiled, guess you're making me stay a little longer. I kicked the wheelbarrow over, grabbed the two handles and pushed it. It scraped across the floor. Doesn't seem right. I lifted it up on my end and pushed it with the wheel rolling. Ah, that's how it goes. I pushed it around and around. "Hey Ruah, hop in and go for a ride." He jumped in and barked as I went faster and faster until it flipped over on its side. Ruah jumped out and I dropped on top of it, smacking my head. After the stars cleared, I struggled to get up, "Guess I need some more practice with this thing, Ruah."

We made our way out to the closest field that was covered in rocks and stones. I shrugged my shoulders at Ruah, "Guess we can start anywhere, eh big guy?" I tossed in a bunch of rocks and headed to the fence, which lasted about four steps before the wheelbarrow tipped to the side and dumped everything out. Standing the wheelbarrow back up, I sat in the dirt and sighed, "Ruah, maybe you can do a better job?" He barked, licked my face and began picking the rocks up with his teeth and dropping them back in, which broke my sadness and made me laugh. Rolling myself back up, I joined him and we finally made it to the fence and dumped them out. Back and forth we went for hours. I don't know how many trips we made. We had so much fun working together. We spread the rocks and stones all along the fence like Farmer said.

"You're doing a fine job there, son."

A tall, sharp-looking guy is standing in the middle of the laneway. Seemed out of place in farm country with his shiny black suit and skinny tie. He isn't one of those chasing me. I know what they all look like. Ruah growls. That's the first time I've seen him do that. Must be protective of me.

"Morning, mister."

"Morning, child. You have a fine-looking dog there", as he glared at Ruah. Ruah growled again.

"Oh, he's not mine."

"You don't say. In that case, perhaps you can help me. I'm rather lost. I'm looking for someone that I'm supposed to meet around here for an apprentice position."

"Apprentice? Apprentice at what?"

"I shouldn't really say, as it's a secret only for certain people to know. I've really said too much already."

"Well, how can I help you then?"

"I'm looking for a lad, much like yourself, that I was supposed to meet on this road today, but I guess he didn't show. Now I have to look for an apprentice all over again."

Weird place to be meeting someone for a job interview I thought. Ruah's pulling at my sleeve to go with him back towards the barn. "Stop that, Ruah. How much does this position pay?" I sneered over at all the rocks I've been transporting all morning. Don't really see any future in that.

"A fortune. And fame too. But it's not for everyone."

"If you tell me what it is, I might be interested." Fame and fortune. Now we're talking.

"Well, I don't know. You seem a bit young for what I'm looking for."

"Please, mister, I'm very smart and a hard worker." Ruah barked at me. "Ruah, be quiet." He groaned and sat.

"I need someone who will be very loyal and do what I say."

"I can do that, mister."

"OK, I need an apprentice to teach them how to be a wizard."

"*A wizard!*"

Finally... power, fame and fortune. But. I don't want to leave the alien farm if this guy's a fake. I've already seen what the Farmer and Ehyeh can do. Better test him. "What will I learn," I questioned him, with my one eyebrow up?

"Things like this," as he levitated off the ground and moved sideways to my right, stopped and then to my left and back down. "And this," as money fell from the sky, landed on the laneway and disappeared.

My mouth was hanging wide open. I've never seen anything like this, although, Farmer and Ehyeh do some pretty fantastic things too. And there is that angel dude. Wonder where *he* went off to?

"That's it," I said looking unimpressed, as I crossed my arms, hoping he's got more to show?

He held up his hands, fire and smoke flashed from them, turning himself into a wolf before my eyes. When Ruah barked at him, the wolf yelped and its tail shot down between its legs. The man reappeared quickly, "You should control your dog," he shouts at me.

"Like I said, he's not my dog. He has a mind of his own. You don't seem like much of a wizard, if you're afraid of a dog."

"I didn't say, *I* was a wizard. I *teach* people to be wizards," obviously angry at me now, snarling through his teeth.

"If you're not a wizard, who are you then," I asked?

In a raised, defiant voice, "I am god of this planet. I control legions of armies. Billions of people do my bidding, you puny child. People worship me. I've trained countless wizards and magicians over thousands of years. I can give you fame and fortune. Just step outside that gate and come with me and you'll see." His face is all red. His black eyes bulging at me like one of those frogs I've seen around here.

There was a brief silence. I guess he was waiting for me to bow or curtsey in his presence or something.

I couldn't hold it in any longer. I finally spit out my laughter, "What a loon." I looked at Ruah and back at this guy. "Can I bring the dog," I snickered? That should rile him up.

Never heard a scream quite like that. He disappeared in a puff of smoke.

Smiling at Ruah, "Was it something I said?"

Ruah jumped on me, knocking me over and was licking my face so hard I could barely talk, "What a loser that guy was, eh, Ruah. Who'd wanna follow that goofball," as I rubbed Ruah's face?

Man, this place is infested with aliens.

CHAPTER 5

uah and I laughed all day together as we worked moving rocks. It seemed like he was laughing anyway. Certainly, was a noticeable smile on his face and a snappier bounce to his step.

I saw a bunch of sticks along the way and was thinking to get rid of them too, but Farmer only said, rocks and stones.

We had just finished doing another load when I saw Farmer at the top of the path waving.

"Come," he yells.

"That's us, boy," as I rubbed Ruah's head and he licked my face. We raced up with the wheelbarrow and put it back in the barn. I turned and ran toward the house where Farmer was already at the door.

Wait just a second as I turned and peeked back in the barn. Is it?

Yep, wheelbarrow disappeared. I should've left it at the fence. Have to remember that next time.

We ran up to the house and through the door. Ah, dinner time. Farmer and Ehyeh are in the kitchen but the table's empty. I looked at them, the table, at Ruah, who tilts his head at me, back at the table, I sit. "What's for dinner," I asked?

"What would you want," says Ehyeh?

A picture of my absolute favorite food popped into my head. Hotdogs. Just then, before my eyes, hotdogs materialized. Dozens of them. I slid the chair back. This is spooky. Then I thought, bare hotdogs, what about buns, mustard, relish and French fries? Pop, pop, pop, pop. Each appears as the thought came into my head. I slid my chair further back. I reached out and touched one, then another. Yep, not a mirage. And warm too. I'll ask them later how they do that as I scooched the chair back up and dug in.

Don't know how many I ate before I thought of root beer and it was there too. I tried to keep up to the pile but finally had to give in. No matter how many I ate there were still dozens left. The pile never got smaller. Actually, it looked like it got bigger.

"Uh, I'm so full," I barely got out of my mouth.

"Wonderful," Farmer smiles. "Let's go for a walk."

"A walk? I can barely move," I moaned and settled down into the chair.

Ruah pushed my arm up with his nose, grabbed my shirt and pulled me off the chair. "OK, boy," I laughed, "I'm comin'."

We got outside and that angel was there by the barn. He's a big one alright. I was thinking, where were you when that whacko showed up on the road today?

Farmer asked, "How was your day?" I walked a little quicker when we got next to the angel.

I'm thinking this is a trick question because these aliens already know what I'm thinking even before I'm thinking it. How else do they have hotdogs ready to go so fast? "A strange ali.. uh, guy was on the road today."

"We know. You handled him very well," Ehyeh said. "You resisted him and he fled. Not only that and more important, you were very obedient today with the task we had for you, doing it joyfully. We're very pleased with you, boy."

"Well, Ruah was a big help. He assisted me with that strange guy and with all the rocks. He's a great companion." I looked down at Ruah and he smiles. Definitely a smile.

My mind ponders as we walked further along, "Farmer, who was that guy down at the road today? He said he was a god."

"He is one of many gods. Many follow that one, believing he'll help them," Farmer explained.

"Really? A god? He had a lot of tricks. Said he wanted me as his apprentice to be a wizard."

"Yes, he's always looking for more people to steal from."

"Steal? He said he was going to give me power, fame and fortune."

"All that is an illusion. False gods that entrap the foolish. You were wise to reject him. Be cautious, because he'll come back. He's very crafty. He'll appeal to your weaknesses to capture you," Ehyeh says.

Illusion? Capture me? I don't understand their words. What's wrong with power, fame and especially fortune? How do these guys know so much about gods? "Is it wrong to want what he offers?"

"No. It's wrong to worship such things. These are just things. They are just tools to an end," Farmer said.

"Would you worship a wheelbarrow," Ehyeh asked?

"A wheelbarrow? That's just something to help move stuff."

"Exactly. So is power, fame and fortune," says Farmer.

OK. I know there's some alien, philosophical thing going on here, but I'm not getting it. "But you guys said you'd teach me how you do your stuff, right?"

Ehyeh smiled, "Of course we'll offer it to you. It's our greatest desire to show you the way. We would hold nothing back."

"Awesome. When do we start?"

Farmer laughed, "Start? You've already started. You've learned what doesn't belong in the barn and not only got rid of it, you don't want it back. You learned obedience to follow exactly what we've said, without deviating on to your own path. Doing so, joyfully. You've learned to recognize a very crafty, false god and came against him. These are all no small victories. Most, never learn these things, young man."

Young man? I like that better than, 'boy'. "Yeah, but that's not power."

"They're conductors of power," he says.

"Conductors?"

"Yes, like moving a handle to force water to come out a spout," as we ended up in front of that stupid pipe that spit at me before I arrived at the farm. Farmer pushed the handle up and down, the thing spits and spurts and then water came flying out in a powerful flow. My eyes widened. So that's how it works.

Ehyeh says, "Weren't you thirsty while you were moving rocks today?"

"Yes, but I didn't know there was water right there next to me all day," I said surprised. Could have used that information.

"Life giving water stands next to people all over the Earth every day. They don't know how to access it. No one shows them how," Farmer explained as Ruah jumped around splashing in the water.

Farmer stopped pumping and the water stopped. "Do you understand what we're saying to you, young man," Ehyeh asked?

"Yeah, I think so. Water is around, if you know where and how to get it. The handle is just a tool that can produce power to get water to come to me. Same as the wheelbarrow to move rocks. We don't worship metal thingys or wheelbarrows because they can do that," I say quite proud of myself.

"Nor do we worship people for the same reasons," Farmer adds.

"So, people are just tools?"

"People are different, as they're like a power source themselves. They can generate power on their own and access other power as well. You can decide to move the wheelbarrow on your own or you can access another power to move it in an instant to the other side of the farm and beyond," Ehyeh said.

Now we're getting somewhere. "So, how do I get this power to move stuff and make stuff, like hotdogs and root beer?" If I could do that, at least I'd never go hungry or thirsty again.

Farmer grins, "That's for another lesson. It's getting late and time for you to rest, young man."

"OK. I am tired. Ruah too, right boy?" He barked and started back toward the barn ahead of us.

Sleep will be easy tonight.

Worked all day and not a smudge of dirt on me. Ruah is laying down on the bed next to me licking my hand as I rub his head. I like this place.

"Good night, Ruah. Good night, mister angel." Quiet. Guess he doesn't talk. I'm feeling comfortable with him around. Those people chasing me wouldn't wanna mess with my angel or Ruah.

The fiery sword flashed through the cracks of the walls as he made his way around the barn.

My mind is calm and clear.

Maybe I won't wake up screaming in my sleep tonight.

CHAPTER 6

Someone's poking my forehead.

"Hey, wake up!"

I tiredly open one eye to see a girl standing there.

I'm instantly awake. Now what? "Who are you?"

"I'm Briella," she says smiling. "Have they given you a name yet?"

"Given me a name? Who? Farmer? Ehyeh?"

"Yes, silly. They gave me my name. They said it's mine." She pats Ruah as she's talking to me. I'm sitting up now.

"Well, they did call me, 'boy'. Now they call me, 'young man'."

"Oh, then soon they'll give you a name. If you want one."

"Want one? Who are you again?"

"I told you. I'm Briella. Farmer and Ehyeh live with me on the farm."

"You live here? Where've you been? Haven't seen you before?"

"No, not on this farm. I live on a different farm."

"A farm next door?" Farmer and Ehyeh have another farm?

"I just came over to see you and to introduce myself. See ya later, it's time for breakfast." She turned around and skipped off toward the door.

"Hey, where....," but she just disappeared. Shaking my head, I'm either hallucinating or it's another one of those aliens. Might still be that coma thing.

I hear Farmer call out, "Breakfast."

We ran to the house. I've got questions. As we enter the kitchen, Farmer says, "Morning. What would you like this morning, young man?"

Food? Not right now. "Morning," I say to them as I sit. "There was just a girl in the barn. Said she was from another farm. Is she from next door?"

"What was her name," Ehyeh asks smiling?

I'm sensing he already knows. "Briella, she said."

"Lovely, sweet daughter, isn't she," Farmer says?

Daughter? Looking down at the table my eyes dart back and forth; what's going on around here? I'm mumbling a bit as Ehyeh says, "Are you OK, young man?"

"And that's another thing. She said you named her and that you'll give me a name if I want one. What's that all about?"

Farmer explains, "Those who decide they want to join our family, accept a family name that we offer to them."

"Family?" Now I'm really confused. "Briella's part of your family, but she lives on another farm?"

"Oh, there are many farms," Ehyeh says. "We told Briella about you, so, she wanted to pop over to meet you and introduce herself."

"And then she disappeared," I said in a panicked voice.

"Was that one of the things you were interested in learning how to do," Farmer asks?

I'm sputtering now, "I want to learn all this stuff."

Ehyeh says, "We can do that when you decide you want us as your family."

"I don't know what that means. How do I do that?" I really have to know how to do all of this alien stuff. How can I go back to such a dull life without it?

"It's easy," Farmer starts. "You have to put away your way of doing things in life and accept our family's ways. You have to put total trust in us that we know what's best for your farm."

I rubbed my forehead hard back and forth trying to understand, "My farm? You mean, like this farm would be mine?"

"It's already your farm," Ehyeh clarified, "But we offer much, much more. As family, you get everything we have."

"Everything?" My head is twirling. They had me hooked on learning their stuff. "So, ya mean I just say, I want to be part of your family? That's it? Then you'll teach me and give me your stuff?"

Farmer continues, "Young man, you don't belong to a family to get stuff, as you call it. That's shallow, selfish thinking. A family is relationship, and our family lasts forever."

They must mean forever like a long time. "So, all I have to do is follow your rules and I'm in?"

Ehyeh slapped his hand on my chest, "It's not about rules. It's about taking us in here, in your heart. It's about wanting to have a relationship with us, trusting us, communing with us, knowing we'll never abandon you like your parents did. Would you like that?"

That would be a different life for sure. Ehyeh's hand on my chest was giving me a weird feeling of something in there I'd never felt before. Kinda like when they hugged me before. What is that?

"I ain't never had a family. I'm not sure what to do."

Ehyeh answered me. "A long time ago I died and came back so you could live with me and our family. Just trust us and believe that I am the only way you can get all that we said. Give your old life to me and pick up a new one with us. When you do that, you'll be a different creature."

Died? Different creature? "Um... say huh?"

Farmer adds, "Think of it like this. When a caterpillar decides it wants a new life, it puts itself through a metamorphosis. It has to leave its old life behind if it wants to become a butterfly. There's only one way it can do that. You must decide if you want a new life."

"It's all kinda strange talk for me. Will you guys help me with this meta.. way thing?"

"Of course, we'll show you the way."

No major newsflash to me that my current life sucks bigtime. I don't understand this stuff they're saying but they're the only guys who've ever been good to me. "OK, I'm all in. I want you as my family." I closed my eyes expecting to get smacked by lightning or something. I got Ruah knocking me off my chair and licking my face.

When Ruah and I stopped rolling around playing together on the floor I stood up, "That's it? That was easy. So, now what?"

"Now we give you a name that we've always had waiting for you."

"Waiting for me?" I guess I'll understand what these guys are talkin' about some day.

"Your name is, Ryder."

"Ryder?" Cool name. I love it. "What's next?"

"Let's go down to the pond and do some more."

"The pond?"

We headed out the door and made our way over to the pond. When we got there, they all walked out on top of the water, turned and waved for me to follow.

"I can't walk on water," I yelled out.

Ehyeh yells back, "Who says?"

"Well, nobody can do that." Except you guys apparently.

"Everyone in our family can do it. And you're in our family now, so, step out," Farmer says as he's waving for me to come. I stared at them like they're nuts. Farmer questioned my hesitation, "Can't you walk on ice?"

"Sure, but tha…"

"That's water," Ehyeh stated, "So, come on."

Ruah ran towards me, grabbed my shirt and pulled. I slid down from the grass onto the water and stood there in shock. I walked around a bit, slowly inching toward them, looking down and around. I'm doing it. I get to them laughing in amazement, "I did it!"

Ehyeh put his hands on my shoulders, looked me straight in the eyes smiling and shoved me down into the water, "Welcome to the family."

I thrashed around and around as they watched with their hands at their sides. "I don't know how to swim," I sputtered.

Ehyeh asks, "Why don't you stand up then?"

"How," as water gurgled out of my mouth when I spoke?

"How would you do it if it were ice," Ehyeh calmly asked?

Don't they care that I'm drowning here? I barely get out, "Well, I'd just stand up."

"Do that."

Do that. Yeah, right. I stopped flopping around, put my hands, on top of the water and pushed, to show them it doesn't work.

It worked.

The water held up my hands. I pushed up and my feet stood again on top of the water. They hugged me laughing, "Well done, Ryder."

I ran around spinning on top of the water. This is way cool. I'm a pond-surfer-dude now.

"What was all this about with the water," I asked, as I'm skidding around?

"Look at this as being born into a new life. You're like the butterfly now."

"Cool. Now what," as water dripped from my nose?

"Now," Farmer says, "Would you like Ruah to stay with you from now on?"

"What? Keep Ruah? But, isn't he your dog?"

"He'll stay with you as long as you want him. He's very loyal. He'll never leave you nor let you down," Ehyeh said with his dark, brown eyes looking into mine. Hey, I thought his eyes were blue.

I knelt down and put my arms around Ruah. "Really? Yes, yes, oh thank you, thank you." Ruah rolled around with me and licked my face. "Friends forever, Ruah."

Ehyeh reached down, grabbed a handful of water and splashed me. I ran a few steps, turned, reached down and returned the splash on all of them. We were running around all over the pond doing this to each other. I was laughing so hard I slipped and fell. I was lying on top of the water laughing my head off watching fish looking up at me while Ruah's licking my face.

So, this is what family is like. But what kind of family are we?

Am I an alien now?

CHAPTER 7

We walked back to shore and onto the grass. I'm pumped. Let me see some magician do that. I think not. I spun around shooting with my fingers in the air, quite proud of myself, "Look out wizards, Ryder's in town and he be dan-ger-ous!"

Farmer asks, "Hungry?"

"I'm starving." Never really need to ask a kid if they're hungry. It's a given.

"Let's eat. My choice this time," Farmer said as we made our way laughing with each other back to the farmhouse.

The kitchen table was full of grapes the size of basketballs, cool looking flat bread, huge slabs of what smelled like fried fish, stuff I never saw before and a pitcher full of some kinda red liquid. This is the first time that they've ever sat down with me as I watched Ehyeh make up some plates, and place them before us. We shared a cup from the pitcher which Ehyeh said was wine. Never had that before. He said this was a celebration of my taking on my new life. These aliens sure know how to cook. This food is outta this world. Hard to beat these flavors. Well, all except hotdogs. Nothing beats hotdogs.

Feeling like a stuffed whale again, I pushed myself away from the table, got up, went straight for the door and out to the porch. I don't even look back at the table. I know what I'll see.

Sucking in a deep breath of fresh, farm air, "Thank you both for all of this and for taking me in as your family. Nobody's ever cared about me before. I don't know what to say. I never owned anything before except the clothes on my back."

Ehyeh pats my shoulder, "You've had a life full of pain and torment from many terrible people who didn't love you. You're always welcome in our family."

How did they know what I've been through? Oh yeah. Must be that alien, mind-reading trick. I have to learn that one. Wonder if they know who I'm hiding from? They smile. OK, so they know that too. "So, now what," I asked?

"Now, we do some more work on the farm," Farmer says with excitement. "Let's work on the garden next."

"The garden?" We go around to the back of the house to see a huge piece of land strewn with rocks, dead trees, weeds and dried out soil. This is the garden? "I'll be here for weeks."

"It'll go fast. We're considered exceptional farmers," as Farmer and Ehyeh smiled at each other. Must be an inside joke I thought.

A guy suddenly appeared. Then another. They were popping in all over the place. I think my eyes were popping out more than they were popping in though. I hid behind Ehyeh, "Who are all these guys?"

Ehyeh turns to look back at me, "Angels came to help you."

Great, more aliens, I sighed.

Instantly, Farmer started directing them. They moved rocks away with ease. Could have used these guys yesterday. Dead trees were knocked down and weeds were pulled and all put on a roaring fire. Others were digging up the land and pouring in fresh soil. It was like watching bees flying around. Farmer came up to me and asks, "So, now, what would you like your garden to look like? What do you want in it?"

I couldn't think of what to say after seeing all this. And, I never had a garden or was ever around one. The angels were waiting for further instructions. Farmer and Ehyeh were smiling at me. Ruah was wagging his tail and licking my hand. Finally, I said, "Anything I want?"

"It's your garden," Farmer grins. "We'll walk through it together for many walks and talks."

"Well, I like roses and big oak trees. Pine trees are nice. Stuff with different colors." The angels moved so fast I could barely see anything more than white flashes. Huge plants with leaves bigger than me materialized. Oak trees full of acorns sprung up. Pine trees so tall I could barely see the tops of them. Purple flowers. Yellow and orange ones too. Some colors I don't even know what they are. So bright and shiny. It all quickly fills in. A path that looks like gold dust was right in front of my feet.

The angels disappeared as fast as they'd appeared. Farmer and Ehyeh put their hands on my shoulders, "Ready to see how it looks?"

"Uh… OK," as I take a step forward in shock. A canopy of leaves and flowers were overhead and all around. Roses larger than my head were sprinkled around everywhere.

"And don't forget, you'll still have to decide what kind of insects, birds and animals you'd like in your garden." I'm holding a rose in my hands as Ehyeh says this. The rose melts and moves and forms to my touch like it's alive. The smell from it fills my nose and head. Amazing.

"Huh… animals? You mean farm animals like cows and chickens?"

"If that's what you want in your garden."

I can't think of what garden animals would be. "Let's do insects and birds first. How about bees and butterflies? And hummingbirds? And, I like those birds with the big noses I've seen in pictures. Others that you guys like, I'm sure I'd like too."

They were popping in as fast as I was saying their names. Everything seems to 'pop' around here.

Bees were flitting around from flower to flower, as were the hummingbirds. Other birds with four wings appeared and started singing in the trees.

Such beautiful songs they had. And eagles. Majestic eagles were souring overhead. Some were all white. My mouth was definitely open a lot wider this time.

A familiar orange and black butterfly with white spots showed up and landed on my nose. "Is this...?"

Farmer introduces us, "This is, Ebenezer. He acted on your request and led you to me."

"Acted on my request? I don't get it."

"You asked him to guide you to me, and, here you are."

With my eyes crossed looking at him, "Thanks Ebenezer. You're awesome." He kissed me before moving over to my shoulder to join us on our walk.

My head was constantly swiveling around as we walked, trying to see everything, which was quite impossible. Farmer and Ehyeh laughed, "Slow down, Ryder. Enjoy. Your garden will always be here. And, what have you decided about animals?"

"Well, I do like eleph...," I bumped into the trunk of a huge elephant standing on the path. He roared and I fell backwards. Such huge tusks. He reached down with his trunk, wrapped it around me and put me up on his back. We turned and continued walking with Farmer, Ehyeh and Ruah beside us. I could see the garden so much better from up here.

Birds are flying all around me, swooping, diving, singing. Many landed on the elephant and rode along with me and Ebenezer.

"I want rabbits and kangaroos and panda bears." I was getting the hang of this.

Pop. Pop. Pop.

Farmer and Ehyeh put some strange looking ones in too. One was a deer with antlers that looked like two trees with purple fruit hanging from its branches. One small animal had blue feathers and fur, with rows of flowers along its back.

"Can we put in a hill with a waterfall," I asked? As we came around a bend, I could hear it before I saw it. A beautiful waterfall of many colors dropping into a small pool below. I got a much closer look when the elephant tossed me into it. I came up laughing. Farmer, Ehyeh, Ruah and the animals were laughing along with me. This is a strange and wonderful place for sure.

The water around me was shining like an emerald. The rocks along the edge looked like diamonds and rubies, but they couldn't be, could they? They were too big for that. I climbed out of the pool and sat on a rock that looked like it was made of solid gold. A huge tree with branches that dripped down into the water was next to me. Farmer said it's a weeping willow tree. I closed my eyes, hugged its branches, breathed in the sweet smell of its leaves and smiled. Tears started dribbling down my face. I've never had these kinds of tears.

Farmer, Ehyeh and Ruah sat next to me. "Do you like your garden?"

I wiped away the tears with my sleeve but they decided to keep coming. "Like? Like? It's just beyond fantastic. Thank you so much. How is all of this possible?"

"That's a long story," Farmer says as he wipes away my tears and gives me a warm hug.

Outside the farm, a raven sitting high up in a tree across the laneway was carefully observing all that was taking place. It flies down, lands on the shoulder of a god who appeared in a flash of smoke and started chattering away into his ear.

"Yes, my trap is being arranged for the boy," the god says, as he glares at the gate and fence holding him back. "Keep watch," he commands, as he turned and disappeared.

An always submissive slave, it flies back up to its perch as ordered.

CHAPTER 8

We spent the day walking through and enjoying the garden. All the birds and animals were so friendly. The big nosed bird, Farmer says is a toucan, came and landed on my shoulder. What a funny little guy. As we came to the edge of the garden, I could see the farm beyond it still looked barren and needed work.

"When do we start on the rest of the farm? What are we going to grow?"

"You will grow the most important things ever grown. Overall, you will work on your farm for eternity," Farmer stated.

"Eternity?" Farmer musta meant it'll take a long time. Like when they say, forever.

"This kind of farm is different from the ones you've heard about," Ehyeh said, as we walked along next to a huge rose bush that wound its way up a mighty oak. "These types of farms usually remain a wasteland. On rare occasions, they grow and prosper to provide a vast harvest. We'd like to see your farm prosper."

"For sure. I don't want my farm to be a wreck. What do I have to do?"

"Let's go back to your farmhouse and we'll show you more."

My farmhouse. I liked the sound of that. We made our way back through the garden past the waterfall, the many flowers, animals, butterflies and birds. So many sights, smells, sounds and colors that flooded my senses until that dingy farmhouse came into view through the trees. This place needs some serious repairs. Maybe the angels can whip me up a new mansion. Maybe a landing strip next to the barn for my jet. Why not two jets?

"Two of them I guess would be ridiculous wouldn't it, Ruah," I said out loud? Ruah's bark agreed.

Instead of the usual piles of food on the kitchen table, there were many rolled up papers trimmed in gold with purple ribbons dangling from them. I picked one of them up, "What's all this?" A red, waxy, circular thing that was holding the paper together broke apart. "Oops, I didn't mean to break it."

Farmer held one of them out to me, "These open only to your hand, as this is you."

"Me?"

"Yes. All of these are your titles that you've inherited. You are royalty now," as Ehyeh handed me another one.

"Royalty?" I flopped down in the chair, more confused than ever.

"Once you accepted us as family you became a royal," Farmer continued. "As part of this family, you are now a king, a lord, a priest and joint-heir of everything, not just this farm."

A king? A lord? Over what? "Everything," I barely get out? Oh yeah, they said that before.

"With these titles comes great responsibility. You can't just sit around squandering your titles on yourself. You're not to chase after fame, fortune and power," Ehyeh warned.

"These are just things, like the wheelbarrow, that can help get you to your goals. They're not the goals themselves," Farmer added.

"So, what are my goals as a royal?"

"Your goals are our goals. We've been around forever. We know the best way to achieve the maximum amount of success for your life, if you'll let us guide you," a strange voice advises.

Wait. Whose voice is that? I looked at Ruah as he tilted his head at me, "Yes Ryder, you're hearing me in your head, not through your ears. We'll guide you on the most perfect and successful way for you, if you'll let us. Treasures beyond your imagination are waiting." Ruah's voice is so gentle.

Treasures beyond my imagination? What's better than a mansion, a truck full of cash and two jets? My head droops down. My eyes closed. This is becoming very strange. I have to obey a dog? An alien dog that sends messages into my head?

Ruah continued, "I chose this form as I didn't want to frighten you. I can come to you this way if you like." A great wind suddenly blasted through the kitchen. I'm on the ground, sliding across the floor. Farmer and Ehyeh are just standing there smiling at me. The wind isn't affecting them at all. Then, the entire kitchen is in roaring blue flames, but I'm not being burned. A flood of water roars over me next before Ruah is finally back in the form of a shepherd dog.

I put my hand up, "OK, OK, dog shape is good. What now?"

There's a knock at the door. "Ah, perfect timing," Farmer says as he yells, "Come on in, Briella."

Briella walked in, throws her arms around Farmer, Ehyeh, Ruah and me for hugs, "Hi everyone. I'm ready to show... "

"Ryder," Farmer fills in my name.

"Ryder," she smiled at me. "What an appropriate name for him, Farmer. I'm ready to show Ryder what you've asked of me."

Great. Now I gotta take orders from a dog *and* a girl. An alien girl. Oops. Gotta stop thinking out loud around here. She grabs me by the hand and takes me outside. More like drags. I looked back at the guys for help. They just smiled, as usual. Great.

Briella's long hair flowed behind her as we ran down to the gate where I came in. She runs fast... for a girl. We stopped at the broken-down fence. Yep... a lot of work needed around my farm.

"See this gate," she says with a serious look on her face? "There's this gate and other gates on your farm."

"OK." So, what?

Then she points to a raven sitting in a tree across the laneway. "See that?"

"Yeah, it's a bird."

"It's not just a bird. It's a spy."

"A spy? How's a bird a spy? A spy for who? What's it spying on?"

"Look really close at it."

I look really closely. Yep. It's a bird. "What am I looking for?"

"Be serious. Concentrate."

I stare at the bird. The bird stares back at me. Then I see it. It comes into view. There's a black lizard looking thing inside of it. I blink my eyes a few times. It's still there. "What is that?"

"That's the spy. It's spying on you."

"Me. Why me?"

"It's waiting for you to make a mistake. It's waiting for you to open a gate for them."

"Them? Who's them?"

"It's the enemy. You don't want them on your farm. They'll destroy pieces of it and even all of it, if you let them. They're at war with you now."

"War? I don't understand this. Why do *they* want to destroy my farm?"

"Because you are royalty now, like me."

War? Now I'm in a war? Why did I come to this place? "What if I just stay on my farm and leave them alone, won't they just go away?"

"If you do nothing but sit on your farm, they'd like that, then you'd miss out on your full inheritance. But they'll still try to take over your barn and your farmhouse. They'll try to convince you to leave the family or do things they want you to do. They want you to give up your royalty. They'll try to get you to grow other things on your farm. Things that'll wreck your harvest. They're very nasty."

"Full inheritance? Why are they doing all of this? What'd I do to them?"

"They hate Farmer, Ehyeh and Ruah. They want to destroy everything they build. They want to be in charge. They want to own your farm."

Now I was getting mad. Own my farm? I looked behind at the barn and farmhouse. Yeah, it's a dump. But it's my dump. Nobody's taking it from me. I stared into those serious, deep, dark, brown eyes, "How do we stop them?"

Briella smiles, "Ryder's a good name for you." We leaned on the gate as she went on, "Farmer told you who you are now. You have titles. You also have great power and authority. Much more power than the enemy has. But they don't want you to know that. They want you to be afraid of them. They want you to think they have more power than you."

"I have power?"

"Oh yes. Great power. Farmer probably told you that you're a joint-heir with everything. You just have to be aware of it, learn how to use it and most important, follow what Farmer, Ehyeh and Ruah says."

My head's overloading. Briella looks me in the eyes, "Don't run this farm without them."

"Why would I do that?"

"Most royalty does, once they become part of the family. They think they can run their farm however they want. They even tell other people how to run their farms. The enemy enjoys this activity very much. They encourage it, as they win this way too."

"There's other farms like mine?"

"Everyone's farm is different. Most don't have Farmer, Ehyeh and Ruah on it. Those ones just lay in waste or are run by them," as she pointed to the spy.

"How can Farmer, Ehyeh and Ruah be on all these farms?"

"You'll find out. They're on my farm right now too. I'm just visiting your farm because Farmer asked me to help you. Farmer's requests are part of my responsibilities as a royal."

The bird and the other thing are still staring at us. "OK, I guess I'll understand more as we go along. What are we gonna do with this spy?"

"Farmer wants you to get rid of it."

The raven must have understood what Briella said because it let out a loud squawk and took off. Briella says, "Tell it to stop."

What? I yelled out, "Stop!" The bird dropped like a rock to the laneway, laying there stiff. Well that was cool. "Now what?"

"Tell an angel to take the spy away in chains to prison," Briella says to me like, what else would you do.

I burst out laughing in her face. "What?" That big angel at the barn wasn't there and the angels around my garden were all gone. "What angel?"

"Look around. Concentrate."

I squinted my eyes in all directions until a bunch of forms started to take shape along the fence line. "I see them." Not as tall as the barn angel but easily over double our height. And each with a sword and shield. All in a row at attention. Quiet. Not moving. I didn't fall down in shock so I guess I'm getting used to not being that surprised anymore. "How do I get them to take the spy away?"

"Just tell them. You're royalty. Act like a king. But a nice king."

"Angels, take that lizard-spy thing away in chains to a prison." In a flash of light, an angel shot over, grabbed it out of the bird and disappeared with it. The bird shook a bit, got up and stood there for a while shaking its head before flying away.

Briella spun us around laughing, "You did it, Ryder. You did it."

I don't know how I did it, but it feels pretty good. We ended up falling down still laughing. Looking up at the sky I could see angels clapping. I pointed up. "Briella, do you see that?"

"Oh yes. They're all so happy for you."

"Happy for me? Why?"

"They're always pleased when we follow Farmer's plans."

"Farmer's in charge of angels, right?"

"Oh yes. And Ehyeh and Ruah are too."

"So, why don't they get rid of these enemy things? They're obviously more powerful than them."

"They could get rid of them in an instant, but they want to share their throne with us."

"Throne?"

"Ryder, they told you that you share in everything now. You're family. They want to give us the joy of victory and success and treasures."

"Treasures?" Yeah, let's get back to that topic.

Briella grabbed my hand, "Come on, let's go." We raced up the lane to the house where Farmer and Ehyeh greeted us with hugs. I could hear Ruah in my head, "Well done, Ryder." Briella gave me a kiss on the cheek and a hug and dashed down the steps waving bye.

"Bye, we all say."

"Thanks, Briella," I said as she disappeared in front of my eyes... again. "Where'd she go, Farmer?"

"She went back to her farm."

I blinked at where she disappeared. Gonna like learning that one. The angels were still there along the fence line in a row. I can see them clearly now. My hand went up to my cheek where Briella kissed me. I smiled. I like her.

"Come," Ehyeh said, as he put his arm around me, ushering me into the farmhouse. It's so bright and warm in here now. The paint wasn't chipped and peeling anymore. The furniture was clean. So much happened today, I don't know what to say first. Before I could say anything, Farmer said, "Well done today, Ryder. With your garden, with Briella, with acting on the enemy as guided."

They steered me into a different room to the left instead of where I usually turned to go into the kitchen and I stopped. There're thrones in here. Farmer sat on one, Ehyeh sat on another and Ruah took the shape of what looked like water and fire in motion, mixed together and sat on a different one.

Farmer motioned for me to come towards him. When I stood in front of him, three angels appeared beside me. One was holding a crown, the other had a long red robe or cloak and the third was holding a ring and a club-type thing. The angel handed the crown to Farmer and he put it on my head. It was gold with many jewels in it. It felt kinda heavy. At the same time, the other angel handed the robe-cloak to Ehyeh and he placed it on me. It hung over my shoulders with no sleeves and flowed around me like it was alive. From the last angel, Ruah placed the ring on my finger and put the club in my other hand. The ring had a light or glow shining from it. The club thing was covered in jewels too, like the crown. I was told later that it was a scepter.

"You are a great king and lord, Ryder," Farmer pronounces. "Much is ahead." He points to an empty throne next to them, "This is yours."

I kinda stumbled over and sat, not sure how to act. It's very comfy. "What do I do now?"

"Rest. It's time for you to rest," Ehyeh says.

Not knowing what as a royal I'm supposed to do, I stood, bowed up and down, holding the crown on my head so it didn't fall off and shuffled backwards to leave, heading for the door.

"Where are you going," Farmer asked?

"To the barn?"

"Why?"

"Because… that's where I live?"

"The farmhouse is where you live now and us in here with you, if you still want us," I heard Ruah in my head.

"Of course, please stay here with me and thanks for all of this. But I really don't understand what's happening."

Farmer nods, "All will be revealed to you. Patience."

"Where do I sleep?" A door opened to my left with a bright light shining out from the room. Beautiful was such a small word to describe it. It's an immense room filled with jeweled and gold… everything.

CHAPTER 9

I woke up still wearing my crown and robe, and clutching the scepter close to my chest. Watching the various shades of red on the robe move like waves on an ocean made me laugh. The light from the ring seemed to dance. Then I realized, I'm in the house. Wonder if the guys are here? I jumped off the bed, opened the door and peeked outside. All three of them are standing there like they were expecting me. Ruah tilted his head, "Did you think we weren't here? We'll always be with you. Isn't that what you said you wanted?"

Stepping out, feeling kind of weird wearing all this stuff, "Yes, yes, please don't go." I couldn't imagine my life without them in it now. They all smiled. Oh yeah. The mind-reading thing again.

"What do I do with the crown and robe an...," several angels appeared as I was asking?

"Hand everything to them," Farmer says, "They'll take excellent care of them for you."

I took off my crown, robe and ring and handed them all over to them with the scepter. They disappeared as quickly as they appeared.

I ran over and hugged each of them, "Thank you, guys, so much." This hugging stuff feels good. But it didn't last long.

My stomach, having a mind of its own and no clear sense of timing, started growling to interrupt all this hugging fuss. We all laughed. "What's for breakfast?"

It was a feast. Everything I had chosen over the previous days was here and more. Including my fav... hotdogs.

"What are we doing today," I asked munching?

"Well, we have a surprise for you in the barn."

"A surprise?" Everything so far on the farm has been a surprise. I love these guys.

They say together, "We love you too, Ryder." The thought-thing again. "You love me?"

"Very much. We always have," Ehyeh says as he puts his hand on my shoulder. His eyes are green now.

"Always? You've only known me for a few days?"

Again, with the smiling. A lot of mystery around here but I don't care. Nobody ever told me that they loved me and I sense that these guys really mean it. I don't think love is just a word to them. I don't know if I even know what love means. I don't think I ever loved anyone. It's just a word to me.

They all start walking toward the door. "Let's go see your surprise, Ryder," Ruah said. I ran up to them trying to think what it could be. I could hear all the animals and birds out back in my garden. How could anything beat that?

"Hey." I noticed that someone had been doing some repairs on the barn. The walls don't look like they're falling down anymore. Some of the holes in the roof are fixed. The tall weeds around it are all gone. Maybe that big angel did it?

As I slowed down and stopped to take it all in, the guys disappeared from sight. I ran around the barn and in through the front door to catch up and there it was. A magnificent, white horse rising up on his hind legs, introducing himself to me.

"Wow!" I'd never actually seen a real horse before. "He's mine?"

"He's all yours. Do you like our gift?"

"So cool. Thank you so much. He's awesome. But I never rode a horse before." The horse walked over to me and nuzzled my face. I stroked his chin and long mane.

I heard Ehyeh's voice, "Then, let's go for your first ride." Ehyeh was standing next to another beautiful white horse that glowed. Ehyeh was wearing a bright, purple robe that partially covered some other gold-colored clothes. I was surprised to see him like this. While I was admiring Ehyeh's new look, a few dozen or more angels appeared around me holding what looked like flashes of light, each one having a different mixture of colors.

"What's all this," I asked them?

Ehyeh walked over to me as the angels stepped forward, "This is your armor of light that we created specifically for you. Each one is something different, but each one is extremely important."

The first angel handed Ehyeh a flash of light, that he put in my hand. "This is 'integrity'. As a part of the nobility of this family you can no longer move about without it. You must live a life of decency, honor, honesty, morality and especially humility."

It feels tingly as Ehyeh is talking. When he finished, it melted right into my hand. Woah.

"Next is 'faith'." Ehyeh placed this one in my other hand. "You must have faith in us and all that we have planned for you. That we have only the best for you at all times. Faith that we will never leave you nor abandon you. Faith also in yourself in your power and authority that we've given you."

The melting part is cool. These light-things make me feel kinda stellar.

Each angel stepped forward to hand Ehyeh a different piece of armor that was explained to me before it melted into me.

The last angel stepped up. "This piece ties all the rest together." Ehyeh placed it on my chest. "This is 'truth'. You need this to keep you anchored in reality and away from the lies and traps of the fantasy worlds. Truth must be adhered to. It can't be watered down or mixed with untruths. Untruths can't be tolerated in any form. You must war against untruth."

The last one disappeared into me with the rest. My whole body is glowing now. I felt like a different person. This must be part of that metamorphy-thing they talked about. While I was checking out the light that was flowing out my fingers, Ehyeh put the red robe they'd given me over my shoulders. "This armor is part of you now. It is up to you to make it stronger or make it weaker."

"How does that happen," I asked?

Farmer answered me, "You become stronger and more powerful as you deepen yourself into what has been supplied to you. Should you choose to reject, compromise or even do nothing to develop yourself in any of these areas, you lay yourself open to attack."

"Attack?"

Ruah walked over to me, "Attack from enemies that are many. Dark ways in any form draws them in like blood in the air calls out to wolves. When they sink their teeth and claws into you, they won't show you any mercy. You mustn't let that happen."

"OK, I won't. But you guys gotta help me with all this scary war and armor stuff and what I gotta do cuz I don't wanna mess up."

Farmer smiles, "We're always with you, Ryder. Never fear of that. Now kneel."

I knelt down. Now what?

A sword appeared instantly in Farmer's hand. He gave it to Ehyeh. Ehyeh touched the sword's blade on both of my shoulders. The blade was a bright white light that was moving and had writing on it. It's alive.

"Stand, king Ryder." As I stood up, they each hugged me.

These aliens sure have weird rules before we can go horseback riding.

"Let's go," as Ehyeh jumped up on his horse with ease.

Trying the same thing got me landing face-up on the barn floor. "This armor still doesn't make me a horse-guy. Doesn't this horse come with a manual?" One of the angels came over to assist me, which was him picking me up with one hand, plopping me into the saddle and slapping the horse on the back-end.

We galloped out the barn, around and out behind it. They must have put some kinda glue on my pants because I don't know how I didn't fall off.

Ehyeh smiling, "You have lots of questions?"

"I don't where to start really. I guess an easy one is, what's the name of my horse?"

"He's for you to name."

Thinking, as I leaned forward petting his neck. "How about, Gideon?"

"Great name," Ehyeh says. Do you know what that name means?"

"Not really. Someone told me it was the name of a great warrior."

"That's exactly right. Well done. Follow me." Ehyeh picked up the pace of our ride. I bounced around on top of Gideon trying to keep myself from falling over. Trying to look like a dignified king is harder than it sounds.

We rode along some of the fenced boundary of my farm, including past several closed gates. Angels were all around the fence-line and especially formed up deep in front of each the gates. As we came near the gates, ravens that were in trees on the outside screeched loudly as they scattered away. More spies maybe. They definitely don't like Ehyeh.

"We're those more spies," I asked?

"Yes. They watch your gates. Like Ruah told you, they wait for you to make a mistake. They're always watching and waiting for you to invite them in."

"Invite them in? Why would I do that? Briella told me that they're my enemy. That they want to destroy my farm."

"That's right. They do. Most farms in the world are ruled by them right now or have been destroyed by them, even farms where people are aware of them. Including farms that started out where you are."

"You mean, people who are aware of them let them in to take over?"

"All the time. Many in ignorance but others want to work with them to get wealth and power, like sorcerers. They don't realize they're all being used and on the road to destruction. You will war against and conquer many of them." He slaps my chest smiling, "You'll see for yourself soon enough."

"War? Against sorcerers? They want to destroy my farm too? How do I fight them?"

"Well. It's not much of a fight. All of them put together can't match your power. Look behind us."

I turned to see only scrubby-looking fields full of rocks. OK. I know this one. Concentrate. I blinked a few times, focused and they came into shape. Angels on horses that are on fire. Other angels on chariots wearing armor and carrying all kinds of weapons. As far as I could see on all sides and up and into the sky. They went so far in the distance they looked like wisps of white smoke. Must be billions of them following us. I turned slowly back around, feeling like I was going to pass out. Ehyeh slapped me on the back. "All good, my lord," as he galloped ahead?

"Go, Gideon." Bouncing around like this was making it very hard to look cool, as I glanced over my shoulder to see the angels were still following behind. "Who are all those guys," I yelled over to Ehyeh as we're galloping, my knuckles white, tightly holding on to the reins hoping I wouldn't fall off?

"They're at your disposal. They wait for your commands, great king." Just as he said that it looked like the air twirled around and opened up in front of us. We rode through, coming to a stop on the other side. Rubbing my eyes with my hands I thought, nah, musta been seeing things, cuz my farm is still here.

"You weren't seeing things, Ryder. This isn't your farm."

Ehyeh was right. This place is much nicer. The fields are in better shape, the farmhouse and barn aren't in need of repairs that I can see, there's a humongous garden with mostly palm trees in it surrounding some tall pinkish mountains with five waterfalls. "Where are we? Whose farm is this?"

A familiar voice behind me says, "Hi, Ehyeh. Hi, Ryder." It's Briella's voice.

riella looked so impressive in that dark red robe, her whole body glowing like mine, sitting on a silky white horse.

Now this just added to everything else that blindsided me so far today, so I knew I had to quickly come up with something seriously witty. All my brain would give me was, "Hey, Briella. Nice horse. What's his name?"

"*Her* name is, Shiloh. She's a gift from Farmer, Ehyeh and Ruah."

"Hello, Shiloh. Meet, Gideon," I gestured with a wave of my hand.

Briella leaned over to rub Gideon's head, "You're so handsome, Gideon." Gideon snorted. Obviously, an instant fan of Briella. The horses introduced themselves by rubbing their noses against each other.

Then it came to me, "Hey, how did we end up here? And where is here?"

"This is my farm. Do you like it?"

"It's much nicer than mine, Briella. Mine needs a lot of work. But, how did we get here?" That weird opening is gone. The angels came through with us, unless these ones are Briella's and mine are still back over at my farm. It's hard to keep up.

Ehyeh explained, "We got here because this is where we wanted to go. Sorry it took so long. Didn't want to shock you."

"Shock me? Took so long?"

"Usually, it's this fast," Ehyeh said as they both disappeared. Twisting around on Gideon looking for them, they showed up as little dots in the distance initially, getting bigger as they rode up to me. "And there's this." As fast as Ehyeh said it, Ehyeh and Briella were all around me. I don't know how many of them there were. Then it was back in an instant to just one of each of them.

"And this," they disappeared again. The tap on my shoulder spooked me until I heard Briella giggling, "We're right here."

They reappeared but were almost invisible. When I reached out to touch them, my hand went right through them.

And of course, while they're grinning, I'm getting a headache.

"How are you doing this? It isn't possible."

"After all you've seen, Ryder, you think this isn't possible," Ehyeh asked?

"But, what about reality? The physical world? Science and, and, and gravity and, you know, physics and all that stuff?" I was grasping for words.

"I didn't know you were a science buff, Ryder," Ehyeh said, tilting his head toward me. "So, tell me, what is reality?"

Back to this again. Never finished talking about this the other day with Farmer. "It's whatever you can see I guess," but I didn't know what to think now after seeing them pop around and disappear.

"So, you say, reality doesn't exist for a blind person?"

"Well, I mean, things in the physical. Stuff that's here even if you can't see it."

"Where is, 'here'," Ehyeh continued quizzing me?

"Here," pointing to the ground. "I mean Earth."

"What about the sky and the universe? What about beyond what people haven't seen?"

I looked up, "Yeah, everything up there too."

"How about things all around you that you can't sense with your physical abilities? Does anything exist outside of that?"

My headache was getting worse. "I don't know. I guess there's things people don't know about. We don't know everything."

"Very good, Ryder. All is not what it seems. There *is* more. Much more. Beyond your imagination more. People dismiss the possibility that other dimensions could exist outside of their physical senses and intellect. They choose to imprison themselves in blindness and ignorance to anything going on outside their box. Reality is a living entity. Eternity is a living entity. Embracing only certain portions of them, calling it truth, is living a life of delusion trapped within a fantasy."

"OK," showing confusion. "What does all that mean?"

"It means you have much to learn along the way, young king," as Ehyeh and Briella turned their horses and waved for me to come.

"Let's go, Gideon." I caught up to them trying not to flop around so much in front of Briella.

While Briella was showing me her farm, I decided not to be so freaked out about all this stuff that's going on. I'm just going to see where I end up. I sighed with relief. I'm not going to struggle anymore against all these mystical things. I don't know everything. What person does? Arrogant ones think they do, I guess. Hmmm. Thinking this way musta worked. My headache's gone. Maybe it was the nice ride. I leaned forward and patted Gideon's neck.

Briella's farm is so big. There's rolling hills that drift up to some mountains, that are next to a lake, bigger than my pond. We rode past an old tree that was all dinged up, with no leaves on any of the dead branches. It looked like an ax had chopped into it here and there. There're hunks of it gone and marks all over it, as well as digging in the ground all around it. Must be a tough one to get out.

When we arrived at her garden, the animals came running up to greet us, causing a slight reaction in Briella as she squealed out in joy, jumped off of

Shiloh and commenced the hugging process. She knew each one by name including the white tigers that purred like kittens as she rubbed their heads. Birds, butterflies and bees were flying all around us, so happy that we were here. Being introduced to them all took hours and I enjoyed every second of it.

We eventually continued on, walking our horses through the towering emerald green palm trees and fluorescent, pink flowers that Briella had chosen as her favs, which were the more prominent ones among all the other trees and flowers of her garden. As we went by, they turned and waved their leaves at us. Don't know what kind of reality this is, but I'm going with, as it sure beats the one that I grew up in.

We reached the farmhouse, that looked somewhat like mine only it was in much better shape. Farmer and Ruah were waiting for us on the porch.

"You guys came over to see us," I asked?

"Came over," Farmer replied?

"Yeah. From my farm," as we all sat down in rocking chairs. Nice. Have to get me some of these.

"No. We're always around."

"You're in two places at the same time?" Let's get back to this mystery.

"We're in all the places at the same time," Farmer smiling.

I did see Ehyeh and Briella duplicate themselves when we were riding but what's this now? "You're everywhere? At the same time?"

"Yes. Is that hard to understand, Ryder," Farmer asked as he rests back in his rocker.

"Well yeah. How's that possible?"

Farmer points up to a star twinkling in the sky. "Do you see that star, Ryder?"

Looking up I see it shining away. "Yeah." Must be a trick question.

"Where is its light," Farmer asked, as he slowly rocked in his chair?

Where is its light? Where is its light, as I stare at the floor searching for the answer in my head? "It's all over the universe I guess, as far as it shines."

"So, its light is everywhere from that star for septillions of miles in all directions?"

Septillions sounded like a lot as I pondered, "Yes, but...." Farmer put his hand up to stop me.

"Go over there to see if it's over there," he pointed to the other side of the porch.

Strolling over while watching the star along the way, "Yep, it's over here."

"But it's over here too," he said still rocking. "And isn't it still there when you can't see it? Is it still there when you're asleep?"

Getting back to my rocker, "But light isn't a physical thing. It's a... a...."

"It's a what," Farmer asked? "Does it exist or not?"

Gazing up again at the star, "The light exists, but...."

"But what," Farmer stopped rocking to smile at me? "Hard for you to wrap your head around, Ryder?"

"A little," I responded. It sorta makes sense. "But, how do you guys do it? You're not light."

"Who says," Farmer chuckled? "Look around."

"What?"

"Look around."

Farmer was standing on the roof waving at me. My eyes shot back to the rocking chair where he was still rocking. Out at the front gate, there he was. It didn't matter how fast or where I snapped my head, he's there and here.

I decided to go for it. "Are you guys aliens? Are you here to take over the planet?" There, I got it out. I hope they don't blast me with their ray-guns now that I've exposed them.

Ehyeh explained, "We are alien to most people although we aren't aliens. And it would be nice to take over the planet."

Ha. I knew it. It's all been a trick. But, how do I warn everyone about these guys? "So, what do you want with us?"

"We invite everyone to join our family. We don't force or trick anyone. People must make their own choices to decide not to be human anymore," Ehyeh said. His light, gray-blue eyes looking into mine with concern, "We don't want to see anyone die. We offer eternity with unimaginable power and a royal position. We're godmakers. We offer godship."

Not human anymore? Godmakers? Eternity? Godship? These guys are crackers like that dude on the road. Maybe I can still get out of here before they zap me. So much for going along with everything so I don't get a headache. I folded my arms and looked away. How can I warn the planet about these guys? "But everyone's a human and everyone dies. How can you change that? How can anyone be a god that lives forever?"

"You already are," Farmer responded at the same time a large being appeared before us holding a blazing white book of light that's on fire.

Acting a little shy, I fell backwards, along with my rocking chair and peaked through the slats at it. This angel or whatever it was, looked different than the others I'd seen. It had eyes all over its body, even over its many spread-out wings. It barely fit on the porch it was so big. Now what?

Farmer flipped through the fiery pages of the book that it brought. "Your name's right here. See," his finger pointing on the page.

My feet couldn't resist. They ran over to let me take a look. Yep, there it is. My new name, Ryder, in fiery red words that moved. I stared at Farmer, Ehyeh, Ruah and Briella and back to my name and touched it with my finger. It felt like a shockwave was moving through my body. "How'd it get here," I asked trembling?

"It got here when you accepted us as your family. When you went through metamorphosis to get away from being a human," I heard Ruah respond in my head.

"So where was I before that?"

A being similar to the first one appeared with another book made of stacks of black paper standing up together, that filled the entire porch of Briella's farmhouse. Farmer walked along the book, stopped and spread it open, "You used to be here. We transferred you over."

Everyone was watching at me. I didn't know what to say. The fuses in my head had sorta all melted together. Finally, pointing at the two books,

"My name here means I live for eternity as some kind of a god and over here what was I?"

"Over here you were dead. This is the Book of the Dead," Farmer answered. The beings covered with eyes disappeared taking both books with them.

I don't know if I was more scared when they flashed in or when they flashed out or maybe it was because of what I just found out.

Farmer stared into my eyes, "If you wish to abdicate your throne, you're certainly able to do so at any time."

"Abdicate? What's that mean?"

"You can decide to walk away from this family to run your own life anytime. We'll leave you alone and all the angels will back off from your fences and gates. You'll have to give up all your titles and your inheritance though and go back to the Book of the Dead."

"Does anyone really do that?"

"All the time. They think that once they get into the family, they're safe to do as they please or that they can follow the dark ways. Reality doesn't work that way. You're either in or you're out. You can't be both a caterpillar and a butterfly. If you do decide to leave, maybe some wizard school will teach you how to fly a broom."

Reality can be like hard medicine sometimes... might not taste good, but you better buckle down and swallow it when it can keep you alive. I'm guessing it tastes like candy after a while, if you let it.

Slowly walking over to the rocking chair, I picked it up and dropped into it. I know I'm just a kid, or I was just a kid, but the height of insanity on this planet must be either staying in or taking any kind of a risk of going back into that black book. These guys are the real deal.

"Godmakers? So, that means you guys are..."

Smiles all around.

I'm all in.

CHAPTER 11

"How does this godship thing work," I asked? "Are there rules? Can I blast people I don't like? Can I make money?" I waved and pointed my index finger around like it was a magic wand, making shooting and zapping noises.

Farmer stood up and gave me a big hug, "I love your enthusiasm, Ryder. We just need to point you in the right direction and let you go," he chuckled.

"OK, so what do I do?"

"Right now," Ehyeh says, "we're going to a circus," as he heads down the steps.

A circus. Awesome. I've never been to a circus as I bolted after him. "Aren't you guys coming," I yelled back at Farmer, Ruah and Briella?

"Nope. It's just you and Ehyeh right now." I ran back up, hugged them quick and dashed back to Gideon. I'm so excited.

"See you later," as we waved, heading towards Briella's front gate that the angels were opening up for us. The horses had just barely hit the laneway when it suddenly dropped away as we rose up into the sky. Reaching down to grip Gideon's mane, "What's happening," trying unsuccessfully not to sound freaked out, as I see mountains, lakes and trees passing below us?

"I told you. We're on our way to a circus," as Ehyeh banked off to the left. Gideon followed. I'm glad Gideon knows what he's doing as I don't know how to steer him.

"I thought it was like down the road a way, not up here."

"We'll be there soon. Thought you'd enjoy the ride. Ya know, doing some godship stuff," he grinned. These guys do have a good sense of humor.

We didn't have to go far, which was a good thing because I wasn't on board with the sky-surfing part of this new life just yet. Our horses came down to stop in front of a gigantic building. The people standing and walking around paid no attention to us flying in on our horses. "They can't see us?"

"No. We're in cloak mode," Ehyeh said as he headed up the grass and right through the wall.

"Gideon, did you see that?" He shoved me with his nose directing me to go.

Ehyeh came halfway out of the building with his hand out, "Come on. Follow me." Woah. I hadn't noticed that huge scar on his wrist before. That musta hurt.

Well, I guess going through a wall can't be harder than walking on water so I headed through the crowd towards Ehyeh. All was thumbs up until a man walked right through me, which made me jump over to the side where someone else walked through me. "What the... I don't look invisible," whispering over at Ehyeh as I dashed up to the wall avoiding everyone.

"Ryder, you don't have to whisper, they can't hear you either,"

Ehyeh said as he grabbed my hand and pulled me through the wall. This godship stuff is wild, as I stumbled through to the other side.

Inside the building, hundreds of people were walking around or sitting in rows of chairs facing a big stage with colored lights flashing on it. That must be where all the circus acts come out. Hope we get a good seat.

There was a lineup at a shop that was selling T-shirts, books, coffee mugs, keychains and stuffed dolls that sorta looked like Ehyeh. Seemed like a pretty good moneymaker. Another shop was selling donuts, cookies, sandwiches and coffee, which made my mouth start watering for a hotdog. Digging around in my pockets, hoping that magic bed made me some money, I found nothing, meaning, gonna have to bring out the big guns now. Making an 'I'm brutally starving' smacking sound with my lips and throwing the best sad, hungry, puppy-dog-eyes look I could bring up towards Ehyeh, he laughed, reached down and held up my hand. A nice, warm, juicy, foot-long hotdog with mustard and relish appeared. Ehyeh's a great hint-catcher.

In-between gulping chunks of my dog down I mumbled, "When does the show start?"

"Look around," Ehyeh said.

Chomping away, watching the stage, waiting for the show to start, something else caught my attention. My mouth gaped opened so much the hotdog hunk I was eating dropped out. "What's all this?"

Ehyeh had a very serious look now, "This is part of the circus."

The rest of the hotdog dropped out of my hand, "I don't think I like the circus."

Strange critters, kinda like that one in that spy bird, were inside and on top of people, mixed in with snakes, frogs and other slimy things. There were more of them than people.

Some were vomiting on people; short ones were stabbing them with pointy things, many were biting them all over, while others were going to the bathroom on them. Sexual things were taking place. They were jumping around from one person to the next, like they were having a party. There were black words written on them like 'witchcraft', 'pornography', 'bitterness', 'lying', 'thief', 'backstabber', 'religion', 'adultery' and 'murder'. "Ehyeh? This is a circus? Where's all the clowns?"

"More is coming. Watch and learn," Ehyeh said, as a man came out on the stage, that must be the circus ringmaster. He was talking but my focus was on the black thing that was attached to him. It was bigger than the others, wearing a crown that had the word 'depravity' on it. It was directing the smaller creatures to go to certain people, to do awful things to them.

"I'm confused, what are these things? Who are all these people? Why are we here?"

Ehyeh pointed at the man on the stage, "That man says he knows me. All these people here say they know me, yet, they've willing picked themselves and other gods to run their lives. Their farms."

"These people want these creatures to be doing all this stuff to them?"

"They opened the gates on their farms. Some did it gladly. There are outcomes for every thought and every action. They should know better because we gave them an operator's manual."

A manual? "But, can't you do something," I asked? "I mean, we're more powerful than those creepy things, right?"

"Yes, we are. We can get rid of all them in an instant but these people have given them rights to attack them. We told you that family members, like humans, have options. These ones pretend to be holy but they embrace dark ways."

"Why would they do that? They look like nice people. You said they know you. They even have a manual? What's their problem then? Why don't they walk around with you like I do?"

"No. I didn't say they know me. I said, they *say* they know me. They don't walk with me."

Staring down at my partially eaten hotdog on the floor trying to understand, I looked back up. Nope. All those strange creatures are still there. I shook my head, "What about their farms?"

Ehyeh waved his hand in front of me. One after another, I was taken to their farms for a quick glimpse. Several farms are on fire. Some look like a desert. That one has trees with rotten fruit hanging from it. Many are overrun with snakes and scorpions while the person is either asleep on the porch or busy doing something else. Some look like my farm when I arrived at it. It goes on and on. When it stopped, I frowned, "Could something like this happen to me and my farm if I wasn't careful?" I already knew the answer.

"Your farm would become a wasteland again and your name would go back in the Book of the Dead," Ehyeh answered without hesitation.

I'm not used to such honesty. He put his hand on my chin and raised it up to look me in the eyes, "Don't be concerned about such things, little brother. Be joyful about where you are and the exciting things ahead."

"OK, I will. But how can we help these people?"

Ehyeh smiled, "That's why we're here. Ready to shake things up a bit?"

"Sure. What's up?" Now I'm excited as I rubbed my hands together.

"Let's have you step into their field of vision and you convince them to change their minds about me."

"Me?" This wasn't what I was expecting. "Why don't you appear to them and smarten them up, like you did with me?"

"No. This time I'd like to help you build up your farm. Are you up for it, great king?"

Slight hesitation before I grinned, "Let's do it!"

"Come. Let's go up on the stage next to that entertainer." We walked through everyone, not around, got up on the stage and still no one noticed us. The man here was asking for everyone to agree with him that signs and wonders should appear. Ehyeh had a serious look as the massive crowd nodded and clapped in agreement to the ringmaster's appeal, "Let's give them what they asked for. Make yourself visible to them."

"How do I do that?"

"You're in a dimension that they can't perceive. Move into their limited reality just as you would move from one room to the next. Your mind moves your body to do it. Have your mind tell yourself to make it so."

This is gonna be cool. Closing my eyes, I think, 'they can see me now', which worked pretty fast, judging by all the screaming going on and people falling back, crawling on the floor. The man on the stage was in a rage on his knees in obvious pain, his face almost black looking up at me.

Ehyeh smiled, "The creatures can see you now too. They control the people's minds and bodies to act this way. The creatures know who you are and they're afraid. They don't see me."

Nice. I like this godship stuff. Does get a little noisy though. "What now?"

"Command all the creatures to stop all that they're doing."

My trusty index finger pointed all around and repeated what Ehyeh said. The creatures all froze into place. Everything's quiet. The people on the floor all got up looking confused.

Ehyeh continued, "Now, tell them Ehyeh has sent you. Tell them you're here to release them from their prisons and show them the way to truth. The way to reality."

I did as Ehyeh directed me and waited for an expected warm greeting and hugs all around. After all, they say we're all family and I came here to help them. The man on the stage stood up and stomped over to me, "You're not welcome here, witch," pointing at me in anger.

Angry men ran up on the stage towards me, while people in the crowd were screaming, "Witch!"

Looking at Ehyeh with concern, "And?"

"Blow at them," Ehyeh answered calmly.

Four big, angry guys were almost on top of me with their hands out to grab me, when I blew at them. It was like they hit and bounced off a rubber wall. They all shot up high in the air, but in slow-motion, landing softly at the other end of the stage. The people in the crowd shrieked, "Witch", louder while they stampeded for the exits.

"Ehyeh, what's the matter with these people? Are they nuts?"

"I told you it was a circus. What they ask for and sing for finally shows up and they run away."

One man sitting towards the back didn't run away. Ehyeh pointed at him, "This is the one we're most interested in."

The man stood up, walked toward me and stared up at me on the stage. The thing attached to him was struggling in a net, caught up in my command to stop what it was doing. The man pridefully crossed his arms, "I'm a senior elder here. Prove that you're from Ehyeh."

Something very strange happened to me. I instantly knew all about this man; what he'd been doing and what I was to say to him. Ehyeh had explained everything to me in an instant into my mind without talking. I began.

"Wizard!" This obviously startled him. "You hide who you are from people but you can't hide from Farmer, Ehyeh and Ruah. You have been imprisoning fragments of people's souls in jars in your basement for twenty-three years." This surprised me as the words came out of my mouth. "You control and manipulate people in this city and region from the shadows, to do the bidding of the one attached to you, that I have bound. You have enjoyed afflicting people with lost jobs, broken families, diseases and early death. Any last words before sentencing?"

The man dropped to the floor with his hands over his face screaming in fear, "Yes, yes, I've done all these things. I was driven by this creature in me since I was a boy. I struggled to stop but didn't know how to escape. Doctors told me what I was experiencing was psychosomatic and gave me counselling and drugs, none of which worked. I begged those from circuses, who said they were experts from Ehyeh, to help me. They said I was just imagining things. My efforts to get rid of it only made it angrier. I finally just gave up and followed its commands. I'm sorry. I'll stop all sorcery. I accept and will follow the way of Ehyeh. Mercy please," he screamed out!

"What should be done with your former master?"

"Just take it from me so I can be finally free." When an angel appeared next to it, the creature screamed in terror through the man and violently shook him. It knew what was coming. The angel reached in, grabbed the creature and they disappeared.

The man stopped shaking and slowly stood up shaking his head, "I feel like my head is empty. So many terrible thoughts are gone." He started dancing. "I'm free! I'm finally free!"

I said to him, "Ehyeh is here. He wants you to go and release the soul fragments you've taken and restore them to their owners. Cease witchcraft. Then wait for Ruah to come. He will show you the way."

His head drooped, "But I don't know how to restore them. I only know how to imprison them."

Warrior angels in armor appeared next to him. "These angels will assist you."

"What angels," he replied?

"Just look." Throwing himself backwards to the floor was my indicator that he could see them now. I smiled. I know the feeling.

The man stared at the angels for a while and then quickly jumped up on the stage and hugged me. "This is what I expected from these others. Thank you."

I said, "Thank Ehyeh. He's the one who has come to you."

"Yes. But your obedience has conquered the beast, where others have walked in arrogance or ignorance or cowered in fear," he replied.

He ran out waving, "Tell Ehyeh I will put all back and never follow the dark path again."

The circus was empty now. Coffee was still bubbling in a pot at the store. My poor hotdog had been crushed in the stampede. Fortunately, Ehyeh made me another one before I had to bring out my big guns again. He's very fast.

During our peaceful ride back to my farm I asked, "Ehyeh, who were all those people?"

"They're contras?"

"Contras? What's that?"

"They're people who are pretenders that say they're in our family but develop alternative farming methods. Usually they want to grow only what gives them wealth or pleasure or power. Their farms don't last for eternity. Most are tricked by the god you met by your gate, into believing they aren't contras."

"How can they be so tricked? He was easy to spot. Who is that god I met by the gate anyway?"

"He's the Eater. He eats lives. He eats farms. He especially wants to eat yours."

he pace back was slow. Ehyeh must have known my mind needed time to sort through all that I'd seen. We rode the same muddy road that I had used to escape my captors. Angels opened the gate where I met Farmer; we turned in and rode up to my barn. The word 'home' came into my mind. I never had a home before.

I'm thinking so much about all that happened and what Ehyeh told me that we got right up to my barn before I noticed, "What happened here," as I climbed off of Gideon to admire the changes? The barn walls looked brand new and an addition was off on one side.

"Your farm has had some upgrades," I could hear Farmer say behind me.

I turned, ran over and gave him a bearhug. "I missed you today, Farmer."

"It's nice to be missed, son."

Son? That sounds so good. I hugged him harder. And hugged Ruah. "So much happened today, guys."

"We know."

Of course. These guys are everywhere at the same time. I just didn't see them. "I have so many questions."

"Let's have supper then and talk about your questions," Farmer said.

This was the best supper so far. There were all kinds of unusual fruit. Never saw anything like them. Bright colors. Unusual yet wonderful flavors. "What are these?"

"We got them from your new fruit trees," Farmer said.

"My new fruit trees? What fruit trees?" There were trees right outside the repaired kitchen window that weren't there before. Some of the branches were hanging in through the open window over the counter. There wasn't just one kind of fruit on each tree. Each branch on each tree had many kinds of different fruit on it. "How's this possible?"

Ehyeh handed me another slice of something that was orange and red, "These are also from what you did today with me."

"Today? These trees and fruit grew just today?"

"Your farm doesn't operate in the dimensions you're used to. What you did at that circus and with that wizard produced much fruit and more to come. Your farm is a living entity," Farmer explained.

"I don't understand."

Farmer continued, "That former wizard has restored all the soul fragments that he had imprisoned. Families are already reuniting. Diseases have left people. He's talking to the contras that ran away, telling them about us and the Eater. We are working with him and others on their farms right now. All of that farming builds up your farm, Ryder."

"Wow! That happened already? We were just there. So, that's how it works. Let's do more. I want my farm to be hugely big," as I grabbed another piece of fruit and bit in.

Farmer laughed, "We have much in store for you, son. You'll see."

"Awesome. But what about this Eater guy? How does he fit into all of this?"

I heard Ruah in my head, "There is much to tell on him. Let me put it all in your mind." I instantly received all this information on him.

My eyes blinked at the three of them in disbelief, "He used to have such a huge farm that you gave him and he wanted more? He wanted to replace you guys? That's crazy!"

"He didn't agree with us when we offered godship to people. He considered people to be about as useful as worms, that should be treated as slaves. He became the first contra. He fooled many angels into going with him, convincing them that he would give them great fame, power and riches. You see, it's not just you who fell under the spell of these false treasures."

"Well, in my defense, I was a dumb kid and, I didn't know there were options. The Eater and those angels had no excuses. Then what happened?"

"We had to show them the barn door so to speak. We reduced all their farms to this planet," Ehyeh said.

"That must have gone over well."

Farmer added, "This enraged him more. He wants revenge against us. He steals, kills and destroys. Those in our family he especially hates. He uses lies, traps, diversions, dead-end roads, alternative ways and smoke and mirrors to confuse and dazzle people. All are poisons that keep and lead people to the Book of the Dead. He tricks people into giving their farms to him."

"Why don't you just lock him up somewhere so people can build and enjoy their farms in peace?"

"This moment will come. There are reasons that we don't do this just yet."

"OK. But I'm just a kid. How do I beat him and his army?"

"Many people try to beat him on their own without us and without our strategy," Farmer explained. "Don't do that. Always walk with us under our timing and our strategy and you will always be victorious."

"OK. But, what do we do next?"

"Right now, we're celebrating your victory." A stacked-high, layer cake appeared on the table, made of chocolate, caramel, cinnamon and some special ingredients, they said, that were not found on Earth.

Each bite was heavenly. It instantly pushed all my favorite old and new foods down the list.

Right below hotdogs.

CHAPTER 13

Slouched back in my chair, licking cake residue off my fingers, my stomach bulging out in front of me, my brain was still going through the process of deleting the dumb stuff and lies, and replacing it with truth and reality. How could I have never seen all this before? Was I that stupid? Well, I am just a kid, but still. And all those adults I saw at the circus. How can they be so blind, especially when it's all right there for them to see, reach out and take?

"Thinking out loud, Ryder," Farmer asked?

"I know you guys hear my thoughts. Thanks for showing me all these things. Thanks for setting me free from all the lies."

"We not only hear your thoughts Ryder, we knew about them before you were born," Farmer responded.

I licked some chocolate from around my mouth as I thought about that one. "You guys already know what I'm thinking before I think it?"

"Yes," they all said at the same time.

The tiny wheels in my head are burning and smoking now. "You know the future?"

"Of course," Farmer continued, "it's already there."

"How can the future be already there, if it hasn't happened yet?"

The words barely got out of my mouth and I'm riding Gideon next to Ehyeh and others all in white. Gideon is snorting, as we ride hard towards Earth that's up ahead. Then I was back in my chair with both hands gripping the table. "What was that?"

"You were just in your future," Ehyeh said.

These guys are so calm about this stuff. "You're saying, I just saw what I'm going to be doing in the future? Something I haven't done yet, but I was just doing?"

"That's it," Ehyeh said.

"Can I go into my future and see what I'm supposed to be doing before I do it and skip past all the mistakes?"

"No," Ruah answers. "You don't want to do that. Some things we will reveal to you at certain times during portions of your life here. Other things will remain a mystery. This is for the best for your destiny with us."

Probably a good plan, I guess. Knowing everything in advance would make me like some kind of robot.

"That's correct, Ryder," Farmer answered my thought. "Your free will is very important. The Eater's ways are all along your road. He has many traps waiting for you. When you willingly work with us, you can avoid his traps."

"Can't I just stay on my farm and dodge all the traps? I know Briella told me that's not a good plan, but it does seem safer. I don't want to end up back in the Book of the Dead."

"This is not the destiny that we want for you or anyone. We want you to introduce others to your family so they may take pleasure in what you're experiencing now," Ehyeh replied. "We want you to enjoy defeating the Eater and his army. And we want you to increase your farm. We want you to grow and function as a king and lord. We want you to have your full inheritance. You'll understand more as we move forward."

"Everything you're saying makes sense. I just need to be patient, I guess."

"Yes. Some areas grow instantly, while some areas are a process," Farmer went on. "And, we have certain missions that are best with your hand, while other projects are designed for Briella and so on. Projects interconnect with each other, even though people can't see or understand all the parts and how they fit together. When people do what they want or what others want them to do, their destinies fail or are hindered and they can become a disruption to other farms. The Eater then achieves victory. Do you understand, my son?"

"Yes, Farmer. I think so. I always want to work with you guys."

"You are way ahead of others, as most don't want to work with us or they don't know how. That's where you come in," Farmer stated.

"What do you want me to do? Like I said, I'm all in."

Ehyeh put his arm over my shoulders, "We were at a circus today, Ryder. There are many of these around Earth that come in all shapes and sizes, that follow strange gods. The Eater's in charge of almost all of them. We have shown you how it's possible to be in many places at the same moment. We will show you how to do that, as we did with Briella. We would like you to work with Briella. Would you like to do that?"

I'm thinking they already know that I like Briella.

"That's great," Farmer grinned, "because she likes you too."

I think my face probably turned red. Nothing slips past these guys. "What are we going to do?"

"We'd like you to operate as a multidimensional. You'll move through various dimensions, which includes through time, observing and conducting multiple actions, as we direct, at various locations, within these dimensions. At times, you'll be in conflict with sorcerers and also directly against the Eater and his gods, who all want to destroy you. The Eater has laid traps for you already. People who say they work on behalf of us, will also attack you, as you've already experienced," Farmer explained.

I was mesmerized by all that I was hearing, "That's sounds intense, but how do I do all that?"

"We'll teach you to be an irregular soldier like a guerilla or commando or a covert agent to break people out of prisons, conduct sabotage and attack enemy encampments."

"Oh. Like fighting behind enemy lines," I said excitedly?

"Yes. Sometimes operating openly and sometimes secretly or invisibly. Does all that sound good to you?"

That was like asking me if I'd like to have a plate of hotdogs when I'm starving. Who would want anything else in life? Jumping up on the kitchen table, I stomped around, pounded my chest with my fists and screamed out at the top of my lungs, "I'm an Eater-smashing gorilla! Don't mess with me!"

"We can take that as a yes," they all said as they laughed together?

"I'm so excited to be in your family I could bust wide open. All that you've given me so far is beyond what I can possibly thank you for." I had to catch my breath I was so happy. "Now you want me to move around through time and dimensions to save people and pound on the Eater and his friends. Wow! Just, wow!"

"You understand what we've said about who you are, right," Ruah added?

"Oh yes. You guys are already more powerful than all of them put together. I've learned that much. You also taught me that as long as I walk with you, we can't lose. And, don't head off on my own somewhere, even if it looks good, because there are traps."

Famer corrected me, "Just a slight revision to what you said. *You* are more powerful than all of them put together. Believe it."

"Just load me up, point me at the target and pull the trigger."

Finally, I knew what it was all about.

CHAPTER 14

It was a long night of tossing and turning, excited about all that had happened and imagining about what and where I'd be going next. Thinking about who I really am, not some made up lie I was told all my life. And words like 'immortal' and 'eternal being' and the big one, 'godship', stayed in front of my mind. I slid out of bed early and went to the window. It was still dark outside. That big angel is out there walking around the barn and farmhouse with his flaming sword. Not much of a talker that one. I slapped my face. Twice. It hurt. I'm definitely not in a coma. Turning around from the window, the three of them are here. They never sleep.

"Excited to continue," Farmer broke the silence?

"To the edge of time. And beyond," I answered. Immediately we were suspended in space in front of a raging wall of fire. As far as I can see up and down and, left to right, it was there. It should burn me to a crisp or at least bother my eyes but it didn't. "Where are we?"

"Well, you did say, "to the edge of time and beyond," didn't you? This is a star in another galaxy, as you call it. There are an infinite number of galaxies. All of these physical galaxies fit inside of universes that populate numerous dimensions that fit inside of eternity. This is a large star in this particular galaxy, like the star you call the sun in the Earth's galaxy. Except this star is two thousand times bigger than the Earth's sun. We want you to tell this star to shrink to half its size," Farmer said calmly.

"Say what? How do I get a star to do that?"

"Speak to it. It's alive. The star knows who you are. You must simply believe in who you are," Ehyeh declared like it's nothing.

Simply? These guy's definition of simply, is a lot more different than mine. OK then. I pointed my finger and yelled at it out loud, "Be half your size, star!"

Nothing happened. I said it louder. Still nothing.

"Ryder. You're saying the words but you don't believe them," Ruah says. "The star doesn't believe them either. Speak with your authority and power that we gave you." Ruah looked kinda weird sitting on nothing. Well, I mean, I used to think space was nothing. Standing on space must be one of those godship things like standing on water. Guessing I don't need oxygen out here either.

Concentrating on who they say I am, I see myself sitting on my throne, wearing my crown and robe. My ring is on my hand and my scepter is in my other hand. I am royalty. "Star. Reduce yourself to half your size."

It's responding. It slowly shrunk, stopping far away.

"Excellent," Farmer says smiling, "Now ask the star to increase to double its original size."

As I spoke, it slammed up instantly in front of us. Startled, my hands reflexed up in front of me as I crouched down. When I opened my eyes, my body was shining brighter than the flames that were shooting off from the sun. Turning my hands over and over trying to understand, "What's this?"

Farmer explained, "Remember I told you about how a star's light covers septillions of miles in all directions?"

Still staring at my hands, "Yep."

Farmer puts his hand on my shoulder, "A star is just created light. You are creative light. You are much more powerful."

"But I'm just a kid. Or, I used to be a kid. What do you mean, I'm creative light?"

"Who you are is creative light inside a physical body. A small fleck of you can destroy a galaxy full of stars. It can also create a galaxy," Ehyeh adds. "You just saw what's possible for you with this one star. A star that a few quadrillion Earth's can fit into. Imagine what is possible for you back on Earth."

This is way beyond where I thought I was going. This surely beats chasing after fame and fortune. "Is everyone this creative light?"

"Not exactly," said Farmer. "Think of each person like a dark star. Each person has been given limited powers confined to physical dimensions on Earth. They have certain capabilities within their life orbit. If they become part of our family, then they are no longer like a dark star. They enter into a new existence, like we said, kind of like a caterpillar to a butterfly. However, if they remain like a dark star, then when they physically die, they end up in a death existence. Their farm ends."

"I see. That's pretty easy to understand. You guys must be busy teaching so many people around the world like me and Briella."

They all put their heads down. This is the first time I'd ever seen them sad. Tears started to trickle down their faces. Farmer puts his hand on my shoulder and looks into my eyes, "Very few want to be part of our family, Ryder. Most willingly or in ignorance choose to be part of the Eater's family."

I didn't understand these words. "What?" That didn't make any sense. The Eater and his army don't have powers like these guys? He doesn't have the power to give life.

Farmer continued, "Like we told you, Ryder, the Eater once had enormous powers. He decided that he wanted it all. We have severely restricted his powers to just around Earth. He fools others into thinking that he's all powerful, but he isn't. He offers trinkets to dazzle people. He just uses them and throws them away when he's done. They don't realize that he steals from them. He steals their lives. Soon what little he has left will be taken from him and he'll be gone."

I turned to the huge star in front of me that I just easily shrunk and expanded. "What you're saying doesn't make sense. Are people braindead?"

"This is why we asked for your help, Ryder," Ruah says. "To be a multidimensional. To save lives."

"How does Briella fit into what you want me to do? Is she a multidimensional too?"

"Yes, Ryder," Ehyeh continues, "We want the both of you to work together on many assignments. Actually, she's waiting for us right now at our farm."

"Our farm? My farm or her farm?"

Farmer smiled, "No, Ryder, Ehyeh means our farm. Your farm is yours, but it's connected to our farm. As part of the family, you are entitled to everything that is ours."

These words are still odd to me. "So, what exactly do you mean by, 'everything'?"

"Our farm is eternity and everything in it. You inherited this."

There was no place for me to sit down. I guess I could sit in space. Too much information was pouring in for me to process. I just had a star do what I said, find out that I can create galaxies and now they say I own everything. They can sense my shock. My mouth opens but nothing comes out.

Farmer rests his hand on my head, "Maybe our farm will settle you down." Immediately we're all at an immense garden or is it a forest? The trees must be thousands of feet tall. Flowers as large as buildings. Strange animals walking around. I can see through some that look like water. The colors are blinding. I put my head down and closed my eyes. This isn't settling me down.

Ruah flips my hand up with his nose, "You don't like this part of our farm, Ryder?"

Opening my eyes to answer Ruah there was a lion right in front of my face sniffing me. I fell back and closed my eyes again, "Just give me a second guys."

It was just a second when I heard a familiar voice, "What are you doing down there, Ryder." Briella's here.

Briella was on the back of a white lion. I really like her smile. Jumping up, looking calm, "Hey Briella, whatcha doin'?" OK, that sounded lame.

"Come on, Ryder, get on. Let's go for a ride with Bruce."

The lion's name is Bruce? He looks me in the eye with one of his eyes of blue fire. Can he read my thoughts too? Great. OK, Bruce it is, as I got on behind Briella. We waved to the guys as Bruce headed down a path that looked like it was made of diamonds. It took us quite a long time just to pass the first tree. It must be hundreds of yards across.

"All of this is pretty amazing isn't it, Ryder?"

I'm not sure the word amazing covers this. "Briella? Aren't you even a little shocked with all of what's happening to you?" Maybe I should have manned up and acted like all of this was normal, but it's not normal. It's still freaking me out.

"Oh, yes. I'm still trying to take all of it in. It's hard to keep up with it all sometimes. We're so used to the small world on Earth and being told by adults that there's nothing else. Reality and truth do take some time to sink in." Bruce is taking us past a waterfall now. I can't even see the top of it. As my head twists around trying to see everything, I didn't notice that we were walking on top of the water pool at the bottom of the falls, until the whales breached up and splashed us. It's a big pool.

"Did the guys tell you that all of this is yours? I mean ours?"

"Isn't it fantastic, Ryder. We share all this and more, forever."

"But isn't there more people? I don't see anyone else around."

"Right now, we're going through some kind of special training. Apparently, there aren't that many that are interested in advanced training, even the few that are in our family. Don't you find that weird, Ryder?"

"Very weird. Why would anyone want to miss out on all of this?" A flock of strange birds is now zipping around us changing their shape, color and appearance every few seconds. They stop, suspended somehow around us, so we'll pet them. They have silky feeling fur rather than feathers. "Why are the animals and birds so interested in us," I asked?

"They don't see many of us and they know who we are. That we're most special family members."

"Did they tell you what they'd like us to do, Briella?"

"They said they wanted us to work together as multidimensionals. I don't really know what that means. Something about guerilla or covert-commando stuff."

We're going up a mountain trail now that looked like it was made of purple gems with gold streaks going through it. "That's right. Have they taken you to the star yet," Briella asked, as I gazed around at loose gems that are larger than me?

"Yeah. I was just there. I don't even know how to understand that. Do you?"

"They're showing us how much we can do with them. Without them, we'd go back to our regular life, like most everyone else does or end up working one way or another for the Eater."

"Did the Eater come to you."

"Oh, yes. He said he would make all my dreams come true. It sounded good but I grew up with lots of people lying to me all the time so I told him I'd have to think about it. I never saw him again."

"With me, I wanted fame and fortune. That's the way he approached me. Good thing that I'd already met the guys and saw some things, otherwise he probably would have tricked me into going with him. How did you meet the guys?" The trail was taking us high up a mountain, yet we still hadn't gone beyond the tops of the trees. I leaned back on Bruce to see if I could see the mountain top. Nope. Where are we going, I wondered?

"Just after the Eater approached me, I met Ruah. I was at a place that the guys call a circus. Ruah walked in and right up to me. I wondered why anyone would let a dog wander in here. I bent down and petted him and asked him as a joke if he came here to join the rest of us. Of course, I never expected him to answer me. I could clearly hear him speak to me in my head. He told me I wouldn't find what I needed at the circus. I didn't know what to make of a dog talking to me and that others around me couldn't see him. He told me to follow him if I wanted to find the truth. Then he turned around and walked out."

"What did you do, Briella?"

"I stood there for a while, thinking I must be seeing things. Then he came back in and just looked at me, with an adorable, are you coming or what look on his face. I went outside with him and asked him where we were going. He introduced himself and told me he was taking me to a farm, where the truth was waiting for me."

"And that's when you met Farmer and Ehyeh?"

"Yes. The farm was all broken down like yours was when I met you that day. They asked me if I was hungry and what I wanted to eat. As I said, I didn't trust people so I thought about turning around and going back. Then I heard Ruah asking me why I would want to go back to shadows and lies when reality and truth were standing right here."

"Then what happened?"

"Then everything I said I wanted to eat was all waiting for me when we went in the farmhouse."

"Yeah, isn't that cool, the way they do that." We're still winding our way up the mountain trail. It's so peaceful. "What happened then, Briella?"

"Then it was getting dark and Farmer said I could stay in the barn if I wanted. I wasn't sure about that until Ruah, with that cute little smile of his, promised he would protect me if I was afraid.

I trusted Ruah. We went to the barn and it was so beautiful. The bed was exactly how I had dreamed a perfect bed would be. It had silky sheets and flowers all around it. Oh, I forgot. They also introduced me to my angel."

"Yeah. Me too. What's with him?"

"I don't know yet. I guess we'll be doing assignments with them later. So, Ruah woke me up in the morning and told me it was time for training if I wanted it. I didn't know what he meant by that but I knew I wanted the truth."

"When did you learn about moving through dimensions, appearing and disappearing and multiplying yourself like you did when we went riding with Ehyeh?"

"Well, that came after some incredible meals, joining their family, telling me that the farm was mine, building my garden, and giving me Ruah."

"Wait. Ruah is yours? They said he was mine."

"He's ours and anybody else can have him too."

"Oh. This stuff is confusing. What's this family thing all about, Briella?"

"Farmer told me that Ehyeh is his son."

"Really? I didn't know that."

"He told me he had a very terrible death."

"Yeah, Ehyeh said that. So, he *is* a ghost then?"

"No. Apparently the Eater had the right to hold everyone as his slaves. Ehyeh came here as one of us to confront him and beat him so people could be free to join the family."

"Really? Did he beat him up good? Must have been a good fight. I saw lotsa scars on Ehyeh."

"No, it wasn't like that. Farmer told me that Ehyeh came here to show us in person who we really are. He did that for a while and then he had to deliberately die and come back to life, in order to rescue us and change things back to the way things were before the Eater took over."

"Yeah, they told me about that metamorphy... thing we have to go through."

"Yes, metamorphosis. We give our old life, that's sitting in the Book of the Dead, over to Ehyeh and he exchanges it for a new life in the Book of Life. It's all kind of mysterious or mystical, and hard to understand for me, but I trust them, even when I don't know what's going on."

"Me too. They showed me the Book of Life and the Book of the Dead and told me about eternity. It's all so huge. I never heard about anything any of this stuff on the street. It doesn't make sense. Something this important and people don't even talk about it."

"I know. School didn't mention it and the circus I went to sorta talked about it. That's where I was when Ruah walked in."

"What were they doing there then if they weren't doing what we're doing. Like riding along here with Bruce?" I patted Bruce on his back. Bruce twisted his head and licked my face. "Oh, Bruce. You got me all wet." Then he licked Briella, making us laugh.

Briella continued, "We all used to be quiet and listen to a ringmaster talk mostly, unless we were singing. Then the people gave money."

"Money? You had to pay to be there?"

"Something like that. I guess you paid for them to talk."

"What did they talk about? Did they talk about Farmer and Ehyeh and Ruah and working their farms?"

"No. Mostly they talked about news that was going on in town or in politics. The performers would get very angry if you didn't follow their rules."

"Rules? What rules did they have?"

"Let's see. Well, nobody was allowed to talk except them. I was told that the ringmaster and circus performers were the only ones qualified to talk."

"Qualified?"

"Yes. There were some others like clowns that did certain things but you couldn't do anything unless the ringmaster approved it."

"Did Farmer qualify them?"

"I don't think so. They never told us of any times spent with the guys like we're doing."

"How can people be qualified to talk about the guys if they've never spent time with them?"

"We were told that no one can do anything with the guys until after you die?"

"What?" I almost fell off of Bruce. "That's crazy. How can they talk about the guys and farms and stuff when they don't know anything about it?"

"No one knows any different. Everyone believes what they're told. When I questioned one of their rules, I was patted on my head and told to run along and play. I was so mad."

I'll bet they wouldn't get away with patting Briella on the head now. "So, then what happened?"

"When I was alone, I would yell in the air hoping I would be heard. I wanted answers. I wanted the truth and the meaning of life. I wanted to know what I was doing here. I yelled out, "Is this all there is?" Soon after that, Ruah showed up and I never went back to the circus."

"Yeah. Ehyeh took me to one of those places. They were so messed up. I never knew what those places were. I was never in one before."

"There's lots of them around. The place I went to said that the laws and rules from other circuses were wrong. I was told only our place was right about everything."

"That's funny. Who'd believe that?"

"They all believed it. They got very mad if anyone left and went to a different circus. They called them all sorts of bad names. They warned us not to leave."

"Or what? The big, bad Eater would get them?"

"Exactly. They said anyone who left wasn't under the ringmaster's special protection anymore and were rebellious."

I almost fell off of Bruce again I was laughing so hard. "Rebellious? Special protection? People actually fell for that junk? Sounds like when the Eater tried to con me and scare me into following him."

"Oh, they're very serious about this. I overheard a few of the grownups talking about someone who left, that used to give their circus a lot of money, that they wouldn't get anymore. They said they couldn't even talk to them after that, because of their rules."

"What? They told people who they could and couldn't be friends with. Gimme a break."

"I'm serious, Ryder. One time a family that lived next door to us left the circus and I was told that I couldn't play with their daughter anymore. I was so upset. I cried all the time. We'd always been friends. They ended up moving away because of the way they were being treated."

"I'm so sorry about you and your friend, Briella. That sounds so mean to treat people like that. They said that these were Farmer's rules?"

"They never said. I asked why I couldn't talk to her anymore. They just told me, "That's the way things are, sweetie. You'll make other friends." Ehhhh! I hate being treated like a kid!"

I never saw Briella mad like this before. "But we *are* kids, Briella. Well, sorta."

"I know, but they think we're stupid. We're not."

I couldn't see her face but I could hear Briella crying. I put my hand on her back. "It's OK now, Briella. Me and the guys are your fam now. Look, there's the guys up ahead. We can talk more about this later."

CHAPTER 15

he trail emptied out upon a huge plateau that looked like blue glass, although blue seemed like such a bland word to use. There're angels all over the place. I still wasn't quite used to angels. Some were different colors, even their faces. Others wore armor, had weapons and are standing in chariots with horses that are burning with fire, but they aren't being burnt. Creatures on fire too, that have different heads looking in all directions all over it and many wings. The two with the Books are here. I tapped Briella on the shoulder and whispered in her ear, "Briella, what is this place?"

She whispered back, "I don't know, Ryder. Isn't it beautiful?"

Briella jumped off Bruce, gave him a big hug and kiss, "Thank you, you big handsome Bruce" and then quickly ran over to the guys to give them each a big hug and kiss.

I slid off of Bruce and brushed his forehead with my hand. He leaned forward rubbing against me to get more. He was a monster sized lion, way taller than me. "Thank you, Bruce. You're the best ride I ever got from a lion." And the only one. Bruce walked over to some other lions that were lying by a magnificent throne and laid down. The throne had a rainbow circle around it. The circle's made up of different colored angels that are bowing and speaking in some language that I don't understand. Others are pouring things on big pots of fire that has sweet, smelling smoke drifting up from them. Everything is so intense, my eyes can barely take it all in.

Turning to look out from where we are there are mountains made of gems, trees I've never seen before, rivers and a blue-green ocean in the distance. As far as I can see are angels. I see what looks like small galaxies full of planets and stars spinning around overhead. One thing's for sure, Farmer's farm is way cooler than mine.

I ran over to the guys who were waiting for me. "Well, what do you think, Ryder," Farmer says with a smile? "Do you like our little farm?"

"Like? You guys are funny. I couldn't even imagine a place like this. How long did it take you to build it?"

"Eternity. So far," Farmer says smiling as he brought Briella and me in for a big hug. "Did you enjoy your time with Bruce?"

"Oh yes, Bruce is a wonderful lion," Briella smiled.

Trying to be funny I added, "But he doesn't talk much."

As Ehyeh was walking over he heard me. "That's strange, Bruce usually has a very, dry sense of humor for an angel."

Briella and I both stared at Ehyeh thinking he was joking. When I realized he was serious I said, "Bruce isn't a lion? He's an angel and talks?"

We looked over at Bruce lying next to the throne. He winked at us, the same time we both heard in our heads, "Gotcha!"

"Just when I thought all you're showing me couldn't get any better, it gets much better," I said. Briella was happily amazed too.

"It's all so pretty, Farmer," Briella says. "On the way up, Ryder and I talked about the circuses. About their ways and how strange they are." Briella glared over at Bruce, "And, you, you sneaky Bruce, could have joined in on the conversation."

Definitely a snicker came back at us. Might have been a snort in there too. I'll have to get together with Bruce and have a chat with him some time.

"They do like to make up many laws and rules, even though we've told them in writing what to do," Ehyeh says. "This is nothing new. They've been doing this for thousands of years. They say they represent us, but their fantasies and deviations keep people from being able to stand where you two are standing right now."

"Why do they do what is obviously so ridiculous," I asked?

"People want to do whatever makes them feel good. The Eater knows this, so, he caters to their whims. He enjoys destroying people and taking farms."

"What a dork. Will he be gone soon" I asked?

Farmer answers, "He and his celestial army will be sentenced for their rebellion when we're ready. Those who've died under him and his farm are sealed forever in the Book of the Dead. The ones currently in his people army still have opportunities to escape a similar fate."

All above my paygrade as they say as I marveled at all that's here. Just want to know how I fit into the big picture.

Farmer continued, "This is where you and Briella come in as our farmers. Most people on Earth live their lives in fantasy realms, but all of these realms reside in one place, The Book of the Dead."

Briella and I are both quiet and glued to the Farmer's words. This is what we've been waiting for.

Ruah goes on, "We have special assignments for you, to move people from the Book of the Dead over to the Book of Life."

Ehyeh adds, "And to attack the Eater, his crack troops and encampments, as we direct you. Remember to always work exactly under our plans, as we see and know what needs to be done in order and what needs to be left alone. You may be tempted to attack certain juicy looking areas on your own. Don't do that, as the Eater has many traps set up. Also, by striking out on your own, more fruitful areas that you can't see, will miss the harvest. Stay on the path that we provide."

Angels are gathered around and above us, watching all that is going on. I'm sensing that this is no ordinary event for this farm.

Farmer looks at us intently with a smile, "My precious ones, do you understand these important facts that we're teaching you? They are vital for success, your safety and your farms?"

After we both confirmed that we understood, the angels broke out into cheers and blowing horns. Billions of angels doing this made me very tense. Briella looked the same. What were we getting into that would cause such a celebration? What could we do that billions of angels couldn't do?

The guys knew we were startled and overwhelmed from this outburst. They walked us across the platform where an opening in the air appeared like the one at my farm when Ehyeh and I went riding. We walked through it into a quiet meadow, with rolling hills, a creek and many smaller trees. Taking a seat under one of the trees by a creek, "How did we get here guys? What was that opening we walked through," I asked?

Ruah answered, "That was a portal. You'll be moving through them into other dimensions and to other locations. Briella has been doing some of this already." Briella nodded.

Ehyeh continued, "Right now we're in the physical realm back on Earth. We knew this would comfort both of you from all the excitement you've been through. Soon you'll recognize the various dimensions and how to willingly move through them. This will come easier as you engage in this activity more."

It's so quiet here. I can hear a few birds singing in the distance. I'm much calmer now. I leaned back against the tree trunk with my hands behind my head and my feet stretched out, "Can we relax here for a while, guys?" Ah, this is nice.

"Actually, it's time for a swim," I heard Ehyeh say, as he picked me up and jumped with me into the creek. Standing up wiping the water from my eyes, there's Briella pointing at me laughing. I grabbed her hand and pulled her in. We splashed, dunked, swam and laughed. I really like this family.

Farmer called out, "You two must be hungry? Are you ready to eat?"

Standing in the creek about waist high, I splashed Briella, "I know I am," and rushed to get out of the water. I didn't quite make it. She jumped up on my back and got a piggy-back ride up to the grass where we both dropped down rolling around laughing. That is, until we both saw the huge table set up on the other side of the tree. It sorta looked like the table when I first came to my farm. The table was solid gold with diamonds in it as big as softballs. There were other gems embedded in the table too. Emeralds and rubies, I knew, but some I didn't know what they were.

The top was smooth as glass and totally empty. Briella and I both looked at each other. "Where's the food, Farmer?"

"You know enough by now to be able to make food don't you," Farmer says. "Work together."

Briella and I looked at each other again. Briella says, "What do you want, Ryder?"

"How about some hotdogs?"

Briella said, "Ew."

Not a hotdog lover I see.

"How about some watermelon" she countered?

"OK. I like watermelon too." I didn't. "How do we do this?" The guys were standing there watching us.

"Like we did with the star, Ryder. Let's both concentrate on making hotdogs and watermelon appear."

I wasn't sure. "Yeah, but the star was already there. How do we make something from nothing?"

We thunk on that one for a while until Briella said, "Well, there's molecules, atoms and elements floating around all over the place that we can't see. There're different kinds of molecules that make up everything. They're here, but we just can't see them because they're all spread out. Let's tell the molecules that make hotdogs and the ones that make watermelon, to all come together in piles on the table."

The guys were all smiling, so, I took that as a sign that Briella was right. "How did you know that, Briella?"

"I don't know. I was just thinking and suddenly it was there." Then she looked over at Ruah, "Were you sliding me that tip, Ruah?"

I could hear Ruah laughing in my head, "Why don't you try it and see." Briella and I both nodded at each other at the same time. So, she heard Ruah laugh too.

Briella grabbed my hand and we stared at the table. I don't know what was going on in her head, but I saw myself sitting on my throne again, like when I was in front of the star. I started to see tiny things floating around all around me. They were everywhere. When I concentrated on hotdogs and watermelon, certain ones started to shine. I told them to come together to form hotdogs and watermelons on the table. Nothing was happening. Oh yeah. I have to believe it's going to happen. I looked over at the guys. They told me who I was now. I spoke again, knowing it was going to happen. I heard Briella say the same. I could actually see certain molecules moving around and slam together. Something started appearing on the table. It's working. Briella and I both squeeze our hands at the same time. This is so cool.

We kept focusing on it and they all came in. Hotdogs and watermelons all over the table. Briella screamed, hugged me, kissed me on the cheek and jumped up and down clapping, "We did it, Ryder! We did it!"

The guys came over and congratulated us, "Well done you two," they said! "Well done."

We zipped over to the table, where I grabbed me a hotdog and Briella her watermelon and we slammed them in racing each other to see who could get the most in first, quite proud of ourselves for making them out of thin air, that is, until... we spit them out on the ground coughing and gagging.

The guys were definitely holding back laughter. "What's wrong," Farmer asked, as we were spitting, trying to get rid of the taste?

They already knew what was wrong, but I answered anyway, "This hotdog is terrible. It smells and tastes like someone's wet, smelly sock!"

"This watermelon tastes like a sponge soaked in sewer water," Briella added!

Their laughter finally sprung forth. Briella and I looked at the slop we made in our hands and slowly started laughing too. I don't remember ever having this much fun from a mistake.

Ehyeh explained to us what happened, "You have to be specific when you do things. If you want hotdogs hot and watermelon cool and them to have a specific taste and texture, you have to order them that way. Reality responds accordingly. And..." Ehyeh snaps his fingers to open one of the watermelons to reveal a hotdog in the middle of it. I don't even want to think about how that watermelon-hotdog mess must smell and taste.

Briella's and my face contorted as we both said, "Ew," at the same time and then started laughing again.

Farmer adds, "And if you want plates, forks, knives, spoons and something to drink with a cup to drink it in, you have to do that too."

We both sighed.

Farmer said, "Don't be concerned my great ones. It'll all become easy the more you do it. Miracles will become second nature."

Our heads snapped towards each other, as we silently mouthed the words, "Miracles!" We grabbed each other's hands, jumped up and down, saying it over and over, "Miracles! Miracles! Miracles!"

While we were celebrating, the guys filled the table with steaming hotdogs with mustard and relish on buns and watermelon slices on plates. Crystal pitchers with ice formed, filled with root beer for me and others with lemonade for Briella. There were no surprises this time, as we dug in and chomped with pleasure.

Later, the guys introduced Briella to my favorite cake. I didn't want this day to end.

CHAPTER 16

Over the next several months, Briella and I were training to be God Ops. Short for God Operators. Don't know why but, Briella didn't like being called a guerilla. So instead, we came up with this cool name that the guys approved of. The name seemed to cover all the various dimensional operations and covert activities, that the guys told us we'd be doing. I didn't tell her, but I liked it better too.

We were quite surprised to find out that we were the first ones exposed to what we would be learning. The guys told us that because we were entering a new phase of eternity, a different intensity was required. Briella and I didn't understand all of this or why we were chosen, but we're honored to be the pioneers. Maybe they'll tell us all about it one day.

And, we finally found out what those big angels were doing around our barns. They're both a special breed of angel to assist us in some of our God Ops. They're called, Waster angels.

"Bre, come in a little slower this time, you're zooming in too fast. I want to look up and see you fly in and then drop down like those superheroes do it. You know, with their cape fluttering in the breeze and their one leg bent at the knee." We decided that during God Ops, we would call our robes, capes.

Bre shot off like a bullet and came back like I described and landed right next to me. "You look so cool, Bre, but next time, do it with your hands in fists. Let me show you," as I disappeared and came back slow, landing next to her. "How was that?"

"You're right, Ryder, you look pretty awesome, but I'm not sure we're supposed to play around like this."

"Why not? No sense in hiding good talent." I then popped a bunch of me all around her, took off and came back down slow in a group.

"Ryder? What are you doing? Now you're just being a showoff," Briella laughed, as I landed all around her.

"I know, but this is fun." I then started several sword fights with myself with our training swords, making swishing sounds like I was a swashbuckler. The swords and I were moving so fast we were like a streak of white and red light. "Bring on the super villains. Yeah! Take that! And that!" I was getting into this new life pretty good.

"Ryder, we're supposed to be over at your barn to go riding with Ehyeh right now and we're late."

"Late? How can we ever be late for anything again? Let's step back in time and we'll always be on time." I was feeling mucho playful today.

"You know we're not supposed to do that outside of our Ops from the guys. That secret ability wasn't released to us to cover up our wrongdoings. We're not playing a game ya know."

She was right. "I know. OK. Let's pop over to my barn and apologize to Ehyeh."

We opened a portal, stepped through from Briella's farm and over into my barn where Ehyeh was already by his horse waiting for us.

"I'm sorry, Ehyeh. I got caught up in all the excitement of training with Briella and got us both late for our ride with you. Please forgive me."

"I'm sorry too, Ehyeh," Briella said. "I shouldn't have been late either."

Ehyeh smiled and hugged us, "You're forgiven my dear brother and my precious sister. I love you both. Let's go for our ride."

Much has been sorted out in my head during our months of training. Briella and I are heirs to everything. That's everything in existence in all dimensions. I know. It's hard to believe. Ehyeh is our brother and Farmer is our father. Something to do with our DNA changing when we decided to become part of the family. Not sure how that worked, but hey, I'm still just a kid. A God Ops kid. Still haven't figured out Ruah yet. But that's OK. I don't have to figure him out.

We rode along the hills of my farm, which had grown considerably since I arrived. It's constantly expanding and being upgraded. The barn has had so many changes done to it it's the size of a mountain now with many floors. The farmhouse looks like a chateau, as I call it, because it looks like a picture that I saw one time. Maybe the guys took that design from my memory because they knew I really liked it. They haven't taught us that one yet. My farm chateau is built into the side of an entire mountain range. The pond where I met Ehyeh is now a very large lake, with mountains all around it and my garden has grown so big I haven't even been to all of it yet. And Briella's place? It's even larger and more magnificent than my farm. She calls her farmhouse a palace.

"Did you hear me, Ryder," Ehyeh asked?

"Sorry, big brother, I was daydreaming about all that's been happening since I've arrived. It's so far from where I came from."

Ehyeh laughs and slaps me on the back, "That's because we love you and Briella so much. We bless our family without measure. What I said was, are you and Briella ready to head out on your first Op? Briella said, yes. How about you?"

"Our first Op? Really!" This is what I've been waiting for. I tried to act cool. "I'm ready when you guys say I'm ready." Inside I'm busting.

Briella wasn't doing so well in containing her excitement though. She kept yelling, "Yes, Yes," while pumping her fist and arm in the air.

"What will we be doing," I asked?

"Farmer, Ruah and I would like you to take on the Eater. Let's let him know there's some God Ops in town. What'd ya say?"

Briella stopped pumping her fist. She was motionless. I started coughing and laughing, looking at Ehyeh thinking he was joking. Nope. He wasn't joking. "You want our first God Op to be directly against the Eater," I asked?

"You guys are ready," Ehyeh assured us. "He'll never know you're coming. You'll attack one of his pets. In and out. Sound good?"

"Won't he retaliate against us and our farms," Briella asked a bit concerned?

"He'll try. He'll definitely be mad. That's OK. He's angry all the time anyway. And, he already knows about you two, as he tried to kill off your destinies before and it didn't work. I promise you'll enjoy it."

"Well, this *is* what we've been training for, Briella. Let's hit him where it hurts!"

"You're right, Ryder. I was just a little surprised he'd be our first Op. I know we can do it. What is it we're doing, Ehyeh?"

"Your Waster angels, Adlai and Elkin, will be going with you and your horses, Gideon and Shiloh."

Briella asked, "Are you, Farmer and Ruah coming with us?"

Great question I thought.

"We'll be with you as we're everywhere, but you'll be doing the action. This is a team effort. Let's ride a bit more enjoying your farm and then see Farmer and Ruah back at your chateau, Ryder."

I really couldn't get enough of my farm. I know it was only a small bit of my eternity, but I found it to be more personal to me, at least right now. Briella really loved my farm too.

We had to cross over a long bridge that was made entirely of gold that spanned over a deep gorge leading to the entrance of my chateau. Getting off our horses we passed by the waterfall on either side of the chateau entrance. The waterfall had many colors, that danced as we walked by. I was told it's alive. The mist hit our faces as we got to the massive archway. Just the archway alone was about a hundred feet tall. The front of the chateau looked part building and part mountain. I don't know how Farmer did it. This was quite a growth spurt from my original run-down farmhouse.

When we walked in, there were angels everywhere. Never asked what they were doing. There were rooms in various directions on many levels. Entranceways had rainbows high over them made of gems that flowed like liquid. Some of the walls inside were just waterfalls. I'd been training so much I hadn't explored all of it yet. It was massive and growing all the time. All of it was inside of a mountain in a mountain range. I wonder what's in the other mountains? Room to grow maybe for my farm or things I haven't seen yet?

We made our way through some areas to reach the library. I really like this room. Briella's farm has one too. The room itself has many floors. I can't even see the ceiling. All the walls are covered in books and rolled up papers that I found out are called, scrolls. Farmer said I can take an eternity going through them all. And, I will. After Ruah taught me in one second how to read and write, I really enjoy learning now.

We finally ended up at one of the massive fireplaces in the library. Many people could easily stand up in it. A fireplace is something else the guys knew I'd enjoy. A fire was always roaring in it when we came here to relax and talk about the days training. Not that we needed a fire where we are, in whatever dimension this is, as I've never experienced being cold or hot. A fireplace is just cool. As usual, Farmer and Ruah are waiting for us by our chairs.

We ran up to hug them. "Did you have a good ride today," Farmer asked?

We both couldn't get our words out fast enough. We were so excited about going on our first Op.

The guys started laughing in enjoyment at our enthusiasm.

Farmer still hugging us, "We're so happy that you've both trained so hard and come so far and are willing to step into these arenas."

Briella asks, "Are we like superheroes now, Farmer?"

The guys all laugh some more as Farmer responds, "Superheroes are entertaining cartoons my great ones. You are beyond such small words to describe yourselves. Meagre words can't fathom all who you are. You've chosen God Ops to refer to yourselves and what you'll be doing. That's sufficient."

Just then some angels brought us some drinks and cookies. The cinnamon cookies are thick, moist and chewy and had become one of my favorites! The drink is a creation of mine. I got the idea from the special cake the guys had made for me, with a few upgrades. It tastes like chocolate, cinnamon, maple syrup, peanut butter, caramel, honey, brown sugar and spices. It's great hot or cold. I call it, liquicake. We sat in our plush chairs in front of the fireplace to enjoy.

"What will we be doing," I finally asked?

Farmer answered, "We're having you directly attack one of the Eater's most dangerous pets. It's quite the beast. The decay of death rests upon it. We want you to wound it and set millions of people free from prison. Both of you are ready."

I'm on the edge of my chair. "How do we do that," I asked, as I glanced at each of them slurping my liquicake?

I can hear Ruah, "You'll ride into the place where it currently lurks. Your Wasters will be with you. As it all unfolds, rely on your training and our direction."

Briella asked, "When do we go?"

All of them are smiling. Crumbs fall out of my mouth as I'm in the middle of a bite, "What? Now? You mean, right now," I mumbled through the cookie in my mouth?

Ehyeh slapped me on the shoulder, "Well, your horses are saddled. And you are both anxious to get at it aren't you?"

I guess I thought I'd get to sleep on it a bit. I stood up a little slower than everyone else. All the training I had was going through my mind like a blur all jumbled up, as we walked through the library back to the horses. Would I know what to do, like Farmer said?

When we walked out the front of the chateau, our horses were snorting and stomping their feet in excitement. I wasn't as pumped to get at it as they were, as I still had fog-head. Training was training, but this was the real deal. Briella looks like I feel. I guess puking right now would be out of order.

The Wasters are here in their full armor, with their barn-sized swords in hand. I feel better now.

Ehyeh walked up with a surprise for us. He had two, dark, ruby red swords with scabbards and belts in his hands. He handed one to each of us, "I forged these swords for you from my blood. You'll be guided on how to use them. They'll never fail you."

"Thank you, Ehyeh," we both say as we happily examined them. We'd only had training swords before. The blades glowed with a blazing, white light inside that reflected in our eyes as we gazed at them. I feel a lot better now.

We strapped on our new swords, mounted up and got set. I could get on myself now like a pro and have become quite the horseman. "Any last words before we take off," I asked them, as I nonchalantly slipped the partially eaten cookie into my pocket?

Farmer says, "My great ones. You're not to kill it. It's not it's time to die. You're just wounding it and setting prisoners free. You'll know more of what I mean when you get there."

"Where is there," I asked?

A portal opened up on the other side of the bridge giving me my answer. It was a much larger one than I was used to, probably for the Wasters to fit through.

This is it.

Taking a firm grip on my sword, I pulled it out of its scabbard and raised it high over my head. I kicked Gideon, who rose up on his hind legs. My cape was very cooperative, fluttering itself perfectly all around me. There's war in my eyes. "The Eater wants me? Well, here I come!" Turning Gideon, we galloped across the bridge and jumped through the portal, quite sure I looked as supremely cool as possible.

I couldn't see a thing over here.

CHAPTER 17

anding on the other side of the portal in almost total darkness I could barely see past Gideon's head. I turned around to see if Briella and the Wasters had followed me through, "Briella? You here?"

She startled me when she rode up beside me. "I'm here, Ryder," she said in a low voice. "Pretty wild exit there, Mr. God Ops guy."

"Did you like it? Was it cool? How'd it look when I swirled my cape open when Gideon rose up, and ya know, when I was swinging my sword around in the air?"

"It was beyond stupendous oh great and wonderful caped, guerilla. I'm pretty sure my heart skipped a beat. Can you do it again?"

Briella was messing with my head. I like Briella.

We both laughed. "Yeah, I guess it was a little superheroesque." OK, back to business. "What are the Wasters doing over there?" We could see their flaming swords swishing around in the cloudy-smoke.

Ah, good, their actions were causing the dark clouds to swirl and clear off, making it easier for us to see. I could see Briella better now. She had her sword in her hand like I did, both of us scanning. The Wasters suddenly stopped what they were doing and disappeared in the smoke. It was so quiet. I could sense something was about to happen. "What are we looking for," I whispered to Briella?

"I don't know." Then she gingerly slapped me on the arm with her sword blade and pointed. It looked like a very large pair of red eyes ahead of us just floating in the dark mist. As more of the fog faded away, its body slowly took shape revealing an enormous black horn sticking out of its head, with smaller horns all over its body. It looked part rhino, part dragon and part porcupine. Safe to say it was much larger than my chateau.

I'm sure we were both thinking, what do we do with this thing. I leaned over to Briella with one eye on the beast, "I think the guys sent us to the wrong place."

Smoke was coming out of its mouth and even out through the horns on its body as it stared at us. Very strange beast indeed. I wonder where the Eater is?

Our little standoff didn't last long when I saw one of the Waster's swords come down in the far distance behind it and cut off part of its horned tail. It let out a deafening shriek as it ran off to the left. The other Waster was waiting for it there and sliced off another piece of it. They had positioned themselves behind it as it was sizing us up. I like these Wasters.

Black blood was splashing out of its wounds now as it turned abruptly and ran straight at us.

I heard Ruah's voice in my head. I knew what we were supposed to do next. I nod at Briella the same time she nods at me, "Let's take it, Ryder," Briella yells! I really like Briella.

She kicked Shiloh and banked off to the left, as I rode off to the right, forcing it to go in-between us. It roared as it came charging at us. Our swords were out, our bodies were glowing, light was flashing out from our chests, our red capes flowed all around us. We're both smiling when it reached us. Just like in training, I was moving so fast it was like the beast was running in slow motion. Black liquid was spewing out of the horns we were slicing off with our swords, as it went by. The light bursting out from my chest was also burning horns off, as I struck it over and over until it disappeared behind us into the fog.

Our horses were snorting in excitement. Briella and I were out of breath from the rush. My sword is covered in the beast's black blood. I yelled out, "Here we are, Eater! Want some," as I scraped the tip of my sword along the ground?"

I was ready for him now. We couldn't hear the beast anymore. He didn't come back for another round.

We rode around looking at the vast number of horns on the ground that were gurgling black blood and gasping like fish out of water, perhaps trying to stay alive. I was surprised we'd cut off so many. What are these things?

"Briella, what was all that? And where are the prisoners that we're supposed to set free? And where's the Eater?"

"I don't know, Ryder?"

When the smoke cleared out, a large hole or portal full of flames opened up in the ground. Now what? The Wasters started swinging their swords down, breaking the horns open that released people that were trapped inside them. Lots and lots of people. When the people poured out, the Wasters tossed the empty horns into the flames. When the last horn went in, the portal closed, leaving a horde of pale and scared looking people covered with massive, black, oozing tumors all over their bodies surrounding us in all directions, as far as I could see. There must be millions of them.

"Who are you," I asked?

Each one we heard from had a strange account of their prison life. People of all ages were here from babies to seniors. Most said they'd been captive all their lives. Many had been in various prisons, moving from one to the next. Others said that they'd willingly walked into their prisons. Most said that they'd enjoyed them, which surprised me.

"Why would any of you walk into a prison? Why would you stay if you could leave," Briella asked, just as stunned as I was?

One old woman walked up to Briella and said, "Remember me?"

Briella looked at her intensely, trying to see around the tumors on her face. "Yes. You're from the circus where I met Ruah. You're all from circuses," as she looked around stunned?

So, that's who these people are, I realized. They're prisoners from various circuses.

"Yes," the old woman continued talking to Briella. "You walked out of prison long ago. I didn't know I was in a prison. It was like my mind was in a haze. I couldn't see or think clearly."

My eyes widened as I realized, the fog from the beast was what blinded their minds. But what's all these black tumors on them? Then I saw the tumors spell out familiar words like 'witchcraft', 'pornography', 'bitterness', 'lying', 'thief', 'backstabber', 'religion' 'adultery' and 'murder'. These were the words I saw on people when I went to that circus with Ehyeh. Some other words were there too, like 'rebellion', 'pride', 'false-seer' and 'wolf'. Must be some kind of diseases afflicting them. But I didn't see the strange creatures on them here. They must have been stuck in the horns when they were thrown down the fire portal. I shook my head trying to understand it all as all these people stared at us.

I looked out over this sea of people. What to say? Then Ruah's voice came to me again.

I yelled out, "Can everyone hear me?" My voice echoed like we were in a canyon. "All of you are free now. Free to do as you choose with a clear mind. You've heard of Farmer, Ehyeh and Ruah.

They're the ones that sent us to set you free. They want you to join their family. Our family. The family offers eternal life. The ways you've been following are the Eater's ways. He has tricked you, trapped you, tortured you, afflicted you with diseases and blinded you from the truth. His alternate ways were leading you to destruction and death."

As I was talking, the portal we came through opened up behind us where everyone could see the golden bridge in front of my chateau and the guys standing on it.

I continued. "All those who want the only way to life can follow us. The guys are waiting to show each of you, how to operate your farms. And, any of you who would prefer to return to the prison comfort of the fog, go and return to your master," as I pointed to where the beast had disappeared.

Briella and I turned our horses and road through the portal with the Wasters along beside us. We dismounted next to the guys and gave them each a hug.

"Well done, you two," they said, "as well as you also, Adlai and Elkin," who both bowed and took positions on either side of the portal entrance.

Briella and I turned around expecting that the people were following us but no one was there. "I'm sorry, guys." I looked concerned at Ruah, "Maybe I didn't say the words you gave me the right way."

"Wait," Ehyeh said.

A few hands poked through the portal and then some feet, slowly at first and then as a steady stream they came. And, when they came, the tumors were no longer on them.

Farmer, Ehyeh and Ruah split off into sets of the three of them and disappeared with each person, heading off to their farms, I guess.

I don't know how long all of it took, but it was all wonderful. Briella and I were hugging each other, laughing and jumping up and down as more came through. I walked over to Adlai and Elkin and stuck my fist up and out for a bump, "Come on guys. Don't leave me hangin'." I was quite sure I saw smiles as they leaned down for the hit.

When the last of them came through, the portal closed, Adlai and Elkin bowed to us and disappeared, which left us alone with the guys.

Briella and I gave our horses each a hug and kiss on the nose before angels led them away, "You were awesome, Gideon and Shiloh. We couldn't have done it without you." They were obviously very pleased with the compliment.

My stomach wanted some attention too. I slipped my hand into my pocket... ah... still here. I nonchalantly shoved the cookie into my mouth when no one was looking.

"Come, my great God Operators. Come," Farmer said hugging us under each arm and walking us to my chateau. Ehyeh was on my other side and Ruah was next to Briella. I just noticed. There're a lot of angels here. A lot. Some angels are clapping and bowing as we walked by them. Others are blowing long trumpets.

"What's all this," I asked as we walked into the chateau?

Ehyeh said, "This is a celebration for what you've done. You've wounded a great, pet monster of the Eater's and rescued millions from its prisons. Recognition is due. Come." We walked along a gold and jeweled pathway, covered in flowers that were falling from above.

We made our way through to the back of the chateau into my garden, walking between rows of animals who've been standing here waiting for us.

Past all of them, along the beach of my lake behind the mountain chateau we made our way. Briella and I looked at each other wondering what's up. "Where are we going guys," I asked?

"It's a surprise. You'll see," Farmer said.

We passed some pine trees that gave off such a sweet smell. I've never been over here before. We ended up at a beautiful rolling valley that's full of people that all started cheering as soon as they saw us. The table set up for us looked like it was made of one giant diamond. The cheering of our names went on for quite a long time.

"Ryder! Briella! Ryder! Briella!" It's deafening.

Farmer raises his hands to speak. His voice rumbled across the valley. "Eternal ones. Two of our family have just returned from a great battle. They wounded the Eater's great pet known as, the Heretix."

Thunderous cheering erupted again as Farmer said this name. Who is this beast I wondered? Why didn't we kill it? Maybe we can have another go at it tomorrow?

Farmer continued, "Not only that, but their attack has released twelve million, seven hundred and eighty-three thousand, six hundred and forty-three people from the Heretix' prisons, allowing them to freely become part of our family and grow their farms."

The intensity of the crowd's roar and angels blowing horns across the valley almost knocked Briella and me over. We had to hold on to the diamond table.

Farmer motioned for us to sit. As we sat, Ehyeh spoke, "Great ones. Enjoy the celebration with us."

It was an amazing feast. Many strange looking foods appeared on the tables across the valley. A quick smile came to Briella and me when, appearing on our table, were stacks of hotdogs and watermelon. And, liquicake. Briella liked liquicake, but she enjoyed her fruity-veggie drinks more.

Too bad. Some people live and others just exist, I say, when it comes to hotdogs and liquicake.

While we ate and drank, many people are dancing and playing musical instruments. I leaned over to Farmer, "Who are all these people? This is the first we've seen any others?"

Farmer spoke over the celebration so Briella could hear, "These are eternal ones that have accomplished many incredible missions for our family over thousands of years. Like you, their farms with us rewards them with an abundant harvest for eternity. These ones, unlike you two, have already stepped over from the Earth's physical realm. They're on different missions now."

Briella asked, "Why is there such a big celebration for us? What is this Heretix thing we wounded?" I nodded in agreement, as I bit into another hot dog. These are the best. I think I'm up to number four. Battling dimensional beasts with Waster angels takes a lot out of a kid.

Ehyeh and Ruah are mingling with the crowd. Such laughter and joy. There's no family like this.

Farmer responds, "You two, with your Wasters, have wounded a beast that the Eater has been feeding since we banished him to Earth. The horns on its body are prisons and circuses. When you severed those horns from it, millions of people were released to see reality, rather than a profane fantasy that they were tricked into following. The larger horn on its head we will deal with another time."

I asked, "Is this the Eater's army that we attacked?"

"He has a vast army that helps him feed the Heretix. Some of the army are foolish people from Earth. Others are those who joined the Eater's rebellion against our family and were also banished with him to Earth. This is just one of his pets."

Farmer looked at both of us, put his hand on ours and continued, "At one time, you, Briella, fed the Heretix and you, Ryder, fed another one known as, the Nullifidian."

Our eyes widened. "We did what," I asked? "The Nulli-

what? I never heard of it. How could I feed a thing I've never heard of?" Briella nodded saying she'd never heard of the Heretix before.

Farmer continued, "Well, for example, ignorance of a law doesn't mean a person isn't guilty when they commit a crime, causing them to end up in a prison. Every action causes a counter-action. That's a law of reality. Whether the act is good or evil. Whether a person does something or nothing. Briella, you fed the Heretix through attending one of its circuses. You then entered that prison. Ryder, you fed the Nullifidian by accepting nothing as reality. Nothing is still a prison. Although much of the blame rests with those who taught you both lies, it was still your personal decisions to stay in those prisons. You entered those prisons. Not recognizing or believing that you're in a prison doesn't make it not a prison. Prisons keep people from working their farms. You were in different prisons, yet both of you worked on the Eater's farm."

My head is spinning, "So, we were both in prisons before we met you?"

"Yes. But, not only were you in prisons, your actions helped justify these prisons to others, who viewed them as valid activities because of you and others partaking of them and so, they walked into these prisons to join you. You were both ignorant, foolish pawns in Eater's plans."

Briella slid her chair back from the table and stood up. She stomped over to the side clenching her fists and screamed. When she came back, she was huffing, puffing and frowning, "When do we strike the Eater again?"

Farmer stood and hugged her, "Soon, great one, soon. Now we celebrate our victory."

This settled her down a bit, "OK," she said as she ripped a hot dog in half and crushed it in her hand, "I want this to be the Eater's head!"

That Eater is in for a mess of hurt. Don't mess with Briella. Although, she could have crushed one of her watermelon slices rather than one of these nice, peaceful hotdogs.

As I looked around at the celebration, I stuck my fist out at Briella, "I'm glad we're free from prisons now, Briella." She fist-bumps me in agreement. I think she cracked one of my knuckles.

As I rubbed my hand under the table, "What's this, Nulli-dude," I asked, "And, when do we hit it?"

"The Nullifidian will be a God Op down the road for you two. Your next Op is against, the Traffiker," Farmer said.

The Traffiker? What's this one? I was ready to go tomorrow against it. Briella was still crushing my hot dogs, so I knew she was ready.

It would be a while. The celebration lasted for seven days.

CHAPTER 18

hyeh introduced us to so many eternal ones during the celebration. Some of their stories left me and Briella in awe, like killing lions with their bare hands and standing in fire and not getting burnt. We really enjoyed the ones that were about Ehyeh. We were so amazed to find out all that Ehyeh had done, so we could be in a family for eternity.

Over the seven days, Ruah and I went for long walks by a brook in the valley. He told me that not only was I a prisoner of the Nullifidian, but I was also a prisoner of the Traffiker, which was our next Op. He told me the Traffiker and the people working for it, were the ones that I was running from when I met Farmer. *That* prison I didn't walk into willingly.

Ruah knew this prison had injured me and would have eventually killed me had I not run away. I told Ruah that it bothered me a lot that I couldn't take other kids with me. He removed this guilt and shame from me for being a survivor, as it wasn't mine to carry, he said. He actually did remove it, as I couldn't hear it in my head anymore. Ruah comforted and healed me during these days. Briella joined us later on some of our walks.

"Ruah, who is this Traffiker that we're going after next," Briella asked?

It's so peaceful here by the brook, it's hard to talk about evil and bad guys. Fish that sparkle like gems playfully swim around the rocks of gold.

"This is a prison that Ryder escaped from. It's a complex prison with many branches like a tree. On the Eater's farm, his prince, the Trafficker, has been around for thousands of years, grown from lust and greed and from people who choose to ignore it. This beast traffics in humans, mostly women and children. It needs to be crippled."

Briella turned and hugged me, "Ryder, I'm so sorry you were in this prison."

"Thanks, Bre, but I think I'm OK now. Ruah has healed what was bothering me. I'm ready to bring some justice to it and to the Eater and of course, with you, my hot dog crushing partner."

She smiled, as I wiped away a tear from her eye.

Ruah continued, "You'll be returning to your old prison Ryder, to do a prison break for your friends and others and to teach the Traffiker and the Eater lessons that others have failed to do. Others that decided to build circuses instead."

"We wouldn't build a circus, Ruah," I countered.

"The horns you cut off of the Hendrix were grown by those who said the same thing. Their actions put and kept millions in prisons. The Eater has many traps set for both of you. Be alert."

Briella and I were kind of quiet after that warning. Still don't understand how adults could be that dumb to build a circus?

Ruah taught us so much over these days about who we really are and what was expected of us as family members.

I don't know how we stayed awake for seven days. Time works differently here in this dimension. Farmer said we could spend what seems like years here, but lasts only minutes on Earth. I don't quite understand it all, as with many things I've seen. I haven't seen all the dimensions but all of them are open to me. I'm told the Eater and his group are only allowed in a few of them. And one day, the dark dimensions will be gone. Good riddance. Until then, Farmer, Ehyeh and Ruah allow us, the honor and pleasure of building up our farms through wrecking the Eater and his follower's activities before the final leg of their judgment comes. Farmer calls where we are now, "the place before my wrath."

I asked Farmer again why he doesn't just open all the prisons and set everyone free to work their farms. It doesn't work that way Farmer said. People must choose. To choose, they have to have choices. I thanked him again for showing me the truth. It was rather an easy choice for me.

After the celebration, we made our way back to my chateau. The chateau had become noticeably larger over the last seven days. The mountains around the lake were taller. I could see other buildings now in the mountains, with ornate, jeweled balconies overlooking the lake. The lake was definitely wider, as the mountain range on the other side was further away. My mind still found it hard to wrap around all that was unfolding for me.

I wondered where Briella had gone off to. She'd been gone for a while. Maybe she was off thinking about all that Ruah had taught us.

The guys and I ended up in front of my library's fireplace. Ahhhh. I enjoyed the peace and quiet here. I could spend eternity right here, thank you very much.

I had just settled back in my chair when Briella popped in. I'm still startled by that ability of ours. She grabbed my hand and we were gone. Instantly we were standing at the beach on her lake at her farm. "Look, Ryder, look!"

"OK. What am I looking at?" I was playing with her. I can see how much her farm had grown since I'd been here last.

"Look at how much my farm has grown, Ryder! Isn't it beautiful?" It looked somewhat like mine, only with different shaped, jeweled mountains. And her lake was much greener than mine. She grabbed my hand and ran me into her garden, "Look at these new flowers, Ryder!"

The aroma from the flowers drifted deep inside of me. It was more than just a fragrance. "These are cute, Bre, what are these again," as I touched some of the obvious Rose of Sharon flowers?" I knew they were her favorite. I loved teasing her.

She pushed me into the pond next to the waterfalls. I came up sputtering water just as she jumped in next to me, hitting me again with another load of water to swallow. Fish were jumping up out of the water all around us having some fun with us too.

"Bre, you made me swallow a bunch of water," I said laughing.

"Serves you right for teasing me."

"Your farm is fantastical and full of great awesomeness, Briella. There, is that better?" She splashed me again.

After a bit of back and forth splashing, we had a cease-fire to float on our backs in the pond. Looking up, I couldn't see the top of the falls they'd become so big.

"Ryder, I feel sad for all those people in prisons like we were. I want them to have farms like we have."

"I know what you mean, Bre. The guys have it all planned out. For a couple of kids, we've done pretty good so far. I can't wait until we take a piece out of that Traffiker."

"The guys trained us very well. The Eater will wish he never messed with us."

As I was talking, Briella snuck over and dragged me under the water. I came up sputtering, "What was that for?"

"That was a test to see how alert you are," as she's laughing. "Gotta be alert for the Eater's traps." She jumps out of the pond, "Come on. Let's go, wet-head."

"Wet-head?" Briella was running down the path towards her palace. I did a speed jump and was waiting for her there. As she came into view, "Where've you been, foot-dragger?"

"You, cheater," she laughed.

"No sense in wasting good talent," I replied.

We walked normal speed through the various rooms and halls to get into Briella's library. It was a different layout, but similar in size. She loved fireplaces too. The guys were there waiting for us.

"You two have fun," Farmer said, as he pulled a pond flower off of my shoulder?

"Oh yes, Farmer," Briella answered, as she jumped up on his lap, hugging and kissing him on the cheek. "I showed Ryder how much my farm has grown. It's so beautiful. Thank you all."

"Your welcome," Farmer smiled, "But you have grown your farm through your own planting and cultivating. You're reaping what you're sowing. As I told you both before, every action has a counter-action. A harvest comes one way or the other."

Sitting down in one of Briella's plush, pink chairs, "We were talking about how we want to release more prisoners so they can grow their farms with you guys. Are we going again soon?" I loved this God Ops stuff.

Ehyeh leaned forward, "Ryder. We know that you've been anxious to move against the Traffiker. Certain factors had to align before you could go. The Heretix operates in the open. The Traffiker prefers to lurk in the dark. You're both going tonight."

Yes. I'm going to enjoy this Op. "What do we do with this one," I asked? "Can we kill it?"

Ruah responded, "As with the Heretix, this is a wounding and prison break. I know you were hoping for more, but those who harmed you, Ryder, will reap what they did to you and to many others around the world. You and Briella will be their harvesters."

Briella and I smiled at each other. I'm going to give this one a brutal thrashing. I pounded the arm of the chair with my fist.

After we'd gone through our mission briefing, we went over to the stable and weapons room. Angels had our horses ready.

Farmer hugged us, "I know you'll be tempted to go beyond the Op because of the evil you'll see tonight. Don't give in to the temptation. I know they hurt you, Ryder," Farmer said as he put his hand on top of mine, that already had a tight grip on my sword's hilt in anticipation. "Rest into our plan which is the most productive harvest that'll be achieved at this time. Trust us."

My hand released its tight grip from the sword, "Yes, Farmer, I will," I said, as I turned Gideon to catch up to Briella, who's already at the open portal.

We rode through, vanishing to other side.

The Wasters weren't with us this time but that's OK. More for us. Hunting evil was in my blood now.

We're hunting in stealth mode as we moved through various dimensions looking for our prey. We rode past many people, yet they didn't see us. The Heretix people were pale, scared and covered in oozing tumors. These ones around here are chained, torn up, bleeding and looked defeated.

The smell was terribly familiar. I stopped Gideon. "This is it, Bre. We're here."

"Are you sure, Ryder," Briella asked?

I saw one of the guards that I'd escaped from, who'd been chasing me that day I met Farmer. He looked much uglier now that I could see that creature resting inside of him. He was whipping some of the prisoners. The scars on my legs gave me pain, as they reminded me of this treatment. He's one of the nastier prison guards. Funny. He doesn't know he's in a prison himself. My fist retightens its grip on my sword, "Yep, this is the place." I remembered what Farmer said. Gotta ignore this guy, Ryder. Focus on the Op.

We rode past him and many other guards. We followed a trail that was leading us to what looked like a mountain in the distance. Some people were screaming and moaning in pain. Others just stared blankly out into space.

We came upon a mountain that was covered in what looked like large shields. It's the Traffiker. It doesn't see or hear us.

Briella looked up and down at the size of it. "Well, we found it. Now what? The guys didn't tell us what to do when we got here. We've got no Waster angels with us this time to get the ball rolling."

A scroll appeared in front of us and unfolded revealing gold and fire lettering spelling out the details of our battle tactics. It rolled back up and disappeared after we were done examining it. Sounded icky, but it doesn't get any plainer than that.

We got off our horses and walked up to the other people that were sitting in front of the Traffiker. Looking at each other, we shrugged and then sat down next to them.

"Ready?" When we came out of stealth mode the beast saw us, smiled, reached down, picked us up with some others and down the hatch we went. It smelled worse in here.

The scroll told us we had to be invited in to get past the many shields protecting it without raising an alarm. As it willingly brought us in, it was now at our mercy. Its interior was soft and weak. It wasn't like the insides of some animal. It was full of people in various cages or cells. The Traffiker was one large prison system made up of many smaller prisons. Nasty place.

We nodded at each other, replicated ourselves and moved in different directions. We smashed our swords through prison doors as we streaked along different levels. Some cells contained many people, some had only one person in it. Almost all that we freed were women and children. We motioned for all of them to come out, directing them to a rally point at the floor of the beast's interior.

We followed the scroll's strategies telling us that some of the cells were to be passed by. I don't know why. Perhaps those in there had to wait for another prison break for some reason. It was very hard to walk by because I knew what they were going through.

I broke open the last cell door at the same time Briella was done far across and above where I was. She formed back into one of herself and jumped down hundreds of feet to where I was. Yes. Farmer's right. We are greater than superheroes.

We both jumped down to the floor where a great mass of women and children had formed and were huddled together waiting. "Go for it, Bre." I'd given the talk about the guys, the farms and eternity at our last hunt. Now it was Briella's turn.

She rose to the occasion. Ruah gave her some good stuff. She spoke of the lies from the Eater, when he said that there's no one to believe in or nothing to hope for. She told them about the guys, our farms, eternity and their farms. She pointed at me telling them that I was once in the Traffiker's prison like they were but escaped to reality. And now it was their turn. She told them love is waiting for them. Even I was mesmerized by her confident voice. Their faces showed a hope I hadn't seen in those from the Heretix.

When the portal opened, we could see to the other side where the guys were waiting on Briella's farm. They said to them, "Come. We are here."

Unlike the hesitancy of the Heretix people, these ones raced to get through. We had to jump up and out of the way. We watched for hours as they moved through the portal. The guys were doing the same as they had done on our other Op, duplicated themselves and taking each one off over to their farms and onto their destinies. It was such a joy to watch and be a part of it. When the last one went through, the portal closed. Now it was time for some serious thumping.

Back into stealth mode we went to set our trap.

We lifted our swords and struck them into the beast's walls. It let out a long, piercing scream. We smiled at each other and at the same time thrust our swords in deeper and twisted harder. I really like Briella.

The sword's seemed to move by themselves in our hands. They knew where the sweet spots were.

Guards, with their creatures attached, burst through doors on each level. They panicked when they saw the empty cells and were scrambling around looking for the escapees. I enjoyed this. They were scared. I heard them say, "The Eater won't like this" and "The Eater's going to punish us!" The beast screamed louder when we slashed our swords again across its insides. The guards were really terrified now. They didn't know why the beast was screaming.

Then I saw him, one of my former guards, who'd taken a personal interest in me. Each guard had their 'special ones', as they called us. It took months of planning to get him where I wanted him so I could escape. His limp told me that I wounded him pretty good when I made my prison break. I jumped up over to him and stared straight into his eyes and his creature's eyes. Briella sensed what I was up to and jumped over behind me, "Don't fall into the trap, Ryder. We're not to deal with the guards and their little buddies. Let the Eater punish them."

"But you don't know what this one did to me, Bre. What they do with all these people." My blood was boiling and I wanted some payback for me and all the women and kids they torture.

"Let it go. Let our trap work. If you do something now, our trap fails."

She's right. Settle down, Ryder.

I stabbed the beast right next to the guard, which caused the side of the beast to violently jerk, smacking the guard down so hard it knocked him out. That'll have to do for now.

Setting our trap was to use our swords and the light from our chests to thrust, slash and burn into it, to make it screech as much as possible. Well... and, cuz we enjoyed terrorizing it of course. The light-show from it all was pretty cool too. Don't know how we were affecting this human trafficking system on Earth with what we were doing but as long as we were putting some kind of hurt into it and saving lives, it all worked for me.

The trap worked.

All the guards dropped down around us onto their faces and started shaking and crying. Finally.

The Eater was here.

CHAPTER 19

he Eater couldn't see or hear us, as he swiveled his head up and down at all the open cells, over at the guard that was knocked out and then at one of the quivering guards, "How many are gone?"

"Millions, my lord."

"Millions? How's that possible," the Eater yelled trying to be heard over the beast still screeching for no apparent reason?

"The how would be me," I answered, as I came out of stealth mode in front of him.

I was a bit surprised that I didn't shock him. He wasn't even mad. I'll have to fix that attitude.

"Remember me," I asked him?

"Of course. You're that stupid toddler that refused my offer."

He was trying to get to me. It didn't work. It's my turn. "Why would I want weak, limited powers like yours? I got a better offer."

With a sly smile, "You think my powers are weak and limited, boy?"

"I know they are. And I can give you a list of what I can do and you can't."

His smile tapered off, as he peered just briefly at the guards who were shocked that I was here and talking to their master in such a brazen way. They're listening to every word that I say. He's in the trap.

"Why don't you go back to your little farm, child. I'll deal with you later," as he turned pretending to ignore me.

"Let's see." I started to count on my hand. "I was standing right in front of your face in the middle of your prison farm here and you couldn't see me, unless I wanted you to. That means, I can move through dimensions that you're barred from. That's number one."

He turned and glared at me.

"Number two. You'll like this one." I instantly duplicated myself all over the inside of the Traffiker. The guards were shocked looking all around at hundreds of me looking back at them. All of my many selves said to the Eater, "You poor thing. You can only be in one place at a time. Tsk, tsk."

In response, he made himself huge, almost filling the inside of the Traffiker. I'm getting to him.

I went back to just one of me and continued, "Nice trick to scare little children. Number three. This is a big one. You might want to sit down. Are you listening? I can go anywhere in existence in an instant. You're stuck on and around this teeny, tiny, little planet. This planet is *your* prison!" I emphasized the word 'your', loud and clear.

He shrunk back down to normal size to face me. He doesn't look pleased. Time to finish up. "I'm sensing some hostility, dude. You definitely won't like number four on the list then."

Briella's sword appeared behind the Eater and slashed a brand tat across his butt. Now he looked surprised.

He turned screaming, as a smiling Briella appeared, "I'm number four, sweet cheeks!" His scream I think was louder than the Traffiker's.

We both transported back to our horses in front of the Traffiker, who was still groaning from all the thrusts and slashes we'd done to it. We got up on our horses, went into stealth mode and waited. The Eater appeared outside holding his butt, twirling around looking for us. He was unaware of our presence as we chatted right next to him.

I looked at Briella with my thumb up, "Bre. Yes?"

"Yep. He'll have that burn scar tat as a souvenir of what we did here."

"Nice! How's it look? He didn't even give me a peek. Not a very nice host." We giggled.

She tapped her sword, "This branded him real nice. Small payback for all he's done."

"Cool. Let's get outta here, Bre."

We turned our horses and left with the Eater still running around shaking his fist in the air mumbling something about how he's going to get us. Yeah, yeah, you're a scary wizard-master. Even Gideon snorted out a laugh. Definitely was a laugh.

"Let's take the scenic way back and savor this one, Ryder."

Sounded good to me. It was daytime now. We made the Earth a little brighter and a little safer last night.

We went through various dimensions on our way back, some we hadn't been through before. Eternity sure is big. We rode up to the bridge in front of Briella's place and got off and took a long time to look around. Words can barely describe it.

The guys were waiting for us up ahead. Excitedly we ran up to greet them, got and gave big hugs all around and commenced to speed talking about all that happened.

Farmer quieted us, "Before we go any further, we have a surprise for you two."

Together we both said, "A surprise?" This fam is awesome.

Ehyeh waved his hand opening two portals in front of us. "You each get to choose one."

What's this? We walked up to the portals and looked in. In the one I was standing in front of, I saw a tropical island with palm trees, fancy flowers, a big hut made of bamboo on the beach, surrounded by an emerald-green ocean. I thought, that's nice. I couldn't see what Briella was looking at in the other portal. She didn't look any more thrilled than I was.

Ruah said, "You're looking in the wrong place you two. Switch."

Briella came over to where I was standing to look. I hadn't moved yet. She screamed, jumped up and down and ran in. I watch her run up and down the sandy beach, into the hut, scream some more, run out and dive into the ocean. Looking over at the guys, "I guess she likes it."

Farmer said, "Well, go on, Ryder, look at your gift."

I walked over to the other portal and gazed at what was perhaps the most beautiful sight that up until now, had only lingered in my imagination. I loved my chateau, my garden, the lake and the mountains of course, but was feeling a bit overwhelmed by it all. But this. This was perfect.

I stepped slowly through the portal into a quiet forest. I could smell the sweet, fresh fragrance of pine and cedar. I inhaled, slow, deep breaths. I couldn't get enough. There're mighty red woods here, like the ones I saw pictures of in the books in my chateau library. I rubbed my hand along their brown, spongy bark. The guys came through as I was staring up at all the trees. "This is exactly like I pictured it in my mind, you guys."

"We know," Farmer says. "We created it to your specifications. Look around, see if we missed anything."

As I walked, I can see and hear many birds. A cardinal, swooped in and landed on a branch near me. I watched a few chickadees flit about and a red-winged blackbird. I'd just been studying about birds in my library. These were some of my favorites. I was introducing myself to them when the smell hit me, mingling with the smell of the pine and cedar. It smelled sorta like liquicake. The guys are smiling as I walked further down the path following the smoke and then there it was.

"You guys got me a log cabin made of stone and logs! It's just like that one I saw in my library!"

"We know. You didn't think we'd give you some measly shack, did you?" They're obviously pleased that I'm so happy.

Smoke was slowly drifting out from the chimney, that was making my eyes water. It wasn't crying, which is what I told myself as I ran around the outside of the cabin, I don't know how many times and then in through the door and up to the crackling fireplace to suck in a huge breath... ahhhh... what a dream come true. My eyes watered some more, while I spun around and around, dropped down to the wooden floor and kissed it, twice, and then hugged it too before getting up. Drifting back over to the door, examining the inside, that was full of beautiful furniture, flowers and a waterfall, my head snapped back. I hadn't even noticed. There's a small lake right in front of my cabin. My eyes watered some more as I ran over and dived in, coming up in front of the nose of a massive moose that was out having a stroll.

I gave the guys, who were at the shore now, a 'what's this' look. Farmer laughed, "You do like moose, don't you?"

"Well, I never met one. And I didn't think I'd ever go swimming with one."

Everyone laughed... except the moose.

Climbing out of the water I hugged the guys, "Thank you so much. This is all way past perfect. I love my chateau, but I really, really, love this place."

"We know, Ryder. We know that you and Briella want your dream spot to relax alone at and so we gave you these new gifts to celebrate your victory against the Traffiker and the Eater. You rescued many people who we're now working with on their farms."

We made our way over to some simple, wooden chairs in front of the cabin, that looked out over the lake and sat. "I'm so glad all those women and children are safe. I know what they were going through," rubbing my wrist where I could still feel one of my chain scars.

Ruah licks the scar, "You and Briella have much to be delighted with. You've saved many lives." Continuing to gaze out over the lake thinking about what Ruah just said, I rubbed my wrist again but couldn't feel the scar anymore. It was gone. Ruah's smiling.

My mind smiled as I thought about how much Briella and I accomplished since we met the guys. Life has eternal purpose on the farm I contemplated, as the songs of the birds from the woods mingled with my thoughts.

Farmer had perfect timing. "Oh good, they're here," as some angels appeared with trays of steaming, warm piles of cinnamon cookies. The smell made my mouth water. I hadn't eaten since well before our God Op. I'd inhaled three of them by the time more angels appeared carrying pitchers of liquicake.

Guzzling back some of it I sorta gurgled out, "What's Briella up to?"

A portal opened in front of us revealing that she was doing about the same thing we were, sitting in front of her bamboo hut in beach chairs with the guys, daintily nibbling pink cookies while sipping some kind of lime-colored, frozen drink in a tall glass with a tiny, paper umbrella in it. Probably tastes like watermelon and lettuce, I chuckled to myself.

We waved at each other and toasted with our glasses, as the portal faded off. It's a bit weird seeing the guys over there with Briella, while at the same time they're sitting here with me. Getting more used to it though.

"Briella's enjoying her new gift, as you're enjoying yours, Ryder," Farmer said. "All the people you saved are enjoying their new gifts too. Gifts of life. Rest and explore your new gift, son, and we'll continue with our next Op, when both of you are ready."

I slammed down another cookie and refilled my glass again.

This could take a while.

CHAPTER 20

 don't know how long I was at my lake cabin. It might have been a few Earth hours or perhaps years. Time is such an imperfect dimension when you're moving in eternal realms.

After swimming in and walking on the lake, hiking all the forest and mountain trails, climbing trees, meeting the birds and animals and eating tons of cookies, I was ready. I realized that people out there needed our help. My feeling must have been mutual, because, as I walked into my cabin, Briella and the guys were looking over a strange display in front of my fireplace.

"Bre!" I was so excited to see her.

"Ryder," she screamed as she ran over and hugged me! "I missed you."

"I missed you too, Bre. Did you enjoy your new place?"

"Oh. It's just so fantastic. It's a dream come true for me. And what about your place, Ryder? It's soooo cute," as she twirled around.

"Bre. It's not cute. It's, its," I was looking for the right word, "manly." I put my hands in fists out in front of me and shook them. The guys laughed.

She slapped my arm, "Oh, you boys and your man caves. My beach island is cute and I don't care if everyone knows it."

"Whose everyone, Bre. Nobody else will ever see it, unless you invite them there."

"Well, I mean," she slapped my arm again, "You know what I mean. Stop teasing me!"

I laughed and faked being injured holding my arm, "OK, OK, I'll tell everyone that your place is cute."

We walked over to the guys to look at what they'd set up. It looked like a small cube glowing on the table, which they said once unlocked, transformed into an eternity-transporting device. I called it a map.

Either we made ourselves small or the map became large, but we ended up being inside of this map, which was where we were going on our next Op.

As we walked through it, the guys took turns pointing out to us the step-by-step plans they wanted us to follow. This Op was different than the other two, in that this beast was just one person. Bre and I had heard of this violent leader, who was followed by millions of people around the world.

Many nations even had a dead or alive bounty out on his head. The guys showed us how all of his decisions and words spread out to infect people all over the Earth. All of this activity had destroyed not only the lives of those who followed him but these followers were instructed to hate and kill others like Bre and me. This was a real, nasty, bad guy.

As I was thinking, that it'll be great when we capture him and turn him in, the next words in the briefing hit us both between the eyes. "Then, you'll have to kill him."

Farmer's words rang in my ears. My eyes shifted to Briella to catch her reaction, which looked about the same as mine. "You want us to kill him?"

"Yes, Ryder," Farmer confirmed.

"But, attacking the Eater and his beasts and releasing prisoners is what I thought we'd be doing. I thought we'd capture this guy and turn him in, then what he's doing will stop." Briella nodded in agreement.

Ruah responded in his always calm voice, "This isn't the most effective strategy."

I was searching for what to say next, "Why don't *you* guys kill him or have one of the Waster angels do it?"

"Because we'd like you to do it." Ehyeh knew we were concerned. "You can certainly decline this Op if that's what both of you decide. Why don't you trust us and wait until the briefing is complete?"

We listening intently to the rest of the briefing of all that pivots around this one man. They're right. It will be his decision to die. Killing him then is the best strategy.

Briella and I trusted the guys. We both felt uneasy with this Op, but we knew millions of lives were at stake. We talked with each other as we were walking to our horses, "Ryder? Do you feel comfortable killing this guy?"

"Like the guys said, it will be his decision to die."

"Yes, I know, but we'll be doing the killing if it comes to that."

"Don't think about it so much Bre. It's just an Op." I couldn't stop thinking about it either.

The angels helped us with our gear and getting ready. The guys saw us off, as the portal opened and we rode through. There's no turning back now.

We rode high over Earth, across an ocean, desert and mountains. Arriving at this Op took longer than the others. We could have gone there in a moment, but the guys wanted us to have more time to come to terms with this one. They were right. Whacking some beast-system was one thing, but killing a person felt different. I knew this Op was necessary though, for so many people's lives, so I focused in on that fact. Briella looked like she went through the same process. Both our minds were locked in now on our mission.

Our horses are very smart. They know where we're going. I reached down and stroked Gideon on the neck, "Good boy."

It all looked just like the map. The horses rode down toward a mountain range where we stopped on a ridge next to a large cave and got off our horses. It's a beautiful, cool night. The stars above looked like waves of smoke from my cabin's chimney. I remember when I was face-to-face with one of those stars. As we walked in, we passed many guards wearing scarves and robes carrying rifles. They don't see us. The creatures controlling them don't see us either. We moved through many areas used for cooking and sleeping. There must be hundreds of soldiers in this cave complex. One room had many weapons and explosives in it. We continued on, just as we did in our briefing.

Deep inside we came across ten armed guards standing in front of a walled area with a locked door. This is the place. The guards were all wearing black, which didn't match the others we'd seen. "The bodyguards," we agreed, as we'd seen from the map.

We walked past them and through the door. Inside was a huge bed, which looked out of place in this cave. There he was, sleeping. He matched his picture in the news. But he wasn't alone. There were two young boys sleeping in bed with him that were younger than me. My hand gripped my sword, just a split second before Briella's hand landed on top of it to stop me.

"Ryder, don't. I know this brings back bad memories for you, but we have to stay on course." Bad memories. Briella had no idea. It hit a nerve. Pigs like this deserve to die. I struggled with Briella but she wouldn't let go. "Ryder, let's stick to the plan." She looked as disgusted as I was, but she was right.

"OK. But I hope he chooses death." The guys didn't tell us about this man's appetites during the briefing. Maybe they wanted to see how I'd react. I nodded at Briella that I was good now, so she let me pull out my sword. The light of Ehyeh's blood, lit up the room. I slapped him on the chest with the blade, introducing myself too hard on purpose. He jumped out of the bed and fell on the ground.

I leaned down to glare at him. His wide eyes kept looking at my sword. I pointed the tip of it at his face, "My name's, Ryder. I already know your name."

He looked past my sword at the door, "How did you get past all my men and my guards?"

"I walked right past them to see you. I have a message for you."

He bowed, thinking I was maybe an angel come to chat with him, "You must be one of the highest one's messengers. I am honored. What message do you have for me, great one?"

"Don't bow to me," I said, trying to contain my anger with a steady, calm voice. He sat back up. "The message is that you are to abandon your black, evil ways. You are to follow the way of Farmer, Ehyeh and Ruah."

His eyes bulged out of his head, his face turning almost as red as my sword. I thought he would explode as he barked at me, "You pagan! You dare to soil my presence with your filthy body and profane words. I'll kill you, you dog!" When he reached for me, I slid back and pointed the sword tip towards his face again. He landed in front of me face down.

"I'm not done with the message," my eyes staring straight into his, "you're not only to accept the Farmer, Ehyeh and Ruah, you are to publicly tell all of your followers that you were foolish. That you led them astray all these years with your false god you call, Yarikh. That they're to lay down their weapons and follow you on the most holy path that you've discovered. The only path that provides true life for eternity."

He looked up at me and laughed, "And if I don't do all of this. Then what heathen?"

"Then you'll die."

He stood to face me, "You stupid infidel. I don't fear death. When I die, I will go to the abode of Yarikh to receive treasures for all who I sacrificed to him."

"Oh yeah. So brave of you to murder innocent, unarmed people, like women, children and babies."

He pridefully smiled, "They are the most pleasant of gifts that I have offered to my lord and to secure my most worthy place at his side. I kill all who refuse to bow to his sacredness."

This disgusting piece of flesh was a living nightmare. Looking down at the sleeping kids, it turned my stomach having to breathe the same air with this monster, but, I had to stick with giving him the guy's offer. Gritting my teeth, "Unless you accept the message, the judgment of death has been decreed."

He wasted no time with his final answer, reaching back, he grabbed his rifle, leaning against the cave wall next to his bed, pointed it at my chest and fired. As the bullets flew out everything stopped. I tapped the bullets, that were suspended in mid-air in front of me, with my finger, "A tad warm."

Bre appeared. "What now, Ryder?"

Stepping away from the bullets to stand next to this horror-show who was frozen in-between time, "Sounds like he's made his choice. Shall we finish up?"

When we released time, the bullets continued on, bouncing harmlessly off the cave wall, at the same moment Briella shoved her sword through his heart.

He dropped the rifle, staggered back to his bed holding his chest, with a shocked expression on his face, perhaps feeling a small portion of what he typically dished out to the weak and innocent. "This is Briella," I said, before I thrust my sword deep into his head dropping him back dead into his pillow. The sound of the gunfire must have brought the guards rushing in with their rifles up, as the terrorist leader never made a sound. A few ran up to him as others searched the room right past us. They slapped and kicked the two boys that were in the bed until they were unconscious, thinking they did something to him.

A doctor ran in to examine him, quickly confirming to everyone that he was dead. Some of the men cried. Others just dropped to their knees in shock. A man who must have been second in charge, commanded the doctor to do tests to see if he was poisoned.

We walked past them all, as they were rushing around with the news and dealing with what had happened. But we weren't done.

Our briefing dictated that we stay here for three days. We didn't understand that part of our Op. We spent the days riding our horses through the mountains. It was very boring and desolate here. Barren mountains full of rocks and dust.

Occasionally we'd ride back to the cave complex to watch the chaos. The doctor had told everyone that it looked like the leader died from a heart attack and a brain aneurism. Actually, he died from the crimes against humanity he was responsible for and for rejecting the offer from Farmer, Ehyeh and Ruah to make restitution. They buried him the same day. The word spread far, as many came to mourn his death.

When the three days were up, Briella and I were sitting on our horses waiting for a signal or a sign that we could leave, when we heard a familiar voice, "Good morning, precious ones. Are you ready to finish this Op?" Ruah came from around a large rock that was next to us.

"Finish? He's dead. Bre and I thought we were done."

Ruah smiled, "Oh no, dear ones. Little has changed with his death. People are meeting right now to choose a replacement leader for the one you killed. All will continue as it has before, if that happens."

"Then why did Ryder and I kill him?"

"Follow me," as Ruah walked past us along the mountain trail. We turned our horses and trailed behind him, ending up where they'd buried the monster under a pile of rocks.

Shaking the dust off my cape after I dismounted, "What are we doing here, Ruah?"

"Clear the rocks off his body."

Hearing that made our noses scrunch up. "Why are we doing that, Ruah. Are we moving the body somewhere else?" I hoped that wasn't it.

Ruah sat down, "You'll see."

Briella came down and we got at it. I was an expert at moving rocks. Some were very heavy and the smell of death was difficult to bear. Finally, there he was. We held our noses as we stepped back. Ruah stood up and walked over to us, "Raise him up."

"You want us to stand him up?"

"No. No. Raise him up. Bring him back from death."

Now I know this part was definitely not in the briefing.

"Raise him? From the dead," Briella said, still holding her nose?

"Yes."

"How," I asked?

"By just doing it."

Just doing it? How do we just do it? "Do we slap him or stick him with the swords again?" Briella was as confused as I was.

"No. No. Haven't you two been paying attention in training? When you spoke to the star, what did it do?"

After a pause, "Well, it shrank and then expanded," we both said.

"Right. So, do that."

I sat down and looked down at the stones and then at Ruah, "You want us to tell him to not be dead anymore?"

"That's it."

"How do you tell him to not be dead? He's dead."

Ruah responds, "How do you tell a star to move and it moves?"

We must have been tired from wandering around here for three days. I stared at the rocks thinking and trying to remember what I said to the star to make it move. Then it came to me. It wasn't *what* I said, it was simply believing what I said. "Briella, the secret is believing what we say, like we did with the star and the food that day."

"Of course, Ryder," she said, smacking her forehead with hand.

We walked over to the body. I had to get my mind right. "Let's do it together, Bre," as I grabbed her hand.

"Body in front of us. We command you to come back to life now," I said.

"Stand up," Briella commanded.

An absolute sense of success came into my mind. I just knew it would happen. Ruah said it would, so therefore, it would. All doubt left me, as it did with the star.

We waited. I thought I saw his chest move. Briella tightened her grip on my hand. She saw it too. His face and hands had many cuts from the rocks that were piled on him. We watched as the cuts disappeared. We heard bones cracking, as they came back into place. Many insects that were crawling all over him, left in a swirl, like a tornado. The smell disappeared. He groaned.

We leaned over his face staring at him. His eyes fluttered open. When he recognized us, I put my hand to my sword, as did Briella. Had to be ready.

His reaction wasn't what I expected. He screamed in terror. We jumped back. The scream lasted quite a while and then stopped. Realizing he was alive, he crawled toward us to hug and kiss our feet. "Thank you! Thank you! Thank you," he kept saying over and over.

I reached down to get him to sit up, "Welcome back sir. We're as surprised as you are. But why are you so friendly towards us now?"

He sat back holding his head silently for a long time. He was crying. Finally, he told us what had happened to him over the last three days. "I was cast into a flaming pit," he started. "Flames were upon me constantly. The flesh on my body would burn off, then reappear and burn off again. In-between the burning, worms were eating me. The pain was unbearable. Strange creatures were laughing at me as they stabbed me. Screams from others filled my ears along with my own screams. There was no escape. I couldn't believe that I wasn't in Yarikh's abode like I'd been told and believed all my life. I remembered what you'd said before I died and so, I knelt down in human waste to beg for another chance. A bright light opened in the darkness and Ehyeh reached his hand down to me. When I reached up to take it, I woke up here with you."

He stretched out and hugged both of us, apologizing in tears for the way he treated us. "I am ready to fulfill the message you gave me. I am a follower of Farmer, Ehyeh and Ruah only."

Three days ago, we plunged our swords into a hideous creature, which I can say was not entirely unpleasant. Now here we are hugging him as a new brother, which I'm enjoying even more. This alien blood in us sure is weird stuff. I patted him on the back, "We understand that you were corrupted by the Eater. He's behind it all. He fooled us too. But now, you're our brother." He hugged us tighter and wept out loud.

I asked him, "Have you met Ruah?"

"No. Looking around. Is the mighty one here? May I see him?"

"You sure can. He's right here." Briella pointed at Ruah.

"Ruah's your dog," he looked strangely at Ruah and us?

"No. He takes the form of a dog. He takes other forms too. You just have to go with it."

The man stared at Ruah. We could tell that Ruah was speaking to him, but we couldn't hear what he was saying. The man sat down in front of Ruah, while we walked over to our horses to leave them alone. After quite some time they both walked over to us. The man walked right by us heading to the cave entrance.

Ruah explained, "Your new brother's farming is starting right now. I've given him instructions on how to proceed. Let's follow."

The guards at the cave screamed and ran into the cave when they saw him. We followed as the man strode in. They couldn't see us. As more men saw him, they ran deeper into the cave. We eventually arrived at a wide-open area where the men that've seen him are screaming at hundreds of men that their leader is alive and was coming. As we came in, they all stared at him in shock. He went straight over smiling to his former elite guards calling them by name, as he hugged and greeted them with a cheek kiss. Many men were slowly backing away.

Ruah tells us, "They think he's a ghost or a jinn."

Briella never heard of that word. "What's a jinn?"

"That's what they call a demon."

The man sat down at the table where they'd been deciding on who'd be their next leader. He was smiling as they stared at him, "Is someone going to bring me some food and water? I haven't had anything in days."

One of his former guards brought him a plate of food and a cup of water and pushed them towards him in fear. They're frozen, watching him eat and drink, until finally one of them says, "How is it that you're alive, my chief?"

The chieftain sat back in the chair smiling, "I have such good news to tell you my friends and brothers." He relayed to them the story of what happened to him, starting with when we came into his room three days ago and his defiance that led to his death. He detailed the horrors that he experienced while he was in the abyss, until he called out to Ehyeh to rescue him, resulting in coming back from the dead. They were all speechless. Then, it got interesting.

"When I awoke," he continued, "I was given knowledge about what happened to me from Ruah. Ruah told me that the evil creed we follow was invented by the Eater to keep us from Farmer, Ehyeh, Ruah, our farms and eternal bliss. We've been following the wrong god for centuries my brothers. I need to warn others so more don't end up where I was."

It was silent for a while as they stared at him, probably processing all the amazing things he said. Surely it was a lot to take in from your leader who you knew was dead for three days and now is sitting in front of you telling you that everything you believe is a lie. That everything you've been doing in life has been leading to your own destruction.

One of them didn't take this news too well. An elite guard lifted his rifle up into the face of the chieftain, "You're a lying jinn, sent by this Eater to deceive us. Our leader is dead." He pulled the trigger. Click. It didn't fire. He backed up, threw the rifle down, grabbed another rifle from one of the other men and pulled the trigger again. Click. Nothing. He was scared and desperate. He pulled a knife from his belt and rushed the chieftain. He didn't see Ruah. Ruah tapped the solid, rock ground, that opened up in front of the man, swallowing him in flames.

Some of the men ran away in terror. Others dropped to their faces screaming out to be saved. The rest stood in shock staring into the fiery hole, where their friend once stood.

The chieftain was saddened at what had happened to this man, as he knew what awaited him. He stood over the hole looking in, "I will tell his family what happened to him so they don't suffer the same fate. Any of you care to join him, jump in." The ones on their faces screamed louder. He had no takers. "Those of you who care to walk into the truth of life, stand here with me now or leave to live your lives waiting for what I went through. What this man will go through for eternity," as he pointed to the hole. They all eventually stood with him.

Demonstration of power is more powerful than words.

Then Ehyeh walked into the room.

CHAPTER 21

hen Ehyeh appeared, there was a mixed reaction of shock and fear. One man fainted. "Don't be afraid my new brothers," Ehyeh said, "I am here to give you what you have been fighting for all these years."

He walked up to each one of them and greeted them with a hug and a cheek kiss. "I will work with each of you to remove the stain of evil that the Eater has afflicted you with. There is much work ahead." Hundreds of angels appeared in the room.

The man who fainted came to, looked around and promptly fainted again. Bre and I couldn't hold back our smiles. "Each of you go now with my soldiers, as they will instruct you on your next steps." Two angels disappeared with each man.

The chieftain was the last one in the room with us. Ruah, Briella and I became visible to him, while Ehyeh walked up to him, to look him in the eyes, "You have just rescued hundreds from the fate that you had a small taste of. Well done. You have followed Ruah's guidance well. As a world leader of the Eater, you are aware of how he used you to accomplish his atrocities and to influence hundreds of millions around the world who look up to you."

The chieftain started crying and dropped to his knees at Ehyeh's feet saying how sorry he was.

Ehyeh knelt down to him, "Do not be ashamed, as you were deceived, like billions in the world are experiencing right now. You sincerely regret and accept responsibility for your actions and have turned from your old life, asking us for redemption and pardon into a new life. In doing so, you have accepted that I have paid the entire penalty for your actions. You are now a new creature, Abarron."

He lifted his head to look at Ehyeh, "Abarron?"

Ehyeh smiled, "Yes Abarron. Your new name befitting a father of a multitude." Ehyeh lifted Abarron to his feet. "As I was saying, hundreds of millions around the world who are mourning your death will hear that you are alive again."

"How will that happen Ehyeh? How will they hear from me? I hide in this cave."

"Your explanation to your men of what happened to you will be spread far and wide beyond this cave. They're the first good seeds of your farm."

"My farm?" Abarron puts his hands to his head, "I don't understand."

"Hundreds of millions of people around the world will soon find out you're alive and that you curse what you once believed and, curse what they were tricked to believe. Most will think what they hear isn't really from you or that if it is really from you, they were lied to about your death and that you are now insane. Some will trust what you're saying and will come to the truth. These will be led to where they each need to go next."

Abarron shakes his head trying to take it all in.

"Ryder and Briella will teach you how to translocate, multiply yourself and be invisible."

"Trans-what," Abarron says?

I whispered to Briella, "I think he's overloading." Briella giggled.

"Once you've accomplished all that, you will appear around the world to meet with skeptical and rebellious leaders and others, to rescue as many as you can."

"But Ehyeh. I'm a hunted man with a price on my head. Won't I be arrested?"

"Yes. Many times. But you will escape."

"But great Ehyeh, many of my own people will consider me a traitor and kill me?"

"Yes, they will. Many times, your words won't be believed and you will be killed. And over and over you will rise again in front of their eyes to demonstrate to them the truth. Train well, Abarron." Ehyeh hugged him and disappeared, along with Ruah.

The last three days took their toll on Abarron, "I don't know what to say."

"It's all a lot to take in, but you'll get used to it," I assured him. "As we're still here, this cave and mountain must be your farm, so, let's get started."

Briella and I worked with him for what seemed like many months. Abarron wasn't the only one benefitting from this teaching process, as our abilities became much more advanced as well.

Farmer, Ehyeh and Ruah came daily to visit and talk alone with Abarron and took him on the same trip to the star that Briella and I had made, to make it contract and expand.

He received a very stunning, spirited horse that he named, Garmon, which fit him well. Garmon took to the battles that we encountered, like a bird does to flight.

After these times, Abarron's farm grew quite a bit. The back side of the mountain opened up transforming into a farm that rivaled Briella's and mine that he called a citadel. A lake of dark, blue waters formed in the middle of the valley between the mountain range, with a lush, garden full of exotic flowers, trees, birds and animals along its base.

Abarron was a quick study and was so pleased with his new life. And, wouldn't you know it, his lake worked just the same as ours when it came to tossing each other in.

The day came when we just knew it was time for us to leave. We all rode out to the edge of his farm to hug and say our goodbyes. When the portal opened up, Briella and I rode through. We looked forward to riding with Abarron again, yet, right now, we were tired and home sick.

I came through the portal at my cabin in the woods. I was hoping I would end up here. I could see Briella at her island hut. This was a new talent that we'd developed while we were gone. We could now see and hear remotely. The guys were waiting for me by one of the red woods. Ahhhh, I missed the sounds and smell here. I closed my eyes to breath it all in before I ran up and hugged each of the guys. We didn't see them as much as usual while we were training Abarron. "I missed you all. It's so good to be back."

"We missed you too, Ryder," Farmer smiled as he hugged me tighter, "although, we're with you all the time, these moments are much more intimate."

The angels brought me some hotdogs and liquicake. "What a perfect welcome home present," as I gobbled and slurped and sloshed all over myself.

Farmer seemed to enjoy my sloppy eating habits as much as he did the first time we met. "You and Briella are such fine teachers. Abarron is setting so many free from their prisons, thanks to you two."

I choked on my hotdog, "Briella and I are nothing without you guys. You're the ones who've given us, and Abarron, so much. Thanks for allowing us to be part of your plans, although I don't understand why you need us."

Ruah walked over to me, "Ryder, don't you know by now why we're doing this?"

"Well. You said it's because you really love us and want to share everything with us and want us to build our farms."

"This is true. Do you know what love is, Ryder?"

"Well, I say, I love stuff, but everyone says that. Before I met you guys, I never felt that anyone loved me. People told me I was stupid and worthless. No one ever said they loved me. I didn't love anyone. Actually, I lived in fear and anger and hate. There're many times I wanted to kill myself, to escape my prison. When the opportunity came, I escaped. They were hunting for me when I met you, Farmer."

"Yes, Ryder, we know," Farmer said. "But now that you've been with us, what do *you* say love is?"

The words just poured out of me, "Love is a living entity. It's not just a word or an emotion or a lustful thing. You guys would never abandon Briella or me. You would never turn against us. Everything that is yours, is ours. It's a bond or a melting together as one that can't be separated. It's an absolute. Love is what human beings hunt for but can never find without you. This is your love towards me." I paused. "My love to you is still a broken thing. I would lay down my life for you guys, but that's not it. More needs to come on my end."

One thing I do love. When the guys smile. I guess they liked what I said, as they weren't saying anything, which was quite rare. "Are you guys OK? Was I close on what love is?"

Farmer started, "You are truly loved by us, son. It's as you say and more. I am so pleased with your words."

"Such common sense is not seen by us that often," Ruah leans up against me. "You're a wonderment and a jewel of great value."

Ehyeh stood, walked over to me, pulled me up and bear hugged me, "My little brother, where did you get such wisdom? Did Gideon give it to you?" Gideon snorts at us as Ehyeh smiles over at him. "No. I think not. Do you keep it in your pockets?" I laughed as he tickled me, while he's patting me down. "No, it's not in there, little brother. I say you're learning all this from love himself. Love is alive as you say and is a great teacher. You are learning well."

"Well, just so you know. I almost burst a blood vessel in my head coming up with that answer," glancing at them out of the corner of my eye. We all started laughing. They grabbed me and threw me in the lake. I came up this time with a duck sitting on my head. "You guys planned this," as I took the duck off and sent him off paddling. We all laughed harder. My love just grew larger.

They all jumped in the lake to join me. We swam around splashing and laughing for such a long time. I love, love.

We came up to shore where angels were waiting for us in a line. I wiped the water from my eyes to have a better look. "What's all this?"

"My brother. These are your conqueror's rewards for victory on your God Op with Briella."

I waved them off, "No, no thanks, you've all given me more than I could ever imagine. The victory and glory of all Ops belongs to you guys." I started walking over to my chair.

Farmer stopped me. "Ryder. Part of love is accepting from those who love you, what they offer to you in love. To refuse is to diminish that love for everyone."

I turned and walked back, "I just don't feel worthy to accept gifts for things I couldn't do without you guys."

"Ryder. Your gift to us is your eagerness to please us and to see you so willing to disregard your own interests to set others free into life. What we present to you here are just symbols in recognition of what you've accomplished."

"You're right. I'm sorry I didn't understand."

The first angel stepped forward. Farmer placed a ring on my finger made from lightning. "This ring was made by Ruah. It recognizes your accomplishments with the Abarron God Op." The next angel had a robe that glowed. "This is a robe made from my robe. It will reveal itself to you, as you continue to wear it." As Farmer put it on me, my eyes opened up to see so many things. It was like I had been blind but now can see. There were so many things flashing before my eyes I started to get dizzy. I closed my eyes and tried again. Too much. I had to take the robe off.

"Farmer. I'm so sorry for taking off your robe. I was getting dizzy. How do I get used to it?"

"You'll get the hang of it, as you did with everything else. It just takes practice."

The next gift was a large chest made of gold and gems. I looked at Ehyeh as I kneeled down to rub my hands over it. "Is this from you, big brother?"

"Yes, my brave brother."

I tried to open it but it was locked. It had a key hole but no key. "It needs a key."

"The key to open it will be given to you after you've completed a future Op."

I jumped up to hug Ehyeh, "My brother, your love for me is more than I'll ever need." I hugged Farmer and Ruah, thanking them for my gifts.

As I was examining my ring and robe, I wondered if Briella got the same gifts. "Yes, she did Ryder," Farmer responded to my thoughts. "She is," he smiled, "extremely keen about them."

"I'll bet. She's probably swimming around her island with her robe and ring on right now." Gideon snorted again. "Oh, I'm sorry guys. Gideon informs me, that she's probably celebrating by riding Shiloh all around her island." I walked over to Gideon, "I'm sorry big fella, you're right. I share these with you too. "Hey guys, can we go for a ride?"

As I said that, I could hear a roaring like thunder. Bolts of lightning streaked down. "Well, I guess we'll have to wait. Sounds like a storm's coming."

The noise of thunder got louder. The trees were shaking. I held on to Gideon wondering what was happening. A chariot of five horses surrounded in fire appeared out over the lake. Farmer says, "Let's go for a ride. I'm drivin'."

All I had was, "Wow!" Then I said, "I call shotgun!"

Heard it in a movie once.

CHAPTER 22

"Y ou join the others, Gideon," Farmer said.

I never saw Gideon move that fast. This must be a dream for him, to ride with Farmer's team. He's earned it.

We all walked out on the water and climbed into the chariot. There's more than enough room. "Shall we give Briella a lift," Farmer asked me?

"Absolutely. Can we sneak up on her and surprise her though?" The smirks told me they liked my idea.

We rode over to Briella's island in another dimension so she wouldn't see or hear us. I stepped out from the chariot, into her dimension and walked over to her hut and knocked, "Anybody home?"

"Ryder," I heard from inside?

She came flying out and knocked me down to the sand she was so excited, "Ryder, look at the new ring I got!"

"Oh, ya mean like this one." I showed her mine. They're identical.

"Did you get Farmer's gold robe too and Ehyeh's secret chest?"

"Sure did. Did you get that other thing?"

She stopped gazing at her ring to give me a puzzled look, "What other thing?"

"Oh. Maybe I shouldn't have mentioned it. Maybe you aren't supposed to get it."

"Get what?"

I got up and brushed the sand off and started walking toward where the chariot and the guys are, "Never mind. Forget I mentioned it." She was running after me so fast she fell face first into the sand.

"Wait, Ryder. What else is there?" She got up running beside me, not noticing that we're walking across the ocean surrounding her island. We walked right up into Farmer's chariot, that I can see but she couldn't.

The guys and the chariot became visible to her as we all yelled, "Surprise!" Briella fell back, splashing into the ocean.

"Now that's what I'm talkin' about," I said to the guys as I leaned up against the side of the chariot waiting for her to come up.

She came up sputtering with a starfish on her head. I looked at the guys, "I think the duck was funnier." Then we all jumped in laughing.

"You guys," Briella said. "You really surprised me. What a beautiful chariot, Farmer." As she examined it closer, the chariot moved. It was alive. It was made of many different kinds and colors of angels. I hadn't noticed until now.

"Are we ready to go for a ride," Farmer asked?

We all rose up out of the water and stepped onto the chariot. Farmer whistled. Shiloh came running out from the other side of the island, out to the chariot, "Join the team," Farmer said, as Shiloh and Gideon greeted each other. We took off leaving Briella's island far behind us riding through many dimensions, portals, past angels, mountains, waterfalls and mighty oceans until we broke through some clouds and could see a city below us.

There were many buildings and people walking around. Nothing looks familiar. "Where are we," Briella asked?

"You'll see," Farmer says, as we landed in a large square with many old columns, statues and ornate buildings. People were all around us, unaware of who just arrived.

We stepped out of the chariot as Farmer acted as our tour guide at this place.

"What are all these columns and statues for Farmer," I asked?

"This is a head circus of the Heretix. This represents the largest horn that you saw on the Heretix' head." Briella and I both pulled our swords out and spun around expecting an attack. "Your swords aren't needed today, you two. We have come to deal with a head ringmaster." Our swords went slowly back in their place. Our hands remained on the hilts.

"This Heretix ringmaster runs all of this," Briella asked?

"Yes. He oversees hundreds of thousands of performers and clowns spread out all over the world in smaller circuses."

As we're talking, a woman ran over and gave Farmer, Ehyeh and Ruah each a long hug. How does she see us? Ehyeh introduced us, "Ryder and Briella, meet Joanna." She gave us a big hug too.

She's very bubbly. "I've heard so much about you two. And I've seen some amazing results from your God Ops." How does she know about us and our God Ops? "You're probably wondering who I am. I'm an old friend of Ehyeh's. We met...", she paused, "A while back," as she and Ehyeh smiled at each other.

"So, are you a God Operator too," Briella asks?

"No. You two are the first ones. I move around a lot. I've lived all over the world doing various things." She didn't look that old. "The guys wanted me to be here to give you some history on this place." She glows when she talks.

As we walked around, Joanna gave us a detailed story of how she came here long ago, before it became the head circus of the Heretix. She told us about so many who were hunted, imprisoned and tortured, including herself. She witnessed entire cities and even nations killed. We listened in shock. How could she have seen and experienced all of this? "And this was all after I walked with Ehyeh."

"When did all of this happen," I asked?

"Over the last two thousand years."

"Two... your two thousand years old?"

"Two thousand and change actually."

"She doesn't look a day over twenty-nine," Ehyeh stated as he squeezed her arm. Briella and I are speechless. "Joanna is what we call, a Perpetual One or Ad for short. She never died."

"Ad?" I didn't know what else to say.

"You two are surprised," Farmer asked?

"Well. Yeah."

"How old do you think *we* are?"

I stared at them. Speechless. Again. Briella had nothing either.

"You two have to shake off this concept of 'time'. Time is just an inferior dimension we made to fit the physical realm. With all you've seen and done with stopping time and time-shifting, we didn't think you could be surprised so easily anymore."

"You're right. It should be easy to shake off that dumb idea that time is unchangeable. And not be surprised with crazy stuff like you guys made time. Come on you guys. We're just kids. Don't get me angry," I said jokingly. "I have a sword and I know how to use it."

Ehyeh put his hands up pretending to be scared, "Settle down my dangerous one. We surrender." It took us all a while to stop laughing. We'd almost stop and then one of us would start it all going again. I love life.

My eyes were still watering from all the laughter, "Tell us more, Joanna."

"The persecution we experienced only made everyone stronger. After a few hundred years of this, the Eater realized his plan to destroy us and our farms wasn't working. So, he devised a new strategy. He came up with… the Heretix."

"Yeah. We met the Heretix briefly," I smiled remembering. "I'm sure it remembers us. We chopped off a few chunks of it."

"Yes. I heard. Well done you two." I like Joanna. "I heard you got the Eater's attention too," as Joanna rubbed her bum smiling.

Briella laughed, "Oh, you heard about that? That was fun."

"Well deserved and more." Then Joanna gave us a serious look, "But, stay sharp though. The Eater will certainly have something planned to seek his revenge."

It was something I knew in the back of my mind, but hearing it brought it back up.

"Then what happened," Briella asked. We were walking throughout the structures that were here, admiring all the paintings, intricate wall hangings, candles, incense and marble statues. I noticed Farmer frown at us. Did we doing something wrong I wondered?

"Most people back then were relieved and happy when the attacks against us all stopped. Until, some of the men were elevated to exalted positions and given elegant robes and treated like royalty by people and the empire. It went to their heads. They replaced the guys with fetishes and charms, like the ones you see stacked up in here. The circus started to take shape. This is when the Heretix was born."

What a bunch a meat-heads. "Really? Then what happened?" I realize why Farmer frowned at us now.

"The rot crept in slowly. Greed. Power. Control. New rules to feed their egos that they said came from Farmer, Ehyeh and Ruah. The Heretix grew bigger and bigger." The guys each dropped their heads at the same time, shaking them. They looked disgusted. "The Heretix grew horns out of its body as circuses and performers all over the world were established with their 'dog and pony shows'. They tricked billions into becoming contras. And killed those who opposed them. This is their main headquarters. The Heretix eventually grew smaller horns out of its head, that spawned more horns with offshoots or growths."

We walked deeper into the circus. There were so many rooms and hallways. Many had walls and ceilings painted with murals. The smell of burning candles and incense permeated the air. I prefer the aroma of hot dogs myself. "What are we all doing here," I asked.

Farmer responded. "The relationship that we have with you, Ryder, Briella and Joanna are what we desire with everyone. We have inheritance waiting for each person that accepts it from us. The Eater doesn't want that. The Eater keeps people from their inheritance through various ways making them contras. Usually it's through attractive substitutes or alternatives, like this place."

"Why did you guys allow this place to start and grow?"

"As we told you, part of our relationship is allowing everyone to choose their own way in life. They can choose a relationship with us or pick a contra way the Eater has for them, which places them in the Book of the Dead."

"But this place isn't really another way, is it? I've heard some of the clowns here talking about you guys."

"Yes, they talk about us, but they don't know us. They tell people that they represent us, but they don't. They've created a beast made of fear, guilt, pride, wealth, compromise, profanity, depravity and lies. The beast you know as the Heretix. The Heretix is a mighty beast made up of numerous circuses run by many ring masters, performers and clowns, all under the government of the Eater's farm."

As Farmer was finished talking, we walked into a large room where a man all in white was sitting on a throne. This must be the ringmaster that we've come to see.

I could see another overlaying him.

CHAPTER 23

We were invisible to all except the black creature wearing a crown that was sitting on the throne with the man in white. It had some chains on it. It stared at us as we walked in, "Why are you here, great lords? It's not my time and I'm welcomed and revered around the world."

Farmer rebuked it. "Don't play the fool with us, Nergal. You know those chains we put on you restrict your actions through this circus. We're here again to see if this puppet will accept more or less chains for you."

Our Waster angels, Adlai and Elkin, appeared in a flash, grabbed Nergal and pulled it away from the throne. They had reduced themselves to a smaller size to fit, otherwise, there'd be a couple of big holes in this roof. The beast struggled as they wrapped it tighter in its chains and stood guard on either side of it. At the same time that Nergal was taken away, the ringmaster screamed, stiffened up like a tree and dropped over, sorta like that wizard I came across where Ehyeh had taken me. His aides ran over to him to see what happened but they couldn't revive him. He started coming around when the doctor arrived, but when he saw us his eyes widened and he fainted again. Well, he is old, I snickered to myself.

When he came around again, Farmer told him to clear the room, as we needed to talk with him. After much convincing that he felt fine, the aides all reluctantly left after being nicely shoved to the door. When he locked the door and turned around, Farmer, Ehyeh and Ruah were sitting on the throne staring at him. The ringmaster nervously dropped down, prostrating himself in front of them. Smart man.

Farmer spoke in a firm and abrupt way I hadn't heard before. "*We* have *not* given you this throne. Who are *you* to sit here saying you represent *us*?"

Briella, Joanna and I turned our heads at the same time to the man. I glanced over at Nergal muffled over in the corner with Adlai and Elkin. This is getting good. I wondered if they had a snack bar here like at that other circus. This stuff makes me hungry.

The ringmaster spoke with a shaky voice, "I was chosen by a sign from you." He was still hugging the floor.

Our heads came back together as Farmer continued, "I gave you no sign. Rather than talking to us directly, you and others that don't know us, made your own decisions. We have brought up these matters with your predecessors. Now, it's your turn. Tell us. Do you think this dunghill you govern, accurately represents us and our kingdom?"

"It's been this way for hundreds of years," he mumbled.

"That is no excuse to sit on a throne of filth. Many people have accepted you like their king. It's in your power to change what others before you have perverted. See that puny god over there in the corner?" The ringmaster shifted his head to look at Nergal, nodded and turned his head away in fear. "That thing is death that reports to the Eater. You've been running a freak show for the Eater. Your circus has kept billions from us and their inheritance. You've introduced them to death."

There was a silence in the room after Farmer's last word fell. This guy acts a lot humbler than Abarron had been with me. I guess the guys can bring that out in someone more than I can. We'll see.

"What do you ask of me?"

"You have the power to turn billions around. You can stand before us and take the mantle that we give you to be one of our kings. Or, you can stay where you are and we'll let Nergal get back at his work."

He didn't hesitate. He stood up, walked over to the guys and bowed, "Forgive me and all that this fake empire has done over the years. I am ready to correct the wrongs.”

The guys went to him for a group hug. We were invited in too. After we were introduced, Farmer gave him a new name. “Welcome to our family, Gabrian!”

Joanna said. “I’ve been waiting for this for fifteen hundred years!”

That statement shocked him, requiring Joanna to explain to him who she was and all that she’d experienced. It was just as riveting to hear for the second time. Much of it made him cry because he had been a part of that horror.

A knock came at the door, “Are you alright, your eminence?”

“Yes. Tell the staff that I will be making an announcement in the square in an hour. Please, set it all up.”

“An announcement, your eminence?”

“Hurry, please.”

Over the next hour, the guys showed him a scroll that he was to read from. It was a very long scroll. We then walked out with Gabrian to the square. Joanna told us that she had witnessed much family blood shed across this square. Their sacrifices are about to produce a massive harvest, she said.

Gabrian walked past the throne that was set up for him. He walked among the crowd that were here to see him perched on it. As he walked, he told them that the kingdom that he and this circus had told them about was real, but they weren’t on the right road to get there.

People gasped and started murmuring in the crowd. We can see an unknown number of creatures crawling all over these people prodding them, poking them, screaming at them to attack Gabrian. The guys didn't stop them.

Gabrian continued. He told them that each one of them had a farm that was theirs for eternity. He said, "Right now, you are all dead sticks on the ground withering away from the vine that gives life." They stood there in disbelieve. Some screamed. Many yelled at him, calling him names. Others threw their beads at him. No one believed him. This circus has a strong following, with a lotta help from all the creatures from the Eater's farm.

Angry circus clowns quickly moved up to usher him away. He disappeared from them and reappeared on the other side of the square. He learned fast.

He walked over to those in wheelchairs and others that had been brought in on cots, commanding them to stand. They all stood up and danced, as the creatures that were crippling them, froze up and dropped off. Joanna smiled at Ehyeh, "This looks familiar." Ehyeh smiled, hugged her shoulder and continued to watch with the rest of us.

A woman with wild eyes ran up to Gabrian screaming, "Witch! Sorcerer!" She pulled a knife out and stabbed him over and over. All of us were a distance away. Briella and I pulled our swords to go help him, but Ehyeh said, "No. Put those away."

"We're just going to let him die?" Briella and I were the only ones concerned. Joanna was just as calm as the guys.

"We knew this was to happen. Watch." Farmer waved his hand. We watched the attack go backwards. Time was being rewound, but just for Gabrian and this woman. The rest of the crowd had witnessed a murder. Now they were watching it being reversed before their eyes. The blood went back into Gabrian's body. He stood back up as the knife lady's strikes were reversed, like seeing a movie going backwards, but just in this section of the movie. Everything else around them moved forward. We didn't know if Gabrian and the lady knew what happened to them until we saw her look at Gabrian, the knife in her hand and then scream and run away.

"What was that?" We knew about going back in time and freezing time, but Briella and I hadn't learned that one.

Joanna cheered, "That was just an awesome display of a select, fragment, time adjustment."

"A select what?"

"A fragment of those few dimensions was edited and reversed. Not only reversed for all around to see, but also for Gabrian and the woman to know they were being reversed."

"Cool!" I didn't know what else to say.

A number of the people in the crowd fainted of course. It was quite a sight. Others ran away screaming. Many crushed forward to touch Gabrian. Demonstration of eternal power exposed the clowns and paper tigers of the circus. Gabrian then floated up above the crowd.

Yes. There was more fainting.

A few of the circus clowns that finally reached him were jumping up and down trying to pull him down. They didn't like what was happening. They don't like losing contras. Gabrian took out the scroll that Farmer had given him, unrolled it and spoke to the crowd while he was floating in the air.

"Each of us is an eternal being. We will live forever." People started cheering.

As they were cheering, Gabrian continued, "There are two books of eternity; The Book of the Dead and the Book of Life. Everyone's name is written in one Book or the other. We are each born with our names written into the Book of the Dead." The cheering abruptly stopped.

"The Book of Life has only one doorway."

The crowd shouted out their guesses. "Surely it's circus attendance?" Some agreed. Another shouted, "Yes. But also doing as the clowns say and revering the sacred objects of old." More people nodded.

Gabrian continued, "The circus is not your god. Circus clowns are not your gods. Candles, beads, statues and buildings have no power. Revering them are wrong paths."

Then he dropped the other shoe.

"You were told to follow rules and laws that my predecessors made-up over the centuries. These fantasy ways are contra to the truth. Those who follow them are cursed!"

People were in a panic. They yelled out, "Cursed? This is what we've been told to do all our lives. We've been lied too? If not these ways, then what can we do?"

"Reject your old life and meet with Farmer, Ehyeh and Ruah to start a new one. Abandon the Eater's ways and those who follow him. Abandon the circus. They are to be no longer part of your lives. Accept your eternal inheritance. Build your farm now.”

Some people responded, “What you say are mysteries. How do we meet with Farmer, Ehyeh and Ruah? We’ve been told that’s impossible. What farms? Where are these farms we’re to build?”

One of the clowns yelled out, “Don’t listen to this madman. He’s an imposter. He’s impersonating the ringmaster.”

Gabrian said, “Let’s see who the imposter is.” Gabrian floated over to one of the many statues overlooking the square, ripped one from its perch and brought it down to the middle of the crowd.”

This made the clowns go crazy, “Look. He’s destroying a statue of Susanna, one of our most revered circus founders.”

Joanna shook her head, “I hang out with Sue. She hates that thing. And, it doesn’t look like her at all.” Bre and I giggled.

Gabrian tells the clown, “If you truly represent Farmer, Ehyeh and Ruah as you say, then put the statue back where I got it from.”

“I have no witch powers, you sorcerer,” he sneered.

“You think wizards have powers greater than Farmer, Ehyeh and Ruah? Greater than those who follow them? What fools do you take everyone for?”

The clown didn’t know what to say. The crowd looked scared and confused. The guys are enjoying the whole thing. Briella and I are loving it.

“Why don’t you ask Farmer, Ehyeh and Ruah to put it back for you,” Gabrian wryly suggested.

Some of the crowd responded. "Yeah clown. If you are who you say you are, then do it." More joined in and chanted, "Do it! Do it! Do it!"

The clown accepted the challenge. He raised his hands in the air and begged Farmer, Ehyeh and Ruah by name to put the statue back to its honored resting place. He commanded. He begged. He screamed. He stomped. The guys just stood there.

Nothing happened.

The crowd laughed at him. The man gave up and collapsed on the ground. Gabrian floated over to him, "Are you done?"

He nodded yes, not looking up from the ground. Gabrian motioned for people to move away from the statue.

What came next no one could have imagined.

CHAPTER

24

The crowd was now surrounding the statue, but at a distance.

"This statue isn't magic. It doesn't take requests," Gabrian mocked. "It's just a piece of stone. Look to the eternal, not what is temporal."

After a pause Gabrian looked over to Farmer who nodded to go. "Farmer, Ehyeh and Ruah, let it be known this day that You alone are to be revered and that I am Your servant, and that I have said and done all these things at Your word. Behold."

Fire fell from the sky like a meteor and consumed the statue and the ground around it. There was nothing left but a black, burnt, smoking hole. Now *that* was cool.

Some of the crowd ran away screaming, others fell on their faces declaring, "None other than Farmer, Ehyeh and Ruah!"

Gabrian pointed to the remaining statues on the columns around them. Each one was leveled with fire dropping from the sky. They exploded like fireworks with sparks of many colors that went high in the air accompanied with bangs and booms.

The crowd roared in approval, as each one was hit.

During the fireworks display, they were beating the clowns, who were running away. The circus was destroyed in their hearts and minds now, just like these statues were destroyed.

Angels came, just as they had with Abarron's men, to take the willing ones to their farms, where Farmer, Ehyeh and Ruah would put them through the paces, as they did with Briella and me.

Then Adlai and Elkin dragged Nergal out to the square. It appeared especially nervous to see Gabrian floating above all the smoldering statues and the angels taking excited people away.

Farmer walked up to it, "What shall we do with you?"

The Wasters removed the chains from its mouth, "I was only following orders, great lord," it explained.

"Yes. And you did so quite cheerfully."

"The Eater expects this behavior or we receive a harsh punishment from him."

"You have little knowledge of harsh punishment. The Eater will receive his reward one day, as will all who choose evil. One day you will harvest the measure of judgment that you have earned. Until then, you will be chained alone, imprisoned in utter darkness."

I gathered from its scream, as the Wasters took it away, that it wasn't overly pleased with this pronouncement against it. Bummer.

Farmer, Ehyeh and Ruah spent more time with Gabrian. We all did. He was told his farm was already quite a success from all that he did today. He hugged each of the guys, thanking them for waking him up and allowing him this opportunity.

We waved bye for now to Gabrian, as Farmer's chariot lifted off. Quite an exciting day.

Joanna was invited to come back with us to Briella's farm. A visitor. This is new.

As Bre was showing her the place I'm not sure which one was more excited. They were jumping up and down, giggling, pointing, laughing, hugging. Girls.

All really was fantastic though. The gardens shimmered more than usual. The animals came to greet Joanna, as did the butterflies and birds. A lion walked at her side everywhere we went. I looked to Farmer and nodded with my head towards it, as to ask, what's with the lion. Farmer told me it was her lion that had been given to her by Ehyeh, two thousand years ago. Didn't see him on the chariot when we came back. Must have been in Joanna's pocket I chortled to myself. He didn't look a day over a thousand.

We ended up by that chopped up, dead, partially dug up, old tree in Bre's garden, that had been here since I'd been given my first tour. I never brought it up as it seemed like Bre would tell me about it one day when she was ready. Bre and Joanna stopped at it. Farmer, Ehyeh and Ruah nudged me along, as I looked back.

Joanna put her arm around Bre as she started crying. "Is Briella OK, guys," I asked?

"She'll be fine, Ryder," Farmer said. "We brought Joanna here to help Briella past this section of her farm."

It was a strange thing that stood out amongst the beauty of everything else. I always wondered why Bre hadn't gotten rid of it.

The guys and I made our way to the palace library. "What a great hunt we had today, wasn't it," I said as I flopped down in one of the plush chairs in front of the fire? The guys agreed but told me it was a limited victory which I didn't understand.

"Ryder," Farmer started, "We did accomplish a great victory today with Gabrian but the Eater and the Heretix always counter-attack."

Ehyeh continued, "Gabrian, naturally, has left the circus, but the clowns under him, for the most part, will remain. They're already declaring Gabrian to be an imposter and insane. They're saying what he did wasn't miracles and wonders, but magic. They're gathering now to choose a new ringmaster."

I sat straight up in my chair, "You're kidding? Didn't those stupid clowns see what happened? Do they honestly think keeping the circus going is a smart thing to do? Who will follow them now?"

"Greed, power, and control are too difficult for them to give up. They're too interested in the treasures of the world, rather than the treasures we have to offer," Ruah said. "Many believe they're doing what's right. They believe they can make up anything and we'll just accept it. They think that following their make-believe ways will bring them to us eventually. Some believe they can live any way they want and we'll just let it go, because we're so loving. They don't understand who we are. They don't understand reality. Even when they know what they're doing is contrary than what we say is true, they continue on the same path. That's why we call them contras. As you can see, contras get hostile when anyone disrupts their version of reality."

I stared down at the floor after Ruah was done. The fire reflected in it, joining the silence in the room as I absorbed what Ruah had just said. People are so dumb.

Dwelling on the foolishness of humanity didn't last long for me, as Bre came running into the library, over to me and gave me a big kiss. On the lips. "Oh Ryder, I'm finally, really and truly full of joy now!" She spun around, went over and hugged and kissed the guys too, but not on their lips, while Joanna was laughing and clapping.

"What's going on," I asked while touching my lips? I had to suppress my smile.

Bre jumped up on Farmer's lap, "Farmer, Ehyeh, Ruah and Joanna knows." Looking at them, "Can I tell Ryder?"

"Of course, you can, Briella. He's your brother," Farmer said.

She jumped down, ran over to me, grabbed my hands and spun me around, "Yes, yes, you're my brother Ryder." Then she reached out, grabbed

Joanna's hand and spun us both around, "And Joanna is my sister." I was getting dizzy. "I finally got that big, dead tree out of my garden Ryder! It's gone!"

"OK. And what was it? Why did it take so long to get rid of?"

"That was my family tree. Well. My Earth family. When Ruah came to me at the circus, I didn't tell you but I was there with my mom and dad and brothers and sisters. My grandparents were there, aunts, uncles and cousins too. I'm the only one that left the circus. When I learned the truth, I came back to give them the good news. They received it about as well as the clowns did where we just were. They locked me in my room and called doctors to examine me. I explained everything to the doctors, who then recommended that I be institutionalized, as they called it."

"Wow, Bre! I didn't know that. What happened?" My lips said that, as my mind said, "Hey. She just kissed me... on the lips!" All three of the guys and Joanna looked at me at the same time and smiled. Oops.

Briella continued, "They took me in an ambulance to some weird place and locked me in a room that had padding on the walls. They strapped me to a bed and wanted to give me some kind of shot with a needle."

I was leaning out of my chair, my eyes wide open.

"I kept telling them that what I was saying was true. They kept saying, "Yes dear, you'll be fine. Just relax." They kept trying to stick me with a needle.

Every time they got close with it, they dropped it on the floor." She looked over at Ruah, "Thanks Ruah. Yes, Ruah came with me in the ambulance and into the room. He made them drop the needle. He said we can leave whenever I say, but I wanted my family to understand what I was saying so they would leave prison like I did. Finally, I realized they weren't going to believe me so I asked Ruah to get me outta there and I disappeared. Well, disappeared from their vision I mean. But I was still there.

The nurse screamed and ran out past my parents and other relatives who were in the hall. The doctor came out, looked at my relatives saying, "She just... she just... ah... disappeared." My parents said "what" and ran into the room. They ran back out and grabbed the doctor, "Where is she? What did you do with her?" I then appeared to them in the hallway."

I started laughing. "Bre, let me guess. People fainted and ran away."

"They did. Then, they tried grabbing me again. I just moved into another dimension with Ruah and watched them scramble around trying to find me. I was so sad. Ruah tried comforting me, but I couldn't get past my entire family being in the Book of the Dead."

"I understand Bre, but what does all that have to do with that dead tree in your garden?"

"The dead tree is my Earth family that refuses to accept the truth. I couldn't bring myself to totally dig it out of my farm. I didn't really want to put them in the past. The guys kept telling me that I was a new creature with new DNA. Their DNA. But

I just couldn't get past that they were no longer my family. It was probably harder because our ancestors started our family's circus. I was expected to be a performer or a clown one day and maybe even a ringmaster."

"What? Bre, no wonder it was so hard for you to deal with all of this."

"Yes, but the guys knew that Joanna would help me and she did," as she hugged Joanna. "She told me about her Earth family long ago and all the imprisonments and tortures she went through from circus clowns and performers that wouldn't accept her. Only the guys and a few others over two thousand years have stood with her. And now us. We're true family!" Bre spun around with her hands out, "I'm finally free and full of joy!"

"I think this calls for hotdogs all around to celebrate." Everyone laughs.

"Oh, Ryder! You and your food," Bre jokingly scolded me.

"What? I thought families like to sit around and ya know, break bread and stuff. In this case, hot dogs."

Farmer interrupts the eyerolling and moans from Bre and Joanna, "Well, Ryder, we do need to celebrate not only Briella's victory but also the victory with Gabrian." Farmer, Ehyeh, and Ruah got up and motioned to the three of us to come with them. We followed them through some long hallways to get to a large room, although the word 'room' didn't quite describe it. It was more like a stadium. As we walked in, the cheers rang out and the trumpets roared.

Farmer leaned over to us, "Your family is here."

CHAPTER 25

he celebration went on and on. Apparently, dealing with Gabrian and Nergal was a very big deal. The hot dogs just kept rolling in. Well, for me anyways. Bre and Joanna teamed up being totally satisfied with various strange looking fruit. They said it was all indescribable. I made a blah sound with my tongue at them as I bit into another dog.

The awards ceremony was the highlight. Farmer, Ehyeh and Ruah each gave such a wonderful recapping of what took place along with speeches of how great we were. Bre and I both felt kinda embarrassed because we mostly were just in attendance on that Op. The guys and the Wasters did all the heavy lifting and also Gabrian.

Next, angels came in three rows with awards and gifts that were handed to the guys and then to us. We received medals, new robes, and chests full of diamonds that we were told will be set into our farms. Each diamond representing a person who moved from the Book of the Dead over to the Book of Life, because of our Op. My family sure knows how to treat members right. Eventually, everyone wanted to hear from us.

Joanna went first.

As she stood, the stadium went quiet. "My family. I'm humbled by these honors that you bestow about me. Walking with Ehyeh on the Earth two thousand years ago, I thought, couldn't get any better. I was wrong. I was gifted with being an Ad..."

I leaned over to Ehyeh, "Big brother, what's an Ad again?"

"An Ad is a Perpetual One, meaning, Joanna hasn't physically died."

"... As an Ad, I've experienced joy upon joy to have been a part of so many farms and destinies. I shared my life with many of you here. These are my greatest treasures. You are my treasures. Each of you. My family." Joanna waves, blows kisses as she sits, at the same time the crowd stands and roars their approval.

When the crowd's applause quieted somewhat, Bre stood and continued, "My dearest new family. So many things have happened to me in such a short time. Reality is much more than I imagined." The crowd laughed. "The Earth's reality is a mixture of lies, false hopes, lusts, difficulties, stress and evil, thanks to the Eater and his slaves. Their roads lead to dead-ends. The road built by Farmer, Ehyeh and Ruah lead to truth, peace, joy, true love and life without end. And real family." Bre looked down at me with those deep brown eyes, placed her hand on my shoulder and squeezed it. I reached up and squeezed her back. "I'm so thankful that I was rescued from the circus and to be with you here now. I love you all." Tears of joy rolled down her cheeks. Joanna stood to hug her. The crowd stood and roared again. Everyone loves Joanna and Bre. Now eyes are all on me.

I swallowed a piece of hotdog, stood and looked around. It's just such a remarkable sight. Angels with trumpets. Banners of many colors. Medals of gold and gems covering my chest. The crowd all in white here to celebrate with us. Farmer, Ehyeh, Ruah, Bre and Joanna are smiling at me. I feel the love deep into my bones. How do I express myself? Words are hard to find.

"Please bear with me everyone. I'm just looking around taking everything in. Ya know, as a kid, I didn't get any chances to speak to crowds. Actually, I was usually beat by my mother, if I spoke up. I never knew my father. When she abandoned me on the street, I was captured, sold to human traffickers, chained up, bought and sold and treated like a wild animal. That's when I found out what real abuse was all about. I'd never experienced any peace or affection. Those were my awards from the Traffiker and the Eater. I'm not saying this to receive any sympathy, as I know we all have horror stories to tell. I say this because to be standing here with the likes of all of you are all the awards I would ever need or want. Thank you all for welcoming me into your family."

The crowd roaring with a thunder. Bre and Joanna jumped up to hug me. Bre's crying, "I never knew you went through all that, Ryder." Then she punched my arm, "You should have told me. Boys!"

I suppressed my ouch. The crowd loved it. As the crowd continued to clap, Farmer rose to quiet them, "Everyone, let's cheer them, as Ryder and Briella are about to head out on their next God Op."

Briella squealed and hugged me again, "I love going on Ops with you, Ryder!"

"I lo... ah... yeah... it's going to be great, Bre." My mind automatically checked me on the 'love' word. Still have some issues to sort through, I guess.

CHAPTER 26

"Bre? Bre? Where are you," I yelled out loud, twirling around in all directions? Nothing. "Must have gone back to her palace to freshen up maybe," I continued to yell out as I walked along. Shaking my head, "Women!"

Talking out to the woods as I walked along, "Searching for you, Bre, through this strange forest on this Op is making me hungry." The woods gave nothing back but silence.

Eyeing an apple orchard over to the left down a small hill I skid down to it looking for a nice juicy one. "Ah, there you are," talking to a perfect one hanging low on a branch. Just one more step...

Snap... wham.

I came to, laying on the ground with my foot stuck in a trap and my head pounding. Rubbing the back of my head with my hand, "What happened?"

"Hey, Ryder. How's your head," a small voice squeaked out behind me?

Twisting around there sat a strange elf-looking creature covered in animal furs, smoking a pipe, leaning back against an apple tree who looked like a tiny version of one of those mountain men you'd see in an Old Western movie.

He has a greasy, black, bushy beard with flies swarming around, going in and out of it, which tells me that's probably where they live. He throws off a very ripe odor, smelling much like the far end of a skunk. A mangy hat on his head made from a dead rat rounded out his scuzzy little outfit. The rat's eyes matched the beady, black eyes of this imp. He tossed me the apple that I'd reached for, "Here. You were after this?"

Catching it, "You know who I am?"

"Of course. You're the infamous Ryder we all keep hearing about."

"Infamous? We? Who's we?"

"We. On this side of the fence. You know, the *bad guys* you're always after," he says proudly. The hat fits him. His voice squeaked like a rat.

"You mean, you're with the Eater."

"Yeah. That's the ticket," his eyes twinkled as he happily puffs away on his long black pipe. "I knocked you out after your leg got trapped, not so much because I had to, but I do enjoy a good thumping," he crowed. Obviously enjoys his work.

"What do you want with me?"

"There's a bounty on your head, kid. And I'm a bounty hunter." He crossed his legs as if to relax more.

"Really? A bounty?" I smiled. Nice to be appreciated. "How much am I worth?"

"Oh, a lot. A nice promotion is coming my way, having you on a stick."

"What's your name, goober?"

"Goober? I like that. My name's, Trapr. I hunt and trap the likes of you for the boss."

"Who's your boss, Trapr?"

"Thought we already covered that. The Eater put a bounty on you and I caught you. He's on his way now, so eat your apple. It's probably the last thing you'll ever get."

I bit into the apple and enjoyed it as I leaned back on my arm, "Really, you seem pretty confident, Trapr."

"I am. I've trapped and stocked the boss's slaughterhouses for thousands of years."

"Slaughterhouses?"

"Yeah. There're slaughterhouses all over the planet. The boss lets us cut wormies out from his herd whenever we want to have some fun. Teasing and killing wormies is our favorite pastime. Some we slaughter before they're born, some we do slowly and painfully when they're old… any way we like. The boss's favorite is getting you wormies to massacre each other. This whole planet is the boss's cattle farm. You worms are the cattle. Except you've been a naughty little worm, rustling livestock from the boss." He shakes his finger at me. "Once I trap your little girlfriend and bring her in for slaughter, I gotta go out and trap all that stock you two rustled and herd 'em back. Can't let any squirt away."

Girlfriend? I like that. "So, we're like cattle huh?"

"Of course, we brand you at birth because all of you belong to the boss's farm."

"Brand?"

He moves his furs to the side to show me the "S" brand on his backside. "See. Like this. The S means I'm one of the Eater's soldiers."

"Really? You sure it doesn't stand for slave or stupid," I snorted.

"I'm no slave you worm. I don't have a W branded on my butt to say I'm a worm," he snaps back.

I waved him off, "Ah go on, I don't have a W on me anywhere, you dingbat."

"All of you get one. You just can't see it with your physical eyes. Even you used to have one, but when wormies like you join Ehyeh, he takes all your black and exchanges it for light. You become a Light-god. Your W brand falls off and is replaced with one of your family's LG brand. Course, we get lots of you back and we just rebrand you again."

"Whatyamean?"

"Well I go out and trap LG's and wrangle them back in to us. My best trap is the circus trap. An LG will start or join a circus and lose their brand when they follow some buffoonery that they made up. We rebrand them with an F and usually set them free."

"F? Set them free?"

"Yes, siree. F stands for Fake light-god. Usually the boss sets them free to trick other LG's into becoming F's. The F's do our work for us. Get it? The boss is so brilliant," hee hee, hee hee!

"You do all this for fun?"

"It's all great fun it is. We love to wreck the lives of the wormies." He stands to do a little song and dance,

"Oh, we chain 'em and we pain 'em,
And we slice 'em and we dice 'em,
Jerkin' 'em around on strings;
We bind 'em and we blind 'em,
And we slash 'em and we dash 'em,
Till they die from our endless stings!"

He twirled and hummed in delight to himself some more.

"What if you can't trap LG's back?"

"We don't get many stubborn LG's when they wander off or get rustled. Most wormies love to live in one twilight zone or another, even when they become LG's. Well, except you and a few others. Wormies are fools and too arrogant and full of themselves to leave a twilight zone."

"What's the twilight zone?"

"Like shopping for a pretty house, wormies buy into a twilight zone of what they say contains moral truth and then think their lives have *meaning* when they live there." He emphasized the word "meaning" in a mocking tone. "We set up pretty twilight zone's all over the world. Some in governments, some in schools, of course lots in circuses and other cracker-bins. They're all really the same though. Wormies can't see that when they're in a twilight zone, they're all really just meat in pens waiting for their turn to die. We show no mercy. We thoroughly enjoy our work and every wormie gets a turnie! It's all so tasty it is." He twirled around doing his little dance again.

"Sounds like you all have fun torturing, maiming and killing us for laughs."

"We do! I really enjoy how scared wormies get before they're slaughtered. The terror in their faces when it comes and then how surprised they are when they end up in the abyss. Especially the shock from the circus wormies." He spun around again, singing,

"Scared, scared, scared,

when they become dead, dead, dead!"

"Yeah, I've lived through some of the nasty stuff that you guys do."

"And the best part of it all is, you wormies always blame the Farmer for everything." He slaps his knee with his hand laughing out loud, "Hee, hee, what a bunch of dummies you all are!"

I took another bite of my apple, "Yeah, you guys are very successful butchers. Slaughtering billions of people as a pleasure sport."

"Thanks for the compliment. We aim to please. Ourselves that is," he chuckled as he sat down and lit up his pipe. "So now that we got all that said, you're probably pretty scared right now, eh kid?"

"Nope. How about you?"

"Scared? Why would I be sacred? You're the one trapped."

"Yes. It certainly looks grim for me," as I bit into the apple again smiling. I detected from the slightly concerned look on his face, that his cheery confidence had drained away. "Tell me, Trapr, don't you regret joining the Eater on his foolish adventure. For someone who's so crafty that they can catch me, the great Ryder, it seems like a very stupid decision to follow him?"

He leaned in, "I am crafty. That's why I joined the Eater. My talents weren't appreciated by the Farmer. He wanted to give all the best goodies to you little wormies, instead of to us. What a joke. Worms are so weak and stupid. Why should you get anything? We're the first born, not you, things," he said with disgust pointing his pipe at me, as he leaned back against the tree rapidly puffing some more on it. The smoke from his pipe smelled like a dead animal.

I'm liking this, "Oh, so, you think *you're* entitled. That's it. You think Farmer's entitled to divvy up his kingdom to a bunch of ungrateful twits like you and the Eater, just because you want it? No wonder he kicked you all to the curb." Now I leaned back and chewed into my apple with a loud crunch directed at him.

Trapr jumped up and pointed at me with his pipe again squinting in anger, "You little worm, how dare you speak to me like that! I might just kill you myself before the boss gets here and just take a pass on getting a promotion."

I laughed, "Nah, you won't do that. The Eater would punish you for disobeying him. You and I both know that, you, wacky, little dipstick." I laughed some more.

Trapr stomped around talking to himself. He knew I was right. "I'm going to look forward to watching what the Eater has planned for you," he barked in anger.

"Did the Eater tell you why he wants me so much or is he too afraid to pass on that little tidbit?"

"The boss isn't afraid of anything. He told us you and that girlfriend of yours have been causing too much trouble and need to be put down like the silly puppies that you are."

"Trouble? If you call branding his sad, wrinkly, ugly butt trouble, then I guess you're right, we are trouble."

He stopped pacing, "What do you mean branding him?"

"Oh, didn't he tell everyone? My girlfriend branded his saggy little butt with her sword. Didn't he show you his new tat? He was bested by a girl," I laughed out loud!

He sat down hard holding his head, then looked at me, "I don't believe you. You wormies always lie."

"Let's ask your boss when he gets here then. We'll see who's lying." Just as I said that, the Eater materialized in front of us in a flash of fire. "Well, well, speak of the devil," I snickered as I sat up to finish my apple.

Trapr jumped up to attention. The Eater circled around me quite pleased to see me in a trap. "Well boy, you aren't so mouthy now I see."

"Oh, I am. You just need to give me a chance." The Eater's grin disappeared in an instant. His eyes shifted around not understanding why I'm not afraid.

The Eater congratulated Trapr, "Well done, my trusted one. My new captain."

"Thank you, my lord, for this honor," as Trapr bowed to the Eater.

"Gimme a break," I said mockingly. "Captain? That's it? That's the big promotion for catching a big fish like me. One who out-crafted the master of evil. Out-foxed the lord of darkness. Butt-branded the wizard of wizards!"

The Eater twirled around. His eyes were on fire. Must have hit a raw nerve. "I'm going to make the rest of your short life very unpleasant boy."

"Really. How do you suppose you can do that?"

"You're trapped, boy. You're mine now!"

"I'm trapped? You guys. Always with the jokes." They both stared at me like I'm nuts. "I'm just poking fun at you. You guys have been quite entertaining, but I guess we should wrap this up."

"What do you mean, wrap this up? Where do you think you're going," he growled?

"Don't you wizards of intelligence wonder where my girlfriend is? I mean, come on, we're always together. How about my horse? And my sword? What about all the angels that hang with me? And, let's not forget Ruah. You remember Ruah don't you slick," looking directly at the Eater? "Can't you geniuses recognize a trap when you see one? And, especially you Trapr. You say you've been trapping for thousands of years. Don't you recognize a trap when you're in one?"

A red-bladed sword appeared in the air behind the Eater. With a slashing sound, another butt-branding is completed. Briella appeared sitting on Shiloh. The Eater howled so loud, apples fell out of the trees before he disappeared in a puff of smoke.

Trapr was jumping up and down and twirling around screaming when it came...

Snap... Wham!

Trapr came to, laying on the ground with his foot stuck in one of his own traps, rubbing his head, "My head hurts. What happened?"

"Hey Trapr. How's your head," I asked?

Trapr looked up to see me standing by Gideon. "I knocked you out after your leg got trapped, not so much because I had to, but I do enjoy a good thumping," I mocked. "I mean, fair's fair right."

"B.. but how did you escape?"

"You trapped one of my other selves. Didn't the Eater tell you that Briella and I can split into numerous versions of ourselves? The version you trapped was the bait," as I tapped his trap with my sword. "We knew where all your traps were. We watched you as you set them. Your trapping me was just a trick. One of the traps you placed over there, we dragged it over here and slapped it on you. How's it fit anyway? Not too tight?"

Trapr's terrified. He tries to run but the trap brings him down.

Briella and I laughed at him, "Hey Trapr, your traps do work pretty good, we'll give you that."

I shoved Trapr up against the tree with my sword, pressing the blade against the side of his neck as he squealed and pleaded with me, "Please don't kill me! I was only following orders!"

"Following orders? Who's lying now? You said it yourself, you're a bounty hunter. You said you enjoy thumping us. You trapped members of my family for thousands of years and turned them over to the Eater to be slaughtered for fun, some of them by your own slimy hand. I don't like that."

As I dug my sword against him tighter, black blood trickled down his neck. "The infamous Trapr has himself been trapped. I find that funny. Don't you find that funny, Bre?"

"Not as funny as branding the Eater again," she laughed.

"Yeah, that musta hurt. His pride mostly."

"How's that tat lookin' these days, Bre?"

"Looks great! It's coming out sweet."

"Imagine that Trapr, you and your boss were out-gunned by a couple of kids."

"Wha... wha... what do you want with me," Trapr stammered?

"Well, wouldn't you know it, there's a bounty on *your* head. Farmer sent us here to trap you and brand the Eater again to collect on the bounty. I guess we're pretty good bounty hunters if we can trap the best in your measly little realm. Whatd'ya think, Trapr?"

"Yes, yes, you're both excellent trappers," he whimpered.

"Strange. I thought you would say that. Well. We'd love to stay and chat with such an important captain such as yourself, but we have other fish to fry. Are you ready?"

Trapr screamed out in fear as two angels appeared and wrapped chains around him. "They're taking you to your own special twilight zone prison that was designed especially for you, where you'll wait for your trial and punishment. And guess who's been appointed as the judge at your trial?" I smiled at him, pointed with my eyes over towards Bre. Bre lifted her eyebrows up and down at him with a smirk. Trapr screamed loader as he and the angels disappeared in a burst of light.

I strolled over to one of the apple trees, ripped off two beauties and tossed one to Briella. She grabbed it and bit in. "Finally. I thought those guys would never leave," I said as I'm trying to figure out how to polish the apple on my cape? "That was fun, eh Bre?"

"Sure was. So," Bre grinned, "I hear I'm your girlfriend."

I tripped over a stick at Gideon's feet, which caused the apple to get crushed against my chest. There's apple chunks and juice dribbling down my shirt. Bre laughed along with snorts coming from Gideon and Shiloh.

I need a hot dog.

CHAPTER

27

his time we came back to my cabin because I wanted to show Bre around. "Now these are what real trees look like," as I rubbed my hand against and slapped the huge redwood tree next to my cabin. "Not like those sad, skinny, silly-looking, palm trees over at your place," I sniffed.

It worked. I turned and ran, with Bre chasing me around several trees, "I'm going to get you, you, you, fat-tree lover!" We were both laughing so hard we couldn't run anymore.

"Ok, you win, you, skinny-tree lover," I said, holding up my hand trying to catch my breath.

We dashed over to the front of my cabin where the guys were waiting for us. "You guys blowing off some steam," Farmer asked?

"I guess we're so happy that this Op was so much fun. We took a bad guy off the field and Bre got to tat the Eater again with her sword."

Bre giggled, "It was all so delicious. All of it."

"That's it. Delicious," I agreed. "Went down like this fresh cookie," as I bit into one that the guys had waiting for us and swallowed it with a loud gulp.

Ehyeh hugged the both of us, "We're glad you're both enjoying building your farms. We have some new surprises for you now." When Ehyeh said surprises, we both stopped eating, stopped laughing and looked all around us. We couldn't see anything. Usually there's new robes or new crowns, along with noticeable farm upgrades. Ehyeh said, "Ok you two, close your eyes. No peaking until I say look."

We both closed our eyes and held hands. Bre was shaking in excitement. We could hear sounds but I couldn't make out what it was.

We heard Ruah say, "Alright, open your eyes."

There were beautiful horses standing in front of us. Their coats, manes and tails were like silk. Bre and I waded through them all, rubbing our hands along them.

"Oh, guys," Bre sighed, "They're beautiful."

I agreed. "Each one is like a different colored gem." Out of the corner of my eye I caught Gideon eyeballing me. "But my favorite gem is still my Gideon." Gideon trotted over and nuzzled my face with his head. Shiloh did the same with Bre.

Farmer continued, "That's not all you two. Look."

We looked past the horses to see two chariots. Wow! This was like icing on the cake. I was blinking like I couldn't believe it. Bre had her hand to her mouth in shock, "These are ours, too?"

They were much like Farmer's chariot, being made up of different colored, living angels. And on the front and sides are various kinds and quite a number of weapons. Some are very strange looking. Farmer will have to show us how they work. One of the angels from each of the charioted reaches down to pull us up into place. We're standing in them still surprised when Farmer asks, "Well. Aren't you going to take them for a spin?"

We both had puzzled looks. "How does it work," I asked, searching around for controls or switches?

Ehyeh said, "Tell the horses to get positioned, work with the angels and direct them where you want to go."

Alrighty then, as I glanced over at Bre in her chariot thinking, I guess we just believe it like before. My head snapped up when I heard her voice in my head agreeing with me. "Bre," I said out loud, "Did we just talk with our thoughts and not our mouths?"

"Yes, Ryder we did. Let's try it again."

We both stared at each other, probably thinking it would work better if we stared hard, I guess. Then I started, "Can you hear me, Bre?"

"Yes, Ryder, can you hear me," she said without talking.

"This is so cool. We don't have to talk with our mouths anymore." Then we could hear Ruah in our heads, "Thought you'd both like that ability." We both grinned over at Ruah, Ehyeh and Farmer.

"Thanks, guys. This is wild," we both said in our minds.

We can hear Ehyeh in our minds, "You can do both, but for now let's practice. Speak to the angels and horses with your minds to have them set up and take you where you want to go."

We did as Ehyeh said. The horses all came over and set up. Gideon and Shiloh took the lead positions. I was thinking to myself it'd be nice to fly over the lake when in a snap we took off so fast it almost threw me out. Bre's chariot was next to mine as we rose high in the air. There were no harnesses or reins. Seven horses around each chariot, not all out in front. We looked like some kind of strange, yet colorful, flying saucers, as we whisked up and down and around over the lake as each thought came from me. I threw a thought over to Bre to give it a try. I could hear her in my head, as she took us over the mountains and trees. This is unbelievable. When I thought that, everything stopped and we started dropping to the lake.

"I screamed over to Bre," what happened as we got closer to the water?

"I don't know, but it looks like we're going for a splash," as we hit and went in.

We both came up out of the water laughing, "What happened?"

"I don't know, Ryder. Maybe we got a flat tire," as she splashed me with her hand.

The chariots and horses were all hovering over the water. "How come they didn't go in?"

"It's because they took control after you lost it," I heard Farmer's voice behind us. Farmer, Ehyeh and Ruah were standing on the water as we twirled around to face them.

Bre and I both pushed ourselves up to stand and walk over. "How did I lose it? We were just flying around and then bam, everything stopped and we dropped."

"That's because you thought what you were doing was unbelievable," Farmer said with a grin. "The angels and horses stopped when you didn't believe what you were doing was possible."

Bre and I looked at each other and started laughing again. "Wow, touchy breaks on these new gifts you gave us, guys." Now we're all laughing including the chariot angels and the horses.

We all walked back across the lake to the cabin, with the horses and chariots trailing us. Quite a sight, I imagine, if Earth people ever saw us. Farmer explained some more of what happened, "When your belief system fails, reality changes. In the physical realm for instance, all may look the same when you speak words or change your mind but repercussions take place immediately in other dimensions."

Bre and I agreed that we were a bit confused.

Farmer continued, "Reality is full of frequencies and vibrations and waves, that you two can't see right now. Earth people not only don't see them, most don't believe they're there. You did a bit of that when you first tried to make hotdogs and watermelon. Words and thoughts have power and are reality that creates an action. Actions can take place in different dimensions. Different words and thoughts of different intensities, effect frequencies, vibrations and waves differently." Farmer could see that we were still confused.

Angels, carrying large jugs, came out from my cabin, walked out to us and poured them out into the lake. The liquids in the jugs were each a different color. The colors just sat there all together in the water as Farmer said, "Now stir the liquids with your fingers anyway you like."

We knelt down and stuck our fingers in, swirling it, pushing it and splashing it. The liquids went in various directions, in many different combinations. We still weren't getting it.

Farmer said, "Look. What do you see?"

Bre answered, "Just the colors of liquid spreading out to where we sent them."

"Exactly," Farmer said. "Do you get it?"

I stood there scratching my head until it hit me, maybe because Ruah snuck the idea to me perhaps. "Our fingers are like our words or thoughts or our actions. When we say, think and do things, these are actions that cause counter-reactions of frequencies, vibrations and waves, that can affect other things. In this case, the counter-reaction is the liquids moving out in various directions to produce a result. Sorta like farming. If you plant good seeds and cultivate them properly you get a good harvest. Bad seed or wrong cultivation gives you bad stuff."

Farmer hugged me, "I knew you weren't just a pretty face." Then he asked Bre, "Do you see now, my gem?"

"Yes Farmer, it makes sense now. Reality is very sensitive to what we say, think and do."

"Yes. You must be careful with your words and thoughts as well as your physical actions, as all produce results that can even be unintended and dangerous."

"Dangerous," Bre questioned?

"Wrong words, thoughts and actions can take a person back to the Book of the Dead," Farmer said matter-of-factly.

That scary thought just came into my mind. I could hear Bre's same thought. I remembered that Trapr told me how people's words, thoughts and actions trapped them into one twilight zone or another.

"Yes, you two. Harness your words, thoughts and actions, to keep them from spreading out like these liquids in the lake here."

When we reached the shore, we had a seat as the chariots and horses went to the side of my cabin to wait for us. What Farmer said and showed us was absolutely unbelievable. Oops. I did it again. I stood up desperate, "Farmer, I just did it again. I said unbelievable in my head. How do I stop all the waves and frequencies and stuff from spreading out against me? I don't want to go back to the Book of the Dead!" I was on my knees now in front of Farmer.

Farmer smiled, "Relax, Ryder. Just quickly admit your mistake. Say you want no part of what you wrongly said, thought or did and move forward. Try not to go off course again. It gets easier as you go along. Make proper frequencies, vibrations and waves part of your life."

Bre asked, "How do we know what's the best things for us, so we don't make mistakes that we're not even aware of?"

"That's a great question, Briella," Ehyeh responded. "Most people never consider that question. They usually go along doing whatever they think is right. Many blindly walk back into the Book of the Dead. What they say, think and do, may look good, but it's not. Some never left that book, thinking or being told by other contras, that they're safely in the Book of Life, when they're not. This is a problem in the circuses. They parade around in their fake world's that they've created, with their whitewashed words, thoughts and actions, thinking all is well. The Eater holds some of the blame too."

"The Eater," we both angrily said at the same time.

"Yes, the Eater," Farmer said with a serious look. He placed his hands on our shoulders, making a point that we pay attention to what he was saying. "The Eater assists people to carry on with their distorted words, thoughts and actions, making them believe they're on the right path. You've both seen examples of the many farms that are run by the Eater and his army. The circuses are death camps and contras are just his puppets. What they do is profane."

"Profane?" I didn't know what Farmer meant by that. "I know that what they're doing is way off course, as you call it, but you're saying that even sincere people who are trying to do right, are running death farms? They're profane? I thought profane was like saying bad words."

Farmer continued, "The definition of profane, is one of those words that people have altered to fit their personal agenda. Same as words like 'good' and 'nice' and 'truth' and 'love', to name a few. People make up their own definitions of words to make them fit their lives, when they should be fitting their lives to the true definitions of the words. Profane has a simple definition. It's anything that people do, that hasn't been initiated by me."

Briella was frowning. "You mean, that all these circuses that people run and go to, are death camps? Isn't some of what they do OK?"

"Call them death camps, death farms, cemeteries or graveyards, they're all profane when they operate even a portion of them under their own hand. One wrong move can profane all the rest." To cement his teaching to us he took us back over to the lake. "Look at the colored liquids that you two moved with your hands. What do they look like?"

We looked out over the water. Some of it was spread out far out into the lake. Most of it had washed up on the shore and was sitting on the beach. "It looks pretty but it's all over the place. It's a mess," we said.

"Exactly. You weren't deliberately trying to make a mess. You weren't trying to fail, but, as you can see, it's as you say, a mess. Now put your hands back in the water and let me guide you."

We did as Farmer asked. As Farmer spoke, we each moved our hands in different ways as he guided us. The colored liquids immediately reacted. Waves from our hands washed the liquid from the beach back into the water. The liquid that had drifted off was coming back. When the liquids came together, Farmer asked us to stop. "What do you see?"

"It's a barn," Bre squealed!

"Yes, it's a barn. Now take one finger and do your own thing again." Bre takes her baby finger and barely touched the water with it. The result was, the barn eventually became unrecognizable.

"Now do you see," Farmer asked?

"I think so," I answered. "So, when people operate their lives under just their own desires, it may look pretty or good to them and some others, but in reality, there are waves, vibrations and frequencies moving them and their farms in wrong or even dangerous ways that they can't see. Ways that can harm other people and their farms too."

"And," Ruah said.

"And, uh, and, if we want to obtain worthwhile, eternal results for our farms and other farms, we need to wait until you help us. We should work with you on when to go, then on how, when and where to move, and when to stop, otherwise, the end result is just a mess."

Bre nodded in agreement as I spoke and added, "These contra-ways all lead to death."

"Very good. You both are very sharp students. The best results are when we all work together as a team," Farmer smiled. Ehyeh and Ruah smiling along with him.

Ehyeh added, "And who's the father of messes and death?"

We both knew the answer to that one. They heard our thoughts.

"Excellent," Farmer said. "Now, you'll find that this teaching relates to our next Op. We go after one of the Eater's favorites. And one that you've been waiting for, Ryder. The Nullifidian."

I jumped up high in the air, "Yes!" Finally.

CHAPTER 28

'd been one of the Nullifidian's many prisoners for years, although I didn't know it. Farmer told us how most people on Earth are its prisoner. Not only its prisoner, but its slave.

After some final tips from the guys, Bre and I excitedly packed our chariots with our traps, weapons and gear and we all roared off.

We took our chariots high over the Earth to get a better picture of what we were up against. This Nullifidian.

"Hey you guys. Our chariots flying in formation is so cool," as I looked over to the guys and Bre, just before we came to a stop over the North Pole.

"It sure is," Bre smiled. "And a person who will remain nameless didn't even once drop any of us into the water along the way."

"Yeah, Ha, Ha. Thanks for the reminder." That was pretty funny though.

"You two have advanced quickly. You'll need that focus on this Op," as Farmer pointed down.

We looked through the various dimensions until it came into view. It made the Heretix look like a flea.

I asked, "How do these things get formed?"

Ruah said that when people keep feeding something, it gets bigger. This one was made up of many heads that looked like dragon heads. Farmer said because of all its heads it had become a hydra. Its body was more like an octopus with twisting arms that spread out all over the planet. It was standing in the icy waters of the Arctic Ocean, but it had tentacles in all the waters and across the continents of Earth.

Bre and I both looked at each other smiling. It wasn't too long ago that we would have been shocked seeing something like this beast. We would have been unsure about our ability to take something like this on. That was then. I looked around at all the weapons on my chariot that Qavvaq taught us how to use. Behind us, billions of angels had our back. I nodded over at the guys who were guiding our every step to victory. Bring it. We're highly trained and experienced God Operators now.

The guys brought us here for not only our on-site battle briefing, but also to show us how the Nullifidian operated. We were told that each head oversaw a different area of the planet. One head oversaw education. One was over governments. Another over the entertainment industry. A real nasty looking one controlled the economies around the world. The beast's main goal was to expand the egotism and self-gratification in people to convince each person, that they were god, so it could grow bigger and take in more slaves. It had worked on me. I didn't believe in anything but myself before I met Farmer, Ehyeh and Ruah. My idols were the rich and famous. Those who dominated and had power. That's what I wanted. It was like a hypnotic drug to me.

We watched how the heads and tentacles maneuvered various creatures under its command to alter laws and societies and people's thinking to adjust to the Eater's will. We didn't see the Eater. Maybe he's at the clinic getting some lotion to put on his burn tats, I laughed to myself. Ah, I love this job.

Farmer was very thorough with his briefing. Such complexity. Trying to figure out how to handle this beast on our own would obviously have been a stupid undertaking. Farmer heard my thoughts and brought it out for discussion, "You're right, Ryder. Many circus clowns and performers try to take on the Nullifidian on their own. They stomp around yelling up into the sky at it, telling it to go away, even though they don't see what they're dealing with or how to deal with it. They end up getting it mad and bringing down its anger upon themselves. They think they're helping themselves and others, but as we taught you with the colored liquids in the lake, personal agendas, no matter how pretty, cause what" … as Farmer turned to me…

"A mess" I said.

Farmer nodded over to Bre, "And" …

"Death," she added.

"Correct. Good intentions are a crafty trap of the Eater's to bring contra-results. He also fools people into thinking their activities against him are working, by pretending to retreat and holding back his hands to draw people deeper into more of his traps. People think they've had victories when all they've achieved is fulfilling more of the Eater's plans and pulled themselves further into his chaos."

I shook my head. I can't believe I was sucked in by all this. What a dork I was. But now, it's payback time.

"How do we attack," Bre asked?

"First, we give you a peak into the future," Ruah said as a portal in front of us opened up next to us. We stepped off our chariots to follow the guys into a large room.

"What is this place," I asked? "I thought we were going to fry up some Nullifidian meat?"

"Patience, Ryder," Ruah continued. "This is the Room of Records. It has everything that happens in eternity in it."

We looked around in all directions. It wasn't *that* big. Hard to imagine it contained eternity I thought.

"No, no, Ryder, it doesn't contain eternity. Here is where the records of eternity are kept."

"What does that mean," Bre asked?

"It means, we're here to show you how the Nullifidian was handled by you two," Farmer said.

"We're going to see now how we fought the Nullifidian in the past," Bre asked?

"Yes, that's it," Farmer patted us on the shoulders. They were all smiling at us again. We'd only jumped a bit before into the future in training.

"We're showing you this room now and this battle as a small gift of love. Soon, one day, more will be revealed to you. Once we show you this battle, enjoy it, as you won't remember it or of being here for a while," Ehyeh said.

My shoulders slumped over, my eyes looked down, "We won't remember being here?"

"One day you will," Ruah licked my face to console me.

I just thought of something, "Hey, have we been here before but we don't remember it?"

"No. This is the first time we've brought you both here. In here are all the details of your life. Every detail, including your thoughts, words and actions. Everybody's life is recorded here for eternity," Farmer explained.

Bre was still confused, "But, how is everybody's lives recorded here, if lots of it hasn't happened yet? Like for people that haven't even been born yet? Are they in here?"

"Oh, yes," Farmer nodded "Everybody and everything are recorded here, right up until the last one."

"The last one?" That hit me a bit.

"There will be a last one at the end of days, but eternity goes both ways. It never started and never ends," Ehyeh added.

I think the wheels in my brain were starting to skid a bit. Looking over at Bre, she gave me the same look. We quickly shook it off though, accepting the mysteries and trusting in the guys. They pulled the record of our battle with the Nullifidian out of a journal for us to witness. Everything was there. The date. Every strike. Every sound. Every emotion that we both had. Even from any angle we wanted to see it. Stop, go back, go forward. Multidimensional. It was fantastic.

"It's time to go. Are you both ready for the battle now," Farmer asked?

As the portal opened, we could see our chariots waiting for us. I looked back into the room as we stepped through. See you again, someday...

ഇരുഇരുഇരു

I shook my head. I can't believe I was sucked in by all this. What a dork I was. But now, it's payback time.

"How do we attack," Bre asked?

The guys were smiling at each other. My head swiveled around and over to Bre to understand why they were smiling. We shrugged our shoulders. Must be an inside joke.

CHAPTER 29

The battle plan that was laid out to us was to seriously wound the beast. This attack, at its weak spot, would weaken it enough so chains it had on its captives would drop off of them. Escape, as usual, was up to them. After all this time I still considered it odd when prisoners and slaves preferred to remain where they were, rather than be free.

Again, we were not here to destroy this thing. It wasn't time we were told.

The army of angels began their assault. Their diversionary strikes were against the tentacles far away from where we were positioned. They needed to restrain themselves, otherwise, any one of them could easily finish this thing off.

Bre and I had to be careful too, because one wrong thought from either of us could turn this mutant into a steamy pile of road-pizza.

It was hard to keep up with all that was happening all over Earth. So many tentacles were being struck by the angels, its heads were swinging around in many directions in an effort to defend itself. As the heads reacted, it exposed what we were after, the spot where their long necks came out of the body in the front. It was the gateway to a major nerve center.

We had to hit it from inside, sorta like we did with the Traffiker.

The guys nodded to us that it was our turn. We were in unity together. We moved our chariots as we were guided. The heads didn't see us coming as we slipped past and below them and into the opening of its body. We came to a stop to see countless flashes and what looked like wires running in all directions. Our thoughts went to the guys, "Where do you want us to begin?"

"Let's do it the way Qavvaq would do it," we heard Farmer respond?

A smile came to our faces. We said together, "That'd be, crush stuff and have fun doing it!"

"That's it," we heard the Farmer laugh.

"Roger that," we both said.

We had many javelins that the chariot angels held out for us. We took the larger ones first and threw them into the crossing points where energy was flashing through. The guys told us these were vortexes. We quickly followed up with smaller javelins that stuck into open points to seal them with a loud explosion. I lost track of how many we threw. We were throwing them as fast as the angels were handing them to us.

The areas we hit went dark. We noticed the beast's movements were slowing down. Probably too dumb to know what was happening to it. We directed our angels to hand us the axes that Qavvaq made for us. These were kinda like boomerangs. When we threw them, they spun around bouncing, cutting, shredding and slashing areas that we didn't hit with the javelins. I was mesmerized watching them move around like helicopters all around us.

Next were the bows. We fired arrows that were alive. They twisted and turned like guided missiles. They hit some primo-looking spots that certainly looked like they needed an arrow put into them. I love this job.

"Hey Bre, watch this." I grabbed three arrows and shot them out together. They zipped off into different directions, each hitting a target and then exploding. Bre did the same.

We continued until the guys told us we were done. We hovered in our chariots in the middle of the damage, admiring our work. "I think this was a very positive meet and greet, don't you, my lady," as I bowed to Briella.

"Yes, great lord. I'm sure it won't soon forget us," she curtsied and smiled. "Nor will the Eater, I'm sure."

A voice came from behind us from where we entered in, "No, I haven't forgotten you."

The Eater was here.

He was standing at the entrance, surveying all the damage. "Oh, look, Bre, it's the great and powerful, Eater," I said sarcastically.

Bre pulled out her sword and tapped it with her other hand, "Come for another tat, have we?"

That startled him, making him take a step back. "You can't escape out of my trap," he said. "I knew you'd come here. You're both mine now." He set some sort of fiery webbing across our escape route.

"Woah," mocking him some more, "He makes the big fire against us, Bre. What shall we do?" I leaned on one of the angels making up my chariot and petted Gideon.

"I don't know, Ryder," Bre giggled. "It looks so scary." She put her forearm up to her forehead pretending to faint.

We hit a nerve for sure. The Eater pointed at us, "If you two are so good, let me see you escape me this time!"

Ah. A challenge. My thoughts took my chariot towards him and the exit. I was still leaning forward, my eyes staring right into his. Bre followed. We got closer and closer. He didn't move. Me, the horses and the chariots went right through him and his fire web like they weren't there. The Eater's and my eyes met, as I went right through him.

He wasn't so fortunate with Bre. He was so upset about me flowing through him and out his trap, he took his eyes off of her to turn around and fling a bunch of arrows, darts, wizzes and bangs at me that I guess he thought would get to me. They all bounced away off my cape and went back at him. I love my cape. As he was dodging his own fire, he forgot a very important lesson. Never turn your back on Bre. Bre's sword hit its mark, to top off the other brands.

I twirled the chariot around to catch the whole thing. Ouch, I smiled, as he disappeared. I saluted him with my backhand, "Bye, dingbat!"

We flew back to the guys who were waiting for us over the Earth. "All good," Farmer asked?

"It was awesome! We hit it with javelins, axes and arrows!"

"And I got the Eater right in the pants over the other tats I gave him," Bre added poking her sword in the air.

"Take a look at what happened," Ehyeh pointed down at the Nullifidian.

We'd been so excited about getting back to the guys, we hadn't looked to see the results of our Op.

One of the heads was drooping down backwards behind it. It was jerking its head trying to get it back in position but it just kept flopping around. Another head kept banging itself against other heads. Many of the tentacles had tangled themselves up together and others were waving around in all directions. We saw angels moving into where these open areas were.

"What does this mean," I asked?

Ruah explained, "It means, that you two disrupted the Nullifidian's strategies in areas it had influenced. The curtain has been pulled back on people's minds over the Earth. Many will no longer see truth as lies and lies as truth. Common sense will be more common, instead of rare. These angels that came with us are moving into these exposed areas to show people the way to us. We don't want them streaming into circuses or similar fool's paradises, thinking they can find the answer there."

Bre and I nodded our heads as we giggled at how goofy the Nullifidian looked. "Not so tough now are you, big dog," Bre shouted.

"Now what," I asked?

"Now you get these," Farmer said, as he handed us each a golden key.

We both stared at them wondering what they went into, then it came to us, "The jeweled boxes that you gave us after the Abarron Op?"

"That's it," Ehyeh confirmed. "Let's go back to your places and see what's in them.

We snapped our chariots around and headed back. Glancing back, the Nullifidian was still struggling. So sad. Not.

When we got back, we quickly jumped off our chariots and ran to our boxes. Mine was on a shelf over the fireplace in my cabin. Bre's was in her island hut. We agreed to meet over at her place. I stepped through the portal hitting the beach at the same time she flew out the door of the hut with her box. The guys were already here waiting for us.

Bre was so excited, "Let's open it at the same time!"

We turned the keys and lifted the lid. I think my eyes opened wider than I'd ever had them. Bre's expression looked the same when I glanced over. I asked the guys, "Wha... how... do we... ah... do with this?"

"Have Qavvaq show you. He's an expert," they all said at the same time.

CHAPTER 30

We're all sitting around a campfire that I fired up in front of my cabin. I'd never had one before, as I'd only ever heard it mentioned by some people when I was a prisoner of the Traffiker. Sure, we had open fires in metal drums under bridges when I lived on the street, but that's not the same.

I liked this campfire as much as my fireplaces… the crackling of the fire, darting up here-and-there, in-between the logs. I know the guys have probably sat in front of gazillions of these through eternity, but they didn't show any sign of boredom. They loved being with Bre and me and we loved being with them.

Ducks paddled in to the shore to join us, along with an assortment of animals from the forest. I guess you could say this was a party. Only Bre and I were the only people here.

"Are we going to be doing more training soon," Bre asked.

I nodded, "Ditto, we want to learn lots more."

As I said that, a deafening crack of thunder struck along with lightning that flashed across the sky. Bre and I jumped back in our chairs. The guys just smiled.

"Wha... was that," we both said together?

"Well, you did say you wanted more training," Ruah answered. "We thought you meant right now."

A portal opened up over the lake releasing a mighty rushing wind in front of wild horses encircling a fiery chariot that roared through and came straight at us like a freight train. The thunder boomed louder, the ground rumbled, the waters of the lake splashed high in the air and the lightning struck right beside us, throwing Bre and I back under our chairs. The horses and chariot stopped just short of the guys, who were still sitting calmly around the campfire like nothing was happening. Just as suddenly as it all came, the wind, thunder and lightning all stopped.

Bre and I peeked out from under the chairs at it, at the guys, then at each other. We hadn't seen anyone but the guys and us on chariots before. Who's this?

The guys stood up smiling as the angels making up the chariot opened up to allow this old man to step out. He struts over to the guys giving them all a group bearhug while yelling into the air, "Ahhhhhh.... I love you guys!" It was a deep, booming voice.

"Same old Qavvaq," Farmer said as they hugged.

Bre and I whispered with our lips to each other, "Qavvaq?"

We noticed Qavvaq looking over at us when we did this. We immediately knew nothing gets by this guy.

He let go of the hug and looked around sniffing with a sour look on his face, "Yep, smells the same."

Smells the same? I sniffed my armpits. What's that mean?

"I see you guys keep your mountains small here." He knelt down, dipped his hand in the lake and took a taste, "Yeah, still tastes like, *water*," as he spit it out and wiped his mouth with his weathered sleeve.

Who does this old geezer think he is insulting my lake and mountains? I started to size this intruder up. The long, snow-white beard, was the first thing that stood out. His hair was also pure white, full and flowing. A rugged face with fierce eyes that burned into you. He wore a mixture of clothes made from metal, leather and furs. Weapons were all over him. There were several strange things strapped to his back that had four blades; a bow, with arrows in a quiver and at least three swords and a few daggers just on the one side. I'm sure there was more I couldn't see. He was rugged and intimidating.

His chariot was covered in short and long spears, nets, chains with steel balls on the ends and some other weird stuff I never saw before. Many, small dark, round things with hair were dangling from many poles sticking straight up along the inside of the chariot.

"So, these are them," he asked the guys with his hands on his hips? He was sizing us up, too.

He walked over to us, snapped us both up off the ground in his arms, squeezed us into his bearhug, spun us around and yelled, "Ahhhhh... the God Ops kids!"

I couldn't breathe. Bre's eyes were getting a little buggy as she gasped for air. When he finally let us go, he put his hands on our shoulders, "Are you two ready to crack some eggs?"

I was coughing trying to catch my breath, "Crack some eggs?"

"Yeah. The guys said you two were tough. You liked smacking bad guys. Ya know, crush stuff and have fun doing it."

Farmer scolded him, "Be easy with them, Qavvaq, they're still a bit new to everything. They need your, special touch."

Special touch? From this old poop, I thought. Like a whirlwind, he turned and tapped me with one finger on the arm. I hit the ground with a thud. Qavvaq looked down at me with his hands on his hips, "I don't know guys, this one looks a tad puny. And he thinks strange things about his instructor. The girl looks tough though."

Great. He reads thoughts, as I struggled to get back up.

He looked me in the eyes, "Did you want this old poop to teach you some things or would you rather sit this one out and let your girlfriend protect you when the going gets tough?"

My face turned red. There's that girlfriend word again. "I want you to teach me, sir," I muttered.

"What was that," Qavvaq said, putting his hand to his ear leaning towards me?

"I said, I want you to teach me, sir."

"Outstanding. Any questions before we get started?"

"Yes," I said. "Who are you," as I rubbed my arm where he tapped it?

He laughed, as he put his arm around my shoulder and then Bre's. "Let's sit by this great bonfire you made, Ryder and I'll fill you in." He knows my name?

It was a great story.

He told us that he lived on Earth long ago. He was a great warlord, although, he didn't start out that way. He grew up in a small community of hunters where he learned to trap and hunt from his father. All was peaceful then, he said. As he got older, the tribe started getting attacked from outsiders making them scatter and hide to survive. Qavvaq said he lived off the land as he'd been taught, while also becoming very skilled in defeating those that wanted to kill him or take him prisoner. His reputation attracted many followers. A small group soon grew into an army. His army switched from being the hunted to being the hunters. Qavvaq wanted to destroy these bad ones to bring life back to the peaceful times.

They were successful for a time until other tribes formed allegiances to come against Qavvaq.

"Great battles raged. We became as heartless and ruthless as those we had formed up to stop," Qavvaq said. "We became mindless destroyers."

His army was moving to the next village to destroy it, when they came upon a man in the middle of the road. He told us this man stopped our entire army. "We all fell over with a word from his mouth."

Bre's and my mouth were both wide open in awe, "One man stopped you and your whole army," I said.

"Yes."

"How's that possible?" Then it hit me. I looked over at Farmer who was smiling.

Qavvaq put his arm around Farmer, "Yes, Farmer and I met on a road just like you, Ryder. He smartened me up!"

"Then what happened," Bre was as excited as I was?

"My army didn't know what happened. They couldn't see Farmer. Only I could see and hear him. He explained to me that I'd become evil. That I had a choice to make to continue on my path to my death and destruction or accept a path with him. A path of love and peace." I remembered growing up in love and peace. This is what I'd wanted all along for me and everyone, but I'd grown into a monster that just wanted power now. Looking around at all my men lying on the ground, I couldn't dispute or match this man's power. As a power-hungry madman, I accepted his offer, thinking I'd trick him along the way and just take what I wanted from him later."

Bre and I started laughing at such a silly thought.

He nodded his head, looking into the bonfire, "Yeah, I know. I was a stupid fool back then. Over time, my head cleared itself of the nonsense, the more Farmer, Ehyeh, Ruah and I were together."

We looked over at Ehyeh and Ruah, "Oh, so you met them back them too, eh?"

"Absolutely! They gave me a new name and made me an Ad."

"An Ad? You mean a Perpetual One, like our sister, Joanna," Bre asked?

"There's a few of us around on special assignments."

"But," I wondered, "You said you were on Earth long ago. You just came through that portal. What happened? Why did you leave? Where've you been?"

He chuckled, "These ones are very inquisitive," Qavvaq said to the guys.

"Yes, Qavvaq. That's one of their strengths," Farmer answered.

"Well, Ryder and Briella, I became a different kind of warlord. I was still battling, but against evil again now, to release prisoners and slaves into freedom and for many years it was working out but as time went on, evil ones rose up into armies united against me. I wasn't fighting individual armies anymore. They marched against my army for a great war which we lost. My army and territories of peace were lost. They took me prisoner."

Bre and I both said, "Whaaaaat," at the same time, as we squinted over at the guys.

"I know," Qavvaq continued, "I didn't understand it either. I yelled out into the air for Farmer to explain it to me. When Farmer appeared to me that night in my prison, he told me that this time, people had chosen evil over love, despite being shown and offered the difference. Our war for now, was done in the physical dimension. At that time, I didn't see or move in other dimensions. It wasn't allowed for that assignment. Farmer congratulated me on a job well done, but people on Earth, he said, had made their decision so they had to die with it. Then he disappeared."

Bre looked at Farmer and then Qavvaq, "Die with it?"

"Let me go on. The vast evil army killed everyone that didn't join them. I was the only one left. I was brought out to the rock-man and given a final chance to accept their ways or be executed."

"The rock-man?"

"Yeah, in the pre-stone-age we had no weapons beyond sticks and rocks. I was about to get a bashing. Well, the leader was swaggering around in front of me so, it just made sense to give him my answer with a headbutt," Qavvaq chuckled.

"You didn't," Bre laughed?

"Sure did. He went down like a bag of rocks."

"Wow! Then what happened?" This story was getting good.

"It, came."

"It," Bre wondered?

Qavvaq nodded over at his chariot. "Thunder crashed and lightning smashed down, a portal opened, crushing wind blew in and that chariot of fire and horses came down. Everyone fell over.”

He dropped his huge hands down on our shoulders, which startled us, “Just like when I arrived. Thought you’d like a taste of what I got,” he chuckled.

“That must have stirred them up” I said, checking my shoulder for dislocation.

“Yeah, it was quite a scene. Brave men in battle were soon screaming like babies and filling their pants,” Qavvaq laughed with a loud roar as he told us. He was laughing so hard he couldn’t speak. He said to Farmer, “You really did make a big entrance back then,” as Farmer smiled and nodded. After Qavvaq calmed himself a bit he continued, “An angel from the chariot walked over, untied the leather straps holding me, walked me back to the chariot and whoosh, we flew up, just before the bang.”

“Bang? What bang? You’re playing this out, Mr. Qavvaq. Why are you leaving us in suspense? Just tell us, please?” This juicy stuff was exposing my impatience.

“It’s not Mr., it’s just Qavvaq. Well, I was just short of filling my own pants too with all of this. I mean, flying over the Earth was hard to handle, even for a warlord. I had an extremely firm grip on a couple of the angels in the chariot, which only tightened as I watched a meteor hit the Earth. And then another and another. I couldn’t imagine such a sight. When my chariot reached Farmer in his chariot hovering over the Earth, terror was on my face as I watched the Earth and everything on it be destroyed. When it was done, our chariots turned and left. This is the first time that I've been back since then."

"You've been gone for what… millions of years," Bre speculated?

"Actually, right now is my anniversary. It will make it an even billion."

"A billion? Years? You're a billion years old," Bre gasped?

"No. I'm a billion and thirty years old. It's been a billion years since I left," Qavvaq turned to the guys winking, "I thought you told me these guys were sharp." He was teasing us now.

Bre and I both leaned back in our chairs trying to absorb all of this. This taxed my brain for sure. "So, where'd you go?"

"I went to another galaxy that Farmer gave to me as a gift. While I was on my new farm, the guys trained me to become a headhunter. Hunting angels."

"An angel headhunter," we both said?

"A dark angel, headhunter. Ones that go off the reservation that turn bad."

I was thinking, if this guy can take out angels the size of our Wasters, I want what he's got.

"Eventually I received my own universe. It's really nice. You'd love what I've done with the place." Qavvaq leaned back in his chair and took a large swig out of a pouch he carried at his side. Much of it sloshed down his beard onto the cape that partially covered his barrel-shaped chest before it splashed to the ground.

Ruah spoke up, "Qavvaq, you're overloading them with too much all at once. Let them process it in stages."

"OK," Qavvaq agreed. "Let's pick it up tomorrow when we start training. You guys still have tomorrow around here on this puny planet don't you," as he looked around with a pretend sneer on his face?

"He's messing with us, Bre," making us all join him in laughter.

I tossed and turned all night in my cabin so excited about be trained by a billion-year-old angel hunter. I mean, a billion and thirty.

The next day came early when Qavvaq lifted up my bed and threw me out of it. "Time to get up sunshine", he barked. "You wanna be good enough to hunt and kill angels, you better get tough." Bre wasn't given any quarter on the wake-up call either.

Training was intense. We thought we knew what we were doing before but all of it was nothing compared to the level he was taking us to. Qavvaq taught us how to use many weapons and how to trap and hunt. We went trappin' and huntin', to use his words, moving through dimensions we hadn't seen yet, striking targets that Qavvaq had set up and setting traps catching many wild beasts, but we never did hunt any dark angels. We weren't near enough ready for them he warned us.

He was an excellent teacher with a wild sense of humor. I guess a billion years will do that to a person. He was constantly playing tricks on us and joking with us. We tried but couldn't get him back. He moved like we were standing still. He knew what we'd do before we'd think it. He taught us how to do that as well.

He took us exploring to many other galaxies. There're hundreds of billions of them, he said, just in our universe and then he showed us how to go to other universes. We lost track of how many we'd been to. Each was different and beautiful in its own way. The planets we saw outnumbered the galaxies and universes of course.

"There's so much," Bre said as we were coming back from one of our training trips.

"There is. It all makes up the 'E'," Qavvaq added.

"The E," I asked?

"Yes. E for eternity. There's no beginning. There's no end. You'll never see it all. It's impossible. I've been around for a billion years and I've seen only a tiny portion of it and I can move at the speed of creative light."

We landed back at my cabin which was an extension of my farm, as Bre's tropical island was to hers. We both still preferred our little hideaways over the chateau and Bre's palace. When we arrived, the hotdogs were already steaming on the table outside. Huge steaks were here for Qavvaq and Bre had her various fruits. We'd made these while we were still on our way back. Creating all this with our thoughts was standard procedure now.

The usual liquicake was here for me, Bre had her special creation juice drink and Qavvaq drank from his pouch, which he said was a mixed, spice drink that he developed from ingredients he found in different universes. He let us try some once. It was like drinking flames, only hotter. It must be an acquired taste, Bre and I both told him, as we were coughing up a lung. We were being nice. Qavvaq just laughed as he swigged in larger gulps that splashed all over. It fit him.

"Ahhh… another perfect hotdog," as I chomped out loud towards Briella. There's no evolving beyond hotdogs.

"Men and your meat," Briella joked as she tenderly cut her fruit with her knife and fork.

The table was created this time by Bre. Very nice silk cloth with multi-colored gems dangling from the edges. Our glasses were made out of one diamond each. The plates, knives and forks made from emeralds. Bre liked her green.

The guys soon appeared and sat with us. "Training go well today," Farmer asked? He already knew the answer, but talking about it was being sociable.

At times we talked with our thoughts and other times out loud. We enjoyed doing both.

We talked about all we'd done and seen. They enjoyed our excitement. "I have a question. We can zip to anywhere as fast as thought, right?"

"You want to take this one, Qavvaq," Farmer said?

"Sure. You want to know why we bother with walking, riding horses and using chariots, right, Ryder"?

He knew my question before I asked it, "Yeah, I mean, what's the point"?

"Point is, to enjoy the ride, my little brother. Savor the process."

My look told him I wasn't getting it. Then all my hotdogs disappeared. "Hey, what happened?" I stood, twirled around, looked under the table, then looked right at Qavvaq with my hands on my hips, "OK, whatd'ya do with my dogs?"

"They're in your stomach. Isn't that better? No wasted time smelling or tasting the flavors. Just zap 'em in. Can do the same with your liquicake," as he lifted his finger?

I jumped over, grabbed my glass, covering it with my hands, "No, no, I get it, I get it!"

Qavvaq roared with laughter. "You're a sharp student, Ryder. Nothing gets by you."

I took a big swig of my drink and let it slosh all over my face and down my chest. "Ahhhh...!" This *is* better.

As I was learning my new lesson, Bre had finished her meal and drink. A chilled dessert then formed itself in front of each of us. "What's this," I asked as I was sniffing it? "Smells like one of your socks, Bre." It smelled wonderful.

Bre frowned at me, "This, you man you, is something I came up with from ingredients I found while visiting one of the other universes we went to with Qavvaq. I want you guys to try it."

I put my glass down, picked up a fork and threw some in. Qavvaq did the same, as did all the guys.

"Well," Bre wanted to know?

All the guys praised her. Qavvaq asked, "What is this, my mighty sister? It's the best dessert I've had in a billion years!" He gobbled the whole plate down like a starved animal. He was serious. He looked over at my plate as if to steal it. I covered it with my hand, eating faster.

"And, Ryder," she wanted to know, frowning at me?

"Bre. This is beyond fantastical. It is breathtakingly, scrumpishly, jaw-droppingly...," I was hunting for some more made up words when she smacked me.

"Just for that, boyfriend. No more for you."

Everyone else started laughing hysterically. Did she just call me, boyfriend?

She came up with the whole thing in her head, like I'd done with liquicake. She called it, Breezie. Each bite changed its taste in my mouth. It would taste lemony, then switch to a creamy strawberry taste, then over to banana, followed by a tangy blueberry wrapped with peachy, whipped cream and so on. Many tastes were new. Never the same taste twice.

The guys complimented her, "It's a wonderful dessert that you created, Briella. May we have more?" They held out their plates. Bang. A huge slab of it instantly appeared on each of their plates. My plate stayed empty.

I peered over at Qavvaq's plate as if to steal some. He covered his plate with his hand, "Naughty boys get no more," he waved his finger at me as he gobbled, smacking his lips deliberately at me to make me jealous. It worked.

CHAPTER 31

After chasing Bre around the table, tackling her and tickling her until she gave me some more Breezie, we called it a day. Bre walked through the portal over to her island. The guys disappeared. Never knew where they disappeared to. Perhaps to that mountain where Bre and I went to, riding Bruce.

Qavvaq and I talked some more by the bonfire. I never got bored with his stories. "Tell me another trappin' and huntin' story. Pick a real nasty one that you went after." Qavvaq always had good ones, so I got comfortable and waited quietly while he was thinking.

"OK, I'll tell you about the first one I went after outside my farm. Well, ya see, the guys asked me if I'd like to take out this savage angel that was terrorizing universe number 37. I'd already cleared out my universe, which was my farm, so I was getting pretty thirsty to go on a deep, woods safari. I wouldn't have known what to do with myself if I wasn't trappin' and huntin'."

During training, Qavvaq had told us about angels that decide to leave Farmer's farm. They have different reasons for wanting to be on their own. Most eventually come back to the family. Some just isolate themselves off in some corner of eternity, preferring to be alone. Then there's the ones that go bad. They decide to brutally take certain galaxies or universes for themselves through destroying, killing and enslaving. That's when Qavvaq is called in. He hunts them down, traps them and then... well, while he was telling us all this, he brought us over to his chariot to show us the things that were dangling on the poles. They were his trophies... shrunken heads of dark angels he'd taken. How cool is that?

"Was it a big angel? How big was it? How did you get it?"

"Settle down, young Ryder. Let me tell my story."

I could tell part of Qavvaq's training was teaching me patience. A quality that is vital for trappers and hunters. That part was hard work for me.

"I loaded up my chariot with my traps, weapons and other gear and headed out on safari. Huntin' a creature in a universe is a bit different than your huntin' around Earth. It could be anywhere in hundreds of billions of planets in hundreds of billions of galaxies amongst hundreds of thousands of millions of stars."

"Wow!"

"I didn't want to rush the hunt. The hunt was my hotdog," Qavvaq slapped my arm. He liked teasing me. I liked that he liked teasing me.

"How did you know where to start?" He pointed at his nose. "You used your nose?"

"Remember when I arrived here, I said it smells the same?"

"Yeah. I thought you meant I stunk."

Qavvaq laughed some more, "No, I meant Earth smells like I remembered. It stinks of rot. Of death. Of evil."

"Oh." I sniffed in the air. I didn't smell it. Something else to learn.

"I traveled through the universe sniffing around. I could have found it instantly, but I suppress those abilities. Same with the weapons I carry and that I've been teaching you and Bre how to use. We don't really need them. We could toast them all in a flash, but where's the fun it that? I enjoy smelling the panic in those evil gods when they're being hunted. I enjoy the trappin' and the bashin'. I love safari."

"I'm enjoying it all too. I love bashing bad guys. So, you were hunting this angel down and then...?"

"I knew where he'd been because I could see many well-placed traps it had set for prey. Prey meaning me."

"You mean, it was hunting you?"

"Sure was. It knew I'd eventually come to get it. Its traps were very crafty. I left them alone. I didn't want it to know I was here. Until I was ready."

"Then whatd'ya do?"

"Since it had traps set up, it made huntin' it easier. I knew its either regularly going around checking its traps or it knows when one is set off and so, it'll come to investigate. I wouldn't have to track it. It would come to me."

"Nice. I love your stories, Qavvaq. I'm learning a lot."

"That's why I'm here, Ryder. To teach you and Bre how to be more successful. Then, you'll teach others when you become instructors."

"We will?"

"Didn't the guys tell you that? You two are the first of many to come. They didn't call me here, after all this time, just to teach you how to set a trap. They want you to learn how to be instructors."

"Why don't the guys just teach everybody else like they did us?"

"They'll have a hand in it, but they want you and Bre to be a part of eternity. To build your farms. That's why they brought me here. They could have easily taught you what I know, but they're giving me the honor and pleasure of doing it. Not that I need a bigger farm, but I don't know what lies ahead for me. Even after a billion years they still have surprises for me. You and Briella are a very nice surprise for me."

"I don't know if I can be a leader. I'm just a kid. I've got a lot to learn. Who would listen to me?"

"You'll see, Ryder. It'll all fall into place. Just move with the guys and you and Briella will be fine."

I jumped up and hugged him, "Thanks, Qavvaq. You're like the big brother I never had." I respected the guys too of course, but Qavvaq was different.

"Your welcome, Ryder." He looked startled with what I said. Never saw him startled. "Are you ready for the rest of the story?"

"You bet." I sat down, wiping the tears from my face with my sleeve. Sniffing a bit. Qavvaq pretended not to notice.

"I spent quite a bit of time looking over this universe number 37. It was a graveyard of death and destruction from species wars. Galaxies and planets were littered with occupants enslaved in chains of illusion, superstition and madness, much like earthlings."

I was glued to every word. "Didn't Farmer tell you what you were looking for, where to find it and how to deal with it, like he does with us?"

"Nah, he knows that I enjoy safari too much. Like I said, I didn't want it to go fast. He tells me the job. He knows that I'll get the job done his way. That's what you would call entrusting me with the gift of sovereignty. You and Briella will receive that one day."

Never heard that word before. So much more to come in this family.

"So, there I was. After a while I knew what I was huntin'."

"You did? How did you know without seeing it?" He pointed to his nose again. Ah. The nose. I gingerly touched my nose like it would one day be an important tool in my arsenal.

"The wars all around. The death. The insanity of the inhabitants. It reeked of a Watcher gone dark."

I leaned back looking into Qavvaq's face. *"A Watcher? What's that?"*

"It's a high-level angel with great intelligence. This one's specialty was war. It enjoyed starting, enflaming and watching wars like an arsonist loves setting fires to watch things burn. That's what it was doing in that universe. The planets that weren't destroyed became slave plantations to provide a steady supply of livestock for this Watcher's sadistic forms of entertainment. I could see why the guys sent me there."

"How did you get it?"

"Well, now I knew what I was huntin' and that it had set traps. Qlaw agreed with me."

"Qlaw? Who's Qlaw?"

"Qlaw's my huntin' animal. Very keen senses. And good company. When I go out, he comes with me."

"Where's he now?"

"I didn't bring him with me on this mission. He doesn't play well with others. His senses are a hundred times sharper than mine. He'd hate the smell here."

"Oh. What's he like?"

"He was just a little, scrappy, savage cub-beast when I found him one day when I was out huntin'. He's bigger than you and a pure killin' machine. His claws are like your arms. Razor sharp. Teeth like daggers. And he's not afraid to use 'em," Qavvaq joked as he continued, "So, Qlaw and me wanted to have some fun. Bored warlords and killin' machines get like that ya know. Putting our noses together and following the path of planet destruction, we picked out a good place for an ambush. It was a planet that we could see the Watcher had set out a lot of traps around. And, Qlaw's sniffer, being much better than mine as I said," Qavvaq tapped his nose, "told us he'd been here recently checking his traps. More often than at the other places."

The training that Qavvaq had put Bre and I through over the months was getting the best of me. I was starting to nod off. The bonfire and waves splashing in on the beach wasn't helping to keep me awake either.

"Qlaw and I set up our own traps. When we were ready, we knew the Watcher would be coming back when we set off..."

CHAPTER 32

"Mmmm. Then you and mmmm…"

"Ryder! Ryder! Wake up. Are you dreaming again? …"

I still had my eyes closed. "Mmmm. Huh? What? OK, then you and Qlaw were waiting…"

"Qlaw? Who's Qlaw?"

That wasn't Qavvaq's voice. I opened one eye. Bre was standing over me with her arms crossed. I was slumped back in my chair. My head snapped up looking around for Qavvaq. He was gone.

"Why'd you sleep out here, Ryder?"

"Uh, well, Qavvaq was telling me a story about some dark angel called the Watcher that he was huntin' with Qlaw when I must've fell asleep. Where is he?" I stood up twirling around. "I want to hear how he caught the Watcher."

"The Watcher? Qlaw? Maybe you were dreaming?"

"No. He was telling me about this universe, that him and Qlaw went trappin' and huntin' to and that you and me are going to be instructors one day and then..."

"We're going to be instructors? Really? When? Did he say when?" Bre was missing the point.

"Bre, where's Qavvaq? I want to know how he dealt with the Watcher. It's important?"

"I don't know where he is. I haven't seen him since I left last night."

He didn't respond to my calling out to him so I ran around the cabin to check, but his chariot and horses were gone. I rushed back out front, "Bre, Qavvaq's chariot's gone! He's gone!"

"Well. Maybe he went out for a coffee."

I frowned at her. Not funny. "You know he only drinks that fire brew from his pouch." I wasn't in the mood for Bre's teasing. I wanted to know why he left.

I was still searching around, like maybe this was one of his training tricks and he would suddenly pop out at us, when Farmer, Ehyeh and Ruah came walking towards us across the lake. We ran out to greet them. "Morning, you two. Have a good rest," Farmer asked?

"Yes," we both said.

"Good. Qavvaq has trained you well?"

"Oh yes," we both said as we all walked back to the shore.

ॐॐॐ

...After some final tips from the guys, Bre and I excitedly packed our chariots with our traps, weapons and gear and we roared off.

We took our chariots high over the Earth to get a better picture of what we were up against. This Nullifidian...

ॐॐॐ

... "Let's open it at the same time," Bre said!

We turned the keys and lifted the lid. I think my eyes opened wider than I'd ever had them. Bre's looked about the same when I looked over. I asked the guys, "Wha... how... do we... ah... do with this?"

"Have Qavvaq show you. He's an expert," they all said at the same time.

ॐॐॐ

There were small galaxies, full of stars and planets floating in the chest. I looked over at Bre's. She had one too. They were slowly turning and spinning in the chests. We had just each received our own universe. I hadn't even got a grip on my chateau yet, that they'd given us.

"Because you both have done so well, your farms have grown. These are now part of your expanding farms," Farmer said. "Would you like to visit them?"

I couldn't take my eyes off my new farm. It was so beautiful. Well Ryder, I thought, now you have a universe. And you thought you wanted fame, power and fortune one day. I chuckled in my head a bit at my stupidity. Then the thought of one of those Watchers possibly destroying it all one day came into my mind. I got angry. My hand formed into a fist, "That mangey, critter better not come near my universe or I'll crush him and have fun doing it!" I wish I'd stayed awake to find out how Qavvaq dealt with it...

౭౦౭౦౭౦

"Ryder! Ryder! Wake Up. Are you dreamin' again?"

I still had my eyes closed. "Mmmm..."

"Farmer just asked if we wanted to go see one of our planets in our universes."

I cracked open an eye. Everyone was staring at me. I jumped up, "Of course. Let's go see yours first, Bre." That made her clap and scream. Women.

We all went in Farmer's chariot. It was much bigger than ours. The colors of the angels making up the chariot still blew me away. It was an awesome road trip. We laughed and joked all along the way. We were so excited. Qavvaq's right. Savor the ride.

After we'd been in Bre's universe for a while, enjoying all the mind-blowing sights, the chariot slowed down once this very, large planet came into view. This was our destination we were told.

I think Farmer deliberately slowed down so that we could watch Bre jump up and down more, scream more and point at it more.

We landed on a patch that was very tropical. Didn't know that it was possible, but Bre *can* scream louder when she wants to.

We walked around to take it all in. Well... Bre was flashing in back and forth around us as the rest of us walked. Sometimes she disappeared for a while. Usually accompanied by squeals and other woman-type expressions of happiness. I sat with the guys by a lagoon we'd found along the path.

"Farmer?"

"Yes, Ryder."

"I was talking with Qavvaq last night and he told me that he has a whole universe of bazillions of galaxies, planets and stars, that's all his farm. And head-hunts through many universes."

"That's correct, Ryder. What's your question?"

"Is this just a taste of what's to come for Bre and me? I don't know what can be beyond a universe farm. Qavvaq didn't tell us..." I didn't get a chance to finish nor did Farmer get a chance to answer. We heard Bre's happy screams getting closer as she was coming back.

She broke through some palm leaves with a strange looking little bird on her arm. "Look everyone! This is my new friend. Her name is, Tweak."

"How do you know her name is, Tweak," I asked.

"Because I told her," Tweak answered. Tweak looked at Bre, "I thought you said your boyfriend was smart?" Bre turned red.

I jumped up, "Wow, Bre, your new friend talks? Out loud?" I didn't want to say bird in case it wasn't a bird, but just looked like a bird. I walked over to them, "You're beautiful, Tweak?"

Tweak tilted her head at me and then back at Bre, "You're right, Briella. He is pretty smart. And a good-looker, too."

We all laughed, including Tweak.

We spent all day exploring with Tweak as our guide. Tweak's body shimmered in a metallic pink as she flitted around showing us the sights. Her six wings allowed her to move up and down and in all directions. The mountains of many colors were spectacular. Waterfalls were everywhere. The flowers had such unfamiliar aromas. I asked Farmer how big this planet was compared to Earth.

"This one planet on Bre's farm is a hundred times larger than Earth. Yours, we'll see later, is the same size, Ryder."

"Wha... Bre? Did you hear that? Just this one planet is a hundred times bigger than Earth!" It just sunk in on us. We ran over and hugged the guys, thanking them over and over. It soon evolved into a laughter that wouldn't stop. We could hardly breathe.

Ruah finally said, "We're so happy that you like your upgraded farms, but you're the ones that make them grow. When you sow, you reap. Are we ready to go over and visit one of Ryder's planets now?"

I thought I was going to burst from excitement. Bre was just as excited for me. She rushed over, put her arms around me and kissed me on the cheek, "Oh, Ryder, I'm so happy, with my farm, with the guys and especially being with you." She kissed me again. Well, she did tell Tweak that I'm her boyfriend. I hugged her tighter.

I could barely get the words out, "Yes, please, let's go see my new place."

We took some time walking back over to farmer's chariot. Bre's head was twirling around trying to see all that she could before we left. I don't blame her. It really was all a jaw-dropper. Bre asked the guys if Tweak could come with us but they informed her that Tweak was the planet's farm manager, who was responsible for looking after things, under Bre's leadership. She was so happy to hear this but sad to say goodbye for now. I thought, quite a responsibility for a bird, but then I thought, hey, I'm just a kid. Look at what I've been doing.

Farmer's chariot lifted off. We waved at Tweak until we couldn't see her anymore. Farmer was taking it slow so Bre could keep watching her planet as long as possible before we slipped into the next universe.

I could see there was a transition from Bre's universe to mine. Farmer did the same for me as he had with Bre, letting us see many of the sights before taking it slower as we approached my new planet. I can understand why Bre was so excited because I had to hold myself back from screaming myself. Bre grabbed my arm, "Ryder, your planet is gorgeous."

I put my arm around her shoulder, "Gorgeous?" "Bre, let's say my farm is ruggedly, handsome." We both laughed.

"Ruggedly, handsome it is," as she put her arm around my waist while we got closer and closer to it.

Something strange then started to happen to me. The thought of me being in charge of all this was starting to creep up on me. It was an uneasy, nervous feeling. I wondered over to Bre. She said she was feeling it, too.

We landed into a spot that was somewhat like my chateau and cabin areas, except this place was like a forest on steroids.

The mountains here were similar to Bre's at unimaginable heights, yet were made of rubies and gold. Bre's were covered in glowing, green emeralds and pink pearls. The trees here made my cabin redwoods look like small twigs.

The flowers were the same size that we saw at Bre's planet, although mine were more like wild flowers and roses. I like roses. Bre's were more tropical looking. The lake in front of us was like an ocean with waves over a hundred feet tall at least, that splashed up on a sparkling beach of gold and diamond sand that had no discernable end in either direction. Ruah told me they were small waves. I kept shaking my head trying to grasp all of it. I turned and grabbed the guys into a hug, "Why? Why are you giving us all of this? I don't understand?" Bre came over into the group too.

Ehyeh started, "We told you both before. Because we love you. Love doesn't end. It grows. It's unconditional. It's eternal. It's alive. Don't you feel it? Don't you want more?"

"Yes, love, but you've given me so much just with you guys in my life. I don't need planets and stuff."

Farmer said, "That's why our love is stronger and grows. You're not after us for power or fame or wealth. You want just us. The relationship is what matters."

All the trees, mountains and lake were making me dizzy and I started feeling sick. Then it came out, "But this is kinda scary. It's a lot of responsibility. I know we've pounded on lots of bad guys and helped millions of people but this is a universe you're giving me. Just this one planet is way bigger than Earth. How many galaxies and planets are in my universe? What if I make a mistake and something bad happens? Am I responsible for everything in my universe, like Qavvaq is in his?" Panic washed over me as the Watcher flashed into my mind again, making my body tremble and my heart pound like a drum in my chest.

Ruah pushed me down on to my back, his paws landing on my chest, his eyes just above mine, "Ryder, you've got to rid yourself of this fear. It doesn't belong to you. Do you want to get rid of it?"

"Yes of course. But it all..." Ruah covered my mouth with his paw.

"Give it to, Ehyeh. He wants it."

"Give it to, Ehyeh? How do I do that?"

"After all you've been through you have to ask how."

This fear of responsibility was strangling me. It was my enemy. It had to go. "Ehyeh?"

"Yes, Ryder?"

Reaching up I took his hand. Ruah was still standing on my chest. "I give you my fear. And..." I was on a roll. "...I give you all my negative thoughts about myself. I give you the anger, hate and bitterness I have towards all the people that hurt me. I give you all the scars I received in my life. I don't want them. They're yours now."

Ruah stepped off of me and I stood up, "Wow, what happened?" It felt like some kind of sludge had left my head, while something else flowed in to replace it. "Wait." I rolled up my sleeves and pant legs and lifted up my shirt. All the chain and whip scars that I always kept hidden were gone. Standing there being stunned was brief. Unable to contain myself any longer, I exploded off the planet, heading off into the hundreds of billions of galaxies in my universe, screaming, "Bring it!" A blink of light, with a touch of red in it from my cape, would be my introduction to these worlds that I've inherited. More would have to come later, as the guys have me dealing with stuff on Earth right now.

After I took off, Bre was so excited at what happened with me, she asked if she could do the same. She had kept many things bottled up to herself also, that she didn't want anymore, including fear of what others thought about her. She took Ehyeh's hand and gave it all to him like I had, receiving the same relief. Emotional containment was about the same for her as it was for me. None. She took off and quickly caught up to me, "Ryder, this is so awesome! I can't even imagine all that we'll be doing in eternity."

Side by side at the speed of creative light we were two former humans on the journey of life. True life. "I know Bre, it's beyond words." Bre grabbed my hand as we both screamed, "Bring it!"

This continued until we heard the guys in our heads, "When you two are ready, come on back and we'll do a planet tour."

Smiling, we shot back and came down slow next to the guys, just like in training.

I love immortality.

CHAPTER 33

xploring my planet was more awesome than sightseeing at Bre's.

Bre would disagree.

We met Phur, my new farm planet manager that looked like he was made up entirely of fir. Dark, green fir. His name fit him. I could put my hand right into him, like he was made of water or something. It was very weird. He was much larger than any of us. He also talked out loud like Tweak and we became immediate friends. At least he wasn't a bird I thought. Bre smacked my arm with the back of her hand, "I heard that!" I smiled, knowing she would.

As with Bre's planet there was so much to see. We all took a swim in one of the mountain streams that was full of different colored dolphin-type creatures that took us for rides on their backs. They jumped and swam all around us enjoying our company.

As usual, I was getting hungry. My stomach announced itself to everyone. I didn't know if I could make hotdogs here but I figured I'd give it a try.

"OK, everyone. I'm going to set up a place for us to eat now."

A clearing next to a gurgling stream over gold rocks was the perfect setting. The planet's purple clouds made an ideal table and the chairs I custom made for each of us here. The first chair was crafted from a piece of a star that was nearby for Farmer. I didn't know if it was possible until I tried, but I knew it was the right pick for Farmer. The star was very pleased to help me, their new owner. Then, I made one from the tip of the highest mountain on my planet for Ehyeh. It seemed to make sense. One from blue fire and water that flowed together for Ruah was next. He loved it. Phur's chair was growing right next to the table with some other flowers. It opened up to shape itself into a chair as I spoke to it. For Bre. What else? A chair made from one pink diamond. Definitely a tear came down her cheek. Mine, I made to look like the same chair I sat in when I met Farmer. The one that was behind my run-down, old barn. It was just as I remembered.

I was so happy that everyone was pleased with my choices. As I motioned for everyone to sit, pitchers made of red jade full of everyone's favorite drink formed in front of them. Drinks for Farmer, Ehyeh, Ruah and Phur were easy. They all preferred water, which I took from glacier ice on one of my mountain ranges. I surprised Bre with making a fruit and flower drink from items I snuck out from her planet, which got me one of her amazing kisses. I'll have to do stuff like that more often. For me, an upgrade I'd been considering... vanilla shake, mixed with root beer, mixed with liquicake. What can I say? Pure genius is in my blood now.

Plates full of local fruit, wild berries and nuts completed my meal presentation. Bre was ecstatic. "This looks wonderful, Ryder. You know how much I enjoy fresh food like this." The guys were all just sitting there smiling as she and I both took a huge mouthful with the gold forks I'd made. She munched a bit and then spit it all out, "Ewww... this tastes like hotdogs!"

Some of it squirted out my nose when I laughed.

After she stopped chasing me around the table, I assured her it was just a joke and that I put the right taste back in everyone's meals. The guys of course hadn't fallen for it. I can't imagine ever slipping a joke by them. Phur chewed in on it at the same time Bre and I did. He loved it. He'd never tasted anything like a hotdog before. Only Phur and I continued eating the hotdog flavored food, while the rest enjoyed the actual flavors. I was thinking of trying the actual taste, but why risk it.

We talked. We laughed. We ate. We drank. Soothing music came from the mountains, forest, flowers and grass.

I didn't want to really break the party mood, but I was antsy about what was coming next. We'd taken on some very bad monsters and set so many people free to go to their farms and Qavvaq had trained us well for sure, so I was ready for some more action. Or, as Qavvaq would say, "Crush stuff and have fun doing it!"

After we all laughed after Bre's story of how we kept banging into things and each other while learning how to operate our chariots, I slipped in my question.

"Speaking about that, when is our next Op and what is it? I want to smack something with all this explosive courage you gave me, Ehyeh?" Bre nodded and agreed with me.

The guys looked at each other smiling. I threw Bre a thought, "This is going to be good, Bre. I can tell by their faces."

"Next up is the Eater's place," Farmer said. "We're sending you in to give him a little attitude adjustment."

Bre and I jumped up and smacked palms, "Yessssss! No fear!"

CHAPTER 34

We said out goodbyes to Phur. What a jolly bear he is. I'm going to look forward to working with him for eternity. Well, I think he's a bear. Anyway, farmer's chariot lifted off and we were soon back in Earth's universe and dimensions. Where we'd just been, the Eater doesn't go, so, we had to come back to his dinky, little prison to deal with him. Earth. Funny to think this way, but I've seen too much to box myself in to the limitations of that tiny planet anymore.

While we were gone, my chateau and Bre's palace had grown quite a bit more. We were told on the way back that, after this next Op, we'd become instructors of leaders. The mountains of our farms were growing into a school for those we'd rescued.

We'd be directors to assist others, as Qavvaq had done with us, to reach their potential and grow their farms. I missed Qavvaq. I never did find out what happened to him. Back in his universe with Qlaw I guess. He never did show us his universe. I know he hates the stink of Earth so he probably won't come back here. He fiercely prefers his solitude so I don't want to pop in on him unannounced. Hermit-dude likes his space. I'll have to ask the guys if we can get together with him again because I'd like to go on a safari with him and Qlaw some time.

The old Ryder would be nervous, not only about going directly into the heart of the Eater's farm but also becoming an instructor over so many. Not anymore. I slapped my hands together after my cape was in place and thanked the angels for helping me load my chariot. I went over to Gideon and stroked his face, "This is a big Op, Gideon. You're going to love this one. You've always had more courage than me." He nuzzled my face. I wondered why he didn't talk like Tweak and Phur. Have to look into that when we get back.

I got on my chariot and took a last scan of all my gear. Weapons. Check. Traps. Check. Cookies. Check. "Let's go guys," as we pulled up from my chateau. The horses were all around my chariot, the angels tuning into and moving to my slightest thoughts. We were a unit. The people on Earth couldn't even imagine such a thing. If they ever took their eyes off themselves, they could see there's a door wide open in front of them.

I rose up high above the Earth to wait for Bre.

And wait.

It must be a women thing. Not that she was late or that I was early. I smiled thinking of Qavvaq and how he'd enjoy cracking some eggs with us on this mission. I'll crack a few in your honor, I pledged, as Bre's chariot got up next me, "Sorry my hunky, manly, rugged, sweet boyfriend. I had to fix my hair."

I was leaning on my elbows up against one of the angels while I'd been waiting for her. I looked at her through the tops of my eyes, "OK, I know you're just saying all that so I won't say anything about your being late." She smiled and fluttered her eyes. "And... your hair is always perfect, my elegant, charming, glamorous, lovable girlfriend."

She patted her hair, "Why, thank you. You clean up pretty good yourself. Do you think the Eater will notice that we spruced ourselves up for him?"

"I doubt it. I'm pretty sure he's going to be more concerned about how we snuck into his farmhouse."

Our briefing with the guys before we left showed us where to go and how to proceed with this Op. I can picture Qavvaq slapping me on the back, like he did during training, telling me to savor every moment. Relish it. I plan on it, as I gripped the hilt of my sword tighter.

Getting to our target was quite easy. We didn't have to leave Earth. We actually went into it. The Eater kept his farmhouse inside the Earth. Good place for it. I want to make that nit chew some dirt for trying to trick me into being one of his wizards. And, for all the years he had me trapped with the Traffiker and Nullifidian, not to mention all those millions of others we set free. Bre was listening to my thoughts. She added in about the Heretix, tricking her and conning all those circus ringleaders and performers to dance to his tune, stealing people's farms and leading billions into the abyss.

We were pumped.

We came to a stop outside this membrane inside the Earth. It was like a portal but this one was made up of lots of black, smelly creatures.

Bre was holding her nose, "Ewww… what's that?"

It was pretty awful. It smelled like rotted meat and bad eggs mixed together with sewage. "Must be the Eater's farmhouse." I didn't want to block off my sniffer, as Qavvaq calls it, as he told us, "that's vital when you're out trappin' and huntin'."

We waited outside this gate for quite a while. We were waiting for them to open it up for their generals from Earth that we knew would be coming in for a meeting. Like us, the Eater's wizards travelled to have meetings, to receive orders on how to defeat and control governments, economies, circuses and people.

The guys told us the Eater called this meeting, on how they were going to deal with Bre and me. We'd put a huge dent in the Eater's farm production and they wanted to stop us. The guys told us this was to be one of the largest meetings the Eater ever had, next to the one he had about Ehyeh long ago. It was nice to be appreciated.

When the generals showed up, the membrane of beings opened to let them into the Eater's farmhouse. We drifted in along with them in cloak-mode.

The wizards were a weird lot. Some were wearing black robes, others had fancy white robes on and lots of them were dressed in fine clothes and jewelry. Bre recognized a few of them as being world-renowned circus ringleaders. Among the herd there were famous musicians, sports stars, actors and leaders of nations. We were both surprised there were so many kinds of wizards. Must have fallen for the Eater's speech about fame and fortune. I lost track of how many were coming in. The guys were right. This was going to be a big meeting.

We didn't need to follow our noses to find the Eater. We just followed the hoard of mutts that had come to discuss us. All along the way there were bizarre creatures like the ones I'd seen in people at the circuses. They were all bowing as the generals went by. Well. I'm pretty sure they weren't bowing at us, although a few times I bowed and waved back saying, "Thank you. Oh, you shouldn't have. For me? You guys." Bre joined in waving and nodding like a princess going by some adoring fans. This was going to be fun.

We arrived at a huge cavern and took a spot high above them in our chariots. We were in the middle of the Eater's farmhouse.

We watched as the generals mingled, with drinks in their hands, murmuring about us, on how we'd disrupted their farms. "Bre. Sounds like we're famous."

"I know. They ain't seen nothing yet, though." Bre's eyes were glaring at them.

Many creatures flew in past us blowing trumpets announcing the arrival of some huge black creatures. All the musicians, sports stars, actors and politicians bowed when they flew in, so I'm guessing these ones rule them. They certainly looked menacing. They were wearing crowns and their eyes showed an intelligence we didn't see in the Heretix or the Nullifidian.

"These guys must be the dark princes, like Nergal. Ones that left the guys to join the Eater. More morons."

Bre nodded, watching them as they flew by us to set up on either side of a platform at the front.

My stomach started to growl. Both of our eyes looked at my stomach and then around the assembly that had gathered. No one heard it. *"Ryder? Now you're hungry? Men,"* as she shook her head.

"Hey, a guy's gotta eat. My cookies are gone. Do you see a snack bar around here for God Operators? Or maybe a street-meat cart?" Bre just shook her head. "I'll be right back."

I jumped out of my chariot down towards where some of the generals were chatting. It surprised Bre. *"Ryder, where are you going?"*

I landed right in front of this teenaged, space cadet with glasses, holding a broom. Hang on. This dimwit looks familiar as I tilted my head left and right trying to remember. "Bre, help me out. Who is this guy? I swear I've seen his face somewhere."

"I don't know, Ryder. Yeah, he looks familiar. So?"

I drew a blank. Oh, well. Can't be anyone that important. "Hey you little daft wizard, you're about to get educated in what real power looks like." He didn't see or hear me. I leaned over and sniffed him.

Yeah. Qavvaq's right. These muppets all have a special kind of stink.

Wandering around the floor looking for some snacks I could see Bre looking down over her chariot at me with her hands up and out to her sides until finally, my stomach had found its prey.

Beauty. These guys have chips and dip.

I headed over walking right through several of the generals. It was the shortest route.

My hand appeared into their dimension, grabbed some chips, dipped it in the dip bowl and then came back to my mouth in my dimension. I even grabbed some that one of the generals reached for. When his hand got there, the chips disappeared. The expression on his face was awesome. I started snickering as I ate, which dropped some to the ground. I could feel Bre's eyes drilling into the top of my head. I know. I should be serious, but it's so easy. And, I am hungry. I ignored Bre and kept munching. I finally just grabbed a bowl of chips and dip and started walking around, nodding along with the generals as they chatted about Bre and me. I agreed. We are trouble. Yes, you're right general, we are dangerous.

I stopped to push a thought into one of their heads, "And, no matter what we do we can't win."

The general put its hand to its mouth when those words came out. One of the other generals punched it in the face and they started rolling around on the ground fighting. Now, that's what I'm talkin' about.

Others joined in to pull them apart just as the trumpets started to blast again. The whole place immediately dropped to their knees and bowed their heads to the ground. This must be the main attraction. I dumped the bowl of leftover dip on the boy-wizard's head, which oddly made him look more familiar, but I still couldn't place him. The chip bowl I balanced on the head of some old woman in a pointy black hat. I slapped the chip dust off my hands and jumped back up to my chariot.

Bre had her arms crossed now. Her foot was probably tapping too but I couldn't see it.

"What? They don't know that chips and dip are on their heads. Come on, you gotta admit. They do look better. I mean, if the dip fits." I tried to look like I was sorry.

Bre relaxed, "Ryder, we're supposed to be focused. The Eater's coming and you're off feeding your face."

I burped a bit as I looked down at the platform. It really was good chips and dip. "He's not here yet. All is good my sweet princess. He likes the grand entrance for himself." Just as I said that, he strolled in grinning, taking in all of his subjects in their subservient positions. The trumpets blared away as he strolled over and sat on his throne. We glided in for a closer look.

Looking down at him, my thoughts took me back to when he first approached me on the road in front of my farm. Crafty snake with his tricks and fame and fortune act. I almost ended up like one of these slobs cowering around him, like some of these kids that I recognized as famous actors and singers. I shook my head.

"Snap out of it, Ryder," I could hear Bre as a scroll was brought to the Eater. A creature came up on the platform, unrolled it and started reading. It was a list of all that Bre and I had done to the Eater's farm. It detailed what had happened with the Heretix, the Traffiker, the Nullifidian, Trapr, Nergal, with the circuses and former ringleaders and prisoner escapes.

It was a long list.

I looked over at Bre, "Do you think he'd give us a copy of that list? I'd like to hang it in my chateau?"

"I doubt it my cute little beast-basher," she giggled. "Did you notice? No mention of the brand I put on the Eater. Guess they all don't know that tidbit. I'll have to fix that." Now Bre was acting frisky. Nice.

The Eater was getting angrier, the more he heard, until he stood up, bashed the reader to the side and screamed, "Enough! I've heard enough about these two whelps. I want to know how you could allow all this to happen," as he pointed around the crowd. "All of you couldn't handle two children? I want to know what you're going to do about them!" He glared around. All were silent. "Well?"

One of the dark princes next to the platform came forward, "Master. Some of us met before your arrival, in anticipation of your request. We have a plan."

The Eater smiled, "Now that's what I'm talking about. Leaders that can think. You can't leave everything to me, you worthless fools. All that I give you, I expect loyalty and sacrifice in return. What is your plan," as he sat back down on his throne grinning? He did look the part of a wacky emperor.

The dark prince laid out its plan. Have to admit, it did sound pretty good, for a bunch of losers. I looked over at Bre. She nodded with a pretend serious look and then laughed. These guys. They try so hard.

The plan was to lure us in with a crisis. A war. A world war. The dark princes and generals over nations would start a war on Earth between the nations they control, sending the worms, as they called them, to the slaughter. Peaceful nations, where people we helped escape were building their farms, would be invaded and plundered. Their goal was to destroy farms and have millions imprisoned and killed. As this was happening, the dark prince continued, the two predators will surely come.

I nodded over at Bre, "Predators? That's us. I like that term." Bre liked it too.

"When they arrive to stop the war, we'll spring our trap on them, master."

The Eater was intrigued. "How will you know exactly where and when they'll show up in order to trap them?"

"We'll announce in our dispatches, that you, our master, will personally arrive to oversee the great finishing battle. The battle that will bring all of Earth under your feet. They won't be able to resist stopping this battle and attacking you. When they come, our assassins will be waiting."

The Eater stood up, "Assassins?" He looked around smiling. "Where are my assassins?"

"We've chosen two excellent assassins, master. One for each of them." The dark prince waved its hand for them to come in. When they materialized in front of the Eater, both dropped to one-knee, with their heads bowed.

"Look Bre. Fresh meat!"

CHAPTER

35

Bre and I wanted a closer look. We dropped down to the platform from our chariots and circled around these two that were supposed to kill us. They didn't look that dangerous, compared to things we've come against, but never underestimate your enemy. Which is what they were doing with us.

The Eater announced that when the assassins completed their job and the Earth was under the Eater's full control after the war, they'd be promoted to princes and given one of the occupied territories. He pointed out two thrones on the platform that would be theirs. He told the rest of the attendees that they'd all receive more wealth and power. "Let's commence the world war immediately," as he twirled around and lounged back on his throne with a wide grin. Trumpets and cheers filled the cavern.

Just killing the assassins would only result in their replacements being chosen. The war would still go on. It was time to take this party up a notch.

The crowd was still cheering when daggers, that were at the assassin's sides, came out of their sheaths, rose up in the air and rammed down through the top of their heads. It actually did sound like two eggs crackin'. They fell over facing the crowd; their dead eyes staring at all those who'd just a second ago cheered for them.

The silence was deafening.

We quickly tossed special nets over the Eater before he could take off, trapping him against his throne. I wish Qavvaq was here. He'd enjoy that we used his hand-made nets on the Eater.

Next, we smacked the stunned crowd with a burst of light from our chests that smacked them down, anchoring them in place. That one we learned from Farmer.

So far, so good. We came out of cloak-mode, revealing ourselves.

"Whatd'ya think Bre? Are those 'happy to see you', screams or 'I think I just filled my pants', screams? I can't tell?"

"My sniffer tells me they're 'I think I just filled my pants' screams." The smells were quite ripe.

Bre and I pulled up the thrones that had recently become available. Dead assassin thrones. We sat down to stare at the continual screaming, moaning and crying from the crowd that were still pinned down from the blast we hit them with. They were paralyzed in place. Savoring the precious moments, as Qavvaq taught us.

"Settle down, you babies," I said. "I thought you were all brave generals and wizards." Talking at the Eater who was struggling to get out from the nets, "You picked a sorry lot to be your apprentices. Guess they didn't read the fine print when they signed those contracts with you."

He growled at us, "You aren't allowed here! This is my throne room! What right have you to be here," he screeched!

"Come on, big dog. We heard you were having a party. A party about us. We love parties. We showed up and your guards at the gate waved us through. By the way, your chips and dip are quite tasty, I must say."

The crowd had quieted and were now mesmerized by our conversation. The famous Ryder and Briella were here. They'd heard about us, but had never seen us. I guess we were sorta like rock stars to them.

"What do you want," he growled? "You can't stop me!"

Bre answered, "Well, we are a bit surprised that you weren't entirely honest with all of your daffy slaves here. You didn't tell them about your new burn tat."

The Eater stopped squirming. His expression changed from anger to fear.

"Let me fill everyone in. You know, the branding you got from me those times we bumped into each other out there. Why didn't you tell them about that? I mean, I think it's pretty flash. Don't be shy."

Bre stood up and walked over to the Eater. He tried to move away from her but the nets held him tight. She grabbed him by his robe and flipped him around so he was kneeling, facing his throne. His back-end facing the crowd now. The nets moved to her will. She drew out her sword. My eyes were darting back and forth to the crowd and to what Bre was doing. I didn't want to miss any of it.

Her sword slashed across the back of his robe, revealing three burn slashes. First time that even *I* got to see them. I shot Bre a thumb's up.

The crowd all gasped of course, many were shaking their heads and I'm sure more pant-filling was taking place. The dark prince who'd been reading the war plan was lying on the platform near my feet whimpering something. I kicked it in the hoof, "Speak up prince. What're you saying?"

"We weren't aware of your great power. Our master told us that all of your victories were just dumb luck."

"Dumb luck," I laughed. Examining the crowd, "Are all of you that dense? You all believe you're mightier than Farmer, Ehyeh and Ruah? Your great Eater was branded by a girl!" I looked over at Bre who was standing by the Eater, "No offense, Bre."

"None taken, Ryder," as she turned to the Eater and started on him with her sword. He was screaming in agony and embarrassment. His screams made the crowd scream again.

When she turned away, the brand was complete. I walked over to examine it. It was the symbol we'd picked for God Ops. She'd slashed him four times making up an eight-pointed light-flash that resembled us when we burst out from our physical bodies. "Bre, it's awesome!"

"Do you like it?" The Eater was growling now.

"I do believe you caught it perfectly." We both laughed.

We then turned to face the crowd. "You were all tricked by the Eater." I pointed back at him, "This is who he really is. A trapped prisoner running a worthless farm. All of your farms are worthless too. Every one of your farms and each of you, will one day be destroyed." Most reacted with another terrifying scream.

Bre continued, "Unless." The screams stopped as suddenly as they started. "Unless, you abandon the Eater and give up all that he's given you. Give up your fame. Give up your wealth. Give up your power. To start a new farm with the Farmer. A farm that will prosper for eternity."

Many were murmuring. They didn't want to risk giving up what they had.

"All those people who want this new life stand up," I said. The power from us that held them down released some of them. Those still pinned had decided to stay with the Eater.

The Eater sneered at us, "See. Even you two can't take their loyalty away from me." He yelled out at them, "I will reward all of you even more for your wise decision to stay with me."

Bre and I stood in front of all those who preferred their fleeting treasures, "Not today you won't, Eater. They picked the wrong road. Farmer gives them their wish. Let it be so." Light flashed from us opening a portal that sucked them up. In a moment they were gone. Those standing shivered in fear probably wondering what would come next for them. The non-human creatures were struggling in their traps, trying to get free. They would be dealt with another time, the guys told us. Pity. We would have loved to get it all over with now.

Our chariots came into view and down to the floor. "Saddle up," directing all the people who wanted a new life with our family, to load up. The chariots of angels expanded to fit as each person was helped by the angels to get aboard. Once they were all in, we turned to the creatures that were left.

"You beasts were allowed by Farmer, Ehyeh and Ruah to remain on your leashes. Your day of woe is not today." I could see this was a relief for them. I reacted in anger pointing around at them, "Don't be relieved, you scum! Your time will come. Your punishment will fit your crimes!"

Bre turned to the Eater, slapping him on the brand with the blade of her sword startling him. "And you, Eater. Farmer has decided you're to stay on your leash, too. You'll no doubt fill your farm up with willing replacements for the crops we've harvested today. Seems like a stupid strategy though, considering, you know what's coming for you one day." She slapped him again with her sword, "See you soon," as we both jumped off the platform to leave.

On the way to the chariot I stopped. "Wait."

"What's up'", Bre wondered?

"Hang on, I forgot a few things." I shot over to one of the tables and filled two large bags with chips and dip. "Come to me, my little beauties."

Bre shook her head. Then I hopped back up on the platform and relieved the dead assassins of their brain stickers. "Don't want to forget these." Next, I reached down and grabbed the scroll with the list of all of Bre's and my Ops on it. "Wouldn't want to leave this jewel behind. It'll look great, hanging in my trophy room." Turning to the Eater I smirked, "And, one more thing." He shivered, as I headed for him. As I lifted my hand up with a dagger in it, the Eater turned his head, bracing for a strike.

I tapped the Eater on top of his head with it, which flipped his extremely, ornate crown onto and down the dagger to my hand. "Ya know. When we first met, you told me you're a god." My elbow leaning against the arm of his throne as I pointed the dagger in his face. "You're right. You run a farm of crops that have a lot of bells and whistles, but it all comes down to mainly there's just one crop." I stared into his eyes, "Rabies. You run a rabies farm." His eyes tell me he's confused. "Let me explain it to ya, slick. You infect Earth with lies, confusion, sickness and death. With madness. You're not a big dog, you're a mad dog. A mad dog with rabies." He growled at me, baring his teeth. "Nice. Give a guy a little constructive criticism and that's what he gets."

Glancing over at his army of rabid gods still stuck to the floor it was time to hit it. "Welp, gotta fly, mad dog. Wicked party though. Love the tat. Stay frosty." I did a slow-mo jump over to the chariot, making sure my cape was puffed out and fluttering. Enjoy the ride as Qavvaq says.

Bre and those on the chariots heard every word. "Loved the speech. Did you get all the goodies you were after, Ryder?"

"Didn't want to leave the party favors behind, Bre. That would have been just plain rude." We giggled. My humor didn't drift over to our on-board guests, who were still stunned by the whole thing.

When our chariots rose up, we switched into another dimension, although we could still see where we were. Most of the Eater's crew slithered away when we released them, while others tried to pull the netting away from the squirming and screaming Eater. Our traps on him were tight. We delayed his release to add to his embarrassment. This job does have a lotta perks.

When we called back the nets, the Eater slapped the prince's away that were trying to help him and disappeared.

"Oh well," I said. "I guess the party's over."

"Shame. I enjoyed it," Bre said, as she sheathed her sword.

Our guests were still in shock mode. "You guys ready for a great ride?" They still looked shaken. "Don't be afraid, you've come out of a nightmare." I pointed at Gideon, "This is Gideon. Gideon, these are the new guys." Gideon gave them a pleasant welcome snort as we left the cavern. All the creatures we'd seen on the way in, were gone. It's deserted.

We made our way to my farm which was the rally point. When we arrived, Farmer, Ehyeh and Ruah went around introducing themselves to each one. All the newbies were amazed at the size of my mountain chateau. I told them that this was a mere fraction of what their farms could be. It was up to them.

Then Farmer spoke, "Farmers. You've chosen a new path for your lives. A path of life, not death. A path of fulfillment, not emptiness. A path of joy, not cheap thrills. A path of love, not lust. You used to be leaders and teachers of evil. Here, at Ryder's chateau and at Briella's palace, you'll learn how to become, God Operators!"

Farmer placed his arms around us and beamed, "These are your instructors."

"I know we haven't been formally introduced. Everyone, I'm Ryder. This is Briella. I think we've met."

Finally, some laughter.

CHAPTER
36

e've been quite busy since we got back from our last Op. It seems like such a long time ago.

My metamorphosis from being human to... well... you know... has been as dramatic as a caterpillar that once crawled on the ground, must go through during its chrysalis phase in order to become a colorful butterfly that flies the skies.

As a farmer of farmers, I'd look at it like I was once a seed, but after planting and cultivating, the real me was allowed to sprout forth, grow and continually produce fruit... forever.

Sitting on my throne on top of my mountain of authority, I looked out over my lake. Parts of my mountain range looked like ants crawling all over it. There're people everywhere. It's the same at Bre's place. People we helped escape from the Heretix, the Traffiker, the Nullifidian, the circuses and the Eater's farmhouse were here.

It's the first day of school. We're teaching farmers how to not just grow a farm, but how to raise farmers.

We're at recess or, I guess adults would call it a break.

There's a wide range of people here, including lots of kids like Bre and me, many even younger. Farming classes are quite a bit different than what the world considers to be school.

Their initial lessons were with Farmer, Ehyeh and Ruah, who spent time with each of them at their own farms, as they'd done with Bre and me, to show them how worthwhile they are. These early days can be challenging, when they're each shown how they were flimflammed by the Eater out of their true destinies and inheritances.

They find out that the trinkets they thought were valuable and even necessary features of their existence, were really just shallow, empty, meaningless illusions, that had expiry dates, which was death. Realities are not an easy pill to swallow, especially for the older students.

These lessons from the guys were all part of their family relationship building process. The relationship with them is the most important part. Without receiving their ongoing, personal, farming input, people's farms will drift back to where they were or into some other hideous thing.

The next phase of their schooling brings them to us.

"Ouch!" I feigned injury when Bre punched me in the arm.

"Whatcha doin'?"

I picked her up, ran into the lake and dropped us both in. "Morning Bre."

As we both came up laughing, we saw the guys standing on shore. They do move fast for old guys. We waded in and gave them each a hug.

"You two have made great progress with farm school," Farmer started. He looked at us and around all that had grown, like an admiring father.

"Yes," Ehyeh continued, "Students have been telling us how much they love their teachers."

"And, how much fun they have with you," as Ruah watched some lake water dripping from us.

"How do you know all that, we just started," I asked?

"We peaked ahead," they each said smiling.

"You guys are awesome. Thanks for the encouragement."

"We love teaching everyone," Bre squealed as she shook her hair around to get us all wet. The guys accepted her wet gift like a smiling cat laps up warm milk.

"I know I've said this lots of times. We both have. But you guys are the only reason we're here and doing this. I was an escaped prisoner from a human trafficking ring and Bre, a former prisoner of a circus. If you guys hadn't rescued us, we'd have been lost—forever."

Farmer gathered us in for a big hug, "You both rescued yourselves. You made the decisions to come with us. We just made the offer. The same offer we give everyone. And, you both built up your farms. Your harvests are producing even greater harvests."

"It's still so hard to imagine you trusted us kids with all of this responsibility," Bre said, as we all walked barefoot along the beach, the waves splashing in on our feet and onto our jeans. Many colorful peacocks were strutting along beside us.

Ehyeh smiled, "Don't look at age as a requirement for greatness. The world has developed a complex formula for people to follow, in order for a person to be considered great. The world doesn't consider anyone worth listening to, until they've reached the top of some artificial mountain."

"Artificial mountain," Bre asked?

"Yes. One of the Eater's traps. A fake reality of greatness. Such as some circus system saying a person shouldn't be listened to until they approve it. Or, if a person that can throw a ball really fast, like in baseball, then, they should be worthy of being idolized. Do you understand?"

"Like someone who the world says is pretty and can act, should be lavished with wealth and admiration. That they're somehow considered more intelligent than others," Bre added?

"Exactly. The Eater slicks the road with grease so people will worship him," Ruah continued.

Slicks the road with grease, I wondered in my head? Ruah heard me.

"Yes, Ryder. This means, he not only helps certain people obtain positions of influence over others, he fogs up or blinds the minds of people to accept these, his artificial mountains, as guidelines for their own lives. All of these people that you rescued from the Eater's farmhouse on your last Op are perfect examples. They were all leaders of the Eater's artificial mountains. The Eater elevated them to the tops of them."

Squirrels had joined our troop along the beach and a herd of buffalo stopped in. The animals loved getting close to us. It was like a zoo full of people and nature all mingled together. Birds, butterflies and bees flying around us. Fluorescent porpoises breeching and spinning over the water. Trees singing softly. People swarming all over the mountains getting ready for class. I took in a deep breath. I love my farm.

"You're right guys. We dealt a major blow to the Eater's mountain systems when we hit its big shots. It caused great confusion in the world when so many of their leaders and idols just disappeared."

"You and Bre certainly did upset the apple cart," Farmer agreed as he petted a herd of chipmunks that had rolled in.

"But now," the guys stopped and by the looks on their faces, something serious was coming. In an instant, we were transported back to my original farm. I'd almost forgot how rough it looked. We walked as Farmer, Ehyeh and Ruah told us, that they wanted to reveal some of their most cherished secrets to us.

All three of their voices spoke in unison in our heads, "Children. You are both so dear to us. You are precious gems. Each person on Earth is

a treasure of irreplaceable, immeasurable value."
We're slowly walking through the weeds around the
old barn. "We taste great pain when people reject
us. And, most do. Yet, this pain is worth the joy that
we obtain, when people accept our gift of family.
Our gift of an eternal farm with us." We meandered
our way through the dirt and rocks of one of the
fields beside the neglected farmhouse.

"When farms are dead like this one was, it
produces no harvest to supply others. It produces no
harvest for its farmer other than these," as Farmer
pulls up a dried-up weed and tosses it to the wind.
"Farmers of such farms are gods of death." The
words struck hard.

"When you two came to us, your farms were
dead. You finally planted one seed that called out
to us. We came. You allowed us to teach you how
to become real farmers. You then nurtured and
grew your farms. Many farmers expect us or other
farmers to look after their farms. This is a great
loss." I thought about what would've happened if
I had just got my farm and then sat on it doing
nothing. The stuff I would have missed out on.

"You both achieved a greater harvest by setting
other farmers free to do the same. Most who run a
true farm rarely offer their harvest to others and
rarer still, are farmers who provide seed to other
farmers. These are the great simplicities and the
wonderful mysteries of farming." Made sense to me.

"But then, you bravely stepped up your farm
production to accomplish what few ever do." Bre
grabbed my hand. She was trembling. My heart was
racing. Their words are piercing.

A portal opened up. We saw Abarron's enormous farm, with all the farms produced from that farm. It multiplied out so far, we couldn't see them all. "You not only replanted and cultivated your own harvest, but with Abarron, your first graduate student, you taught him to replant and obtain a greater harvest by teaching him to not only be a farmer but a farmer of farmers."

Another portal opened, where we were shown Gabrian's farm of farms. He was doing the same. We both trembled more. It was a mixture of joy and fulfillment. A sense of real purpose.

"These seeds of harvest grew to produce this school, as part of your farm. We couldn't be prouder of you both." They hugged us tight. We hugged them tighter.

I knew the guys were right. It's not rocket science to realize the effect one farmer can make by teaching others how to become farming teachers. One nagging thing crossed my mind though. Bre said it out loud.

"Did we defeat, the Eater?"

"No. He's still out there. His mountains and dark ones are still there. He suffered a great blow that took him thousands of years to develop, but people will always line up to accept his apprenticeship offers. Many will always prefer to satisfy their personal lusts, even when presented with the truth. You witnessed that yourselves when you were at the Eater's farmhouse."

Bre sighed. I looked at the ground feeling the same thing. How can people be so stupid? How long will this go on? I enjoyed helping others, but I just wanted to go to my universe and enjoy its fruits and see what else the guys had for us in eternity. Throwing Bre in the lake once and awhile too was a bonus. I'm tired of the Eater.

Bre heard all of it and smiled. We were on the same page.

Farmer put his hands over our shoulders and drew us in closer as we walked along again. "Our children. Our loves. We love you so deeply. You are both deep in our heart and we in yours. Nothing can separate us. Don't be thinking about the Eater and all those who choose to follow him. Be joyful about these things... that you're here... about all those you've rescued... and about those you're teaching. We must give the Eater credit for all that he's done for you."

We both snapped our heads to look at Farmer with that 'say what' look.

He smiled, "Don't you see? The height of his foolishness is that he allowed you both the opportunity to grow your own farms. The more he came against you, the greater his defeat, the more your farms grew, the larger the harvests. Harvests against himself. Because of him, both of you have a larger portion." We walked through a portal back to the present.

Farmer pointed at all the people that were here at the farm, "The Eater's ways are offering all of these farmers and their farms to grow, harvesting fruit that destroys him. The Eater is his own worst enemy. What's better is, he knows it. But he won't stop himself. He feeds on himself, even though he knows his roads all lead to his destruction. A destruction that will launch, eventually, to your greatest Ops yet when you both turn to your universe farms and more important matters." He winked at us.

Bre and I both looked wide-eyed at other. At the same time a quiet "Wow," came out of our mouths. The Eater is his own worst enemy. All of that hadn't occurred to us. Love helping him shoot himself in the foot.

"We have many more secrets we want to share with you next time," as we arrived back at the beach.

What mysteries lay ahead? We couldn't imagine what could possibly match or even be better than all of what we have now. Greater Ops? Now Farmer, Ehyeh and Ruah were each smiling at us. This is going to be good.

We stopped along the crystal beach to look out over the farm. Millions and millions of people were all around us on these mountains of reality, about ready to get back to class. We had to prepare them for their own God Ops. Break was almost over. The same was going on at Bre's place. There was activity going on all over our farms.

Bre and I jumped up and slapped hands, "Let's crush this!"

"And.." I said?

"Have fun doing it," we both yelled out!

Many classes had to be taught and doing them one at a time obviously wasn't efficient so we split off into our multiselves. Each version of each of us was busy with a different class.

Let's see, I was about equally split up between my place and Bre's place. Ruah was also with us in every class.

Bre and I held classes together. One was a riding class with students that just received their horse partner. Another group was learning to cloak. We took a field trip to a sun, various classes were being held on weapons, how to open a portal, how to build a sturdy trap and one of my favorites, the 'Using your Sniffer for Trappin' and Huntin' class.

There's a lotta work in this kind of farming.

A chariot racing competition was going on over the lake, being judged by our two Wasters. The winner gets to lead Adlai and Elkin and a formation of chariots on a little, what I call, a getting to know you God Op, with one of the Eater's pets known as the Legerdemain and a bunch of broom-jockeys at the academy of wizards and tricksters that it runs.

While this was all going on, I was also in my universe takin' care of business. Phur and I were having a good time planting gardens on various planets. Good news to report on that front... happily, we encountered no difficulties at all, in making foot-long hotdogs with condiments, anytime we want.

We experimented on the condiments. Turns out, Phur prefers mayonnaise, gravy and pickles on his dogs. Who knew that was a thing? Love the Phur.

Bre was at her universe too, working with Tweak. Probably creating new varieties of watermelon to make me taste.

"I heard that!"

Oops! I forgot. We can teleunicom our thoughts across the universes and dimensions now.

"Just teasing, Bre. Love you!"

"Love you too, Ryder!"

Yes, I said the love word out loud. Feels pretty good.

Another one of me is out trappin' and huntin'. When we got back from the Eater Op, I gave all the trophies to the guys. They were so pleased with what we'd done and our honoring them, that they handed most of them back to me, to do with them as I pleased. I sent the daggers, chips and dip by angelic messenger to Qavvaq and Qlaw with a note. A safari invitation was sent back to me almost immediately.

Our reunion was epic. Qavvaq squeezed me so tight I think it punctured a lung. He was wearing the daggers I sent him, in place of the ones he used to carry. He wanted me to come on his next safari, to share in the "application of the daggers", as he put it. I love the Qavvaq.

Qlaw ran to me when I arrived, kicking in my reflexes that made me disappear, thinking it was an attack. I reappeared after I got a familiar whiff of his breath. Turns out, he was just overly anxious to meet the guy that'd sent him the chips and dip. We became even better friends when I told him I knew how to make all that he wanted.

One of the questions I asked Qavvaq was, why Farmer didn't bash all these rogue angels and beasts running berserk in other universes or leash them down to some planet, like he did with the Eater and his army. Qavvaq explained that it was just one of those mysteries that Farmer decided to give them some more rope for some reason.

I wasn't complaining since it just gave Qavvaq and me more meat to carve up.

Our chariots, once full of traps and weapons, flew off together on our safari taking us to a universe that's being pillaged by several Irin, a breed of Watcher angels, that had joined forces into an elite unit. Qavvaq said they'd set up strongholds and were waiting for us. Nice!

Before we left, Qavvaq taught me the fine art of preparing and mounting trophies on my trophy pole that he helped me attach to my chariot. I was a dark angel, head-hunter now.

Qlaw ate chips and dip on the way. I love the Qlaw.

Qavvaq brought some fishin' poles along, saying, "After we're done trappin' and huntin', we're goin' fishin'." He found a secluded fishin' hole, that him and Qlaw discovered when they were huntin' that Watcher from universe number 37. Finally, I'm gonna hear how that hunt went.

While I was huntin' with the boys, Bre joined Joanna at her new universe that the guys gave her. I'm sure they're having as much fun as we are. I love the Joanna.

Bre and I are also each at our special places. Me at my lake cabin and Bre at her island hut. Each of us needs down-time ya know. I leaned back in my chair to munch on some fresh, warm, cookies and some liquicake, while watching that moose wading through the water in front of me. We nodded 'yo' to each other as I tipped my glass to some red-winged blackbirds singing to me from the trees. Does it get any better than this?

I think not.

Right now, I'm also watching Ruah walking up to different people, like he did with Briella, to convince them to follow him. Wonder which ones will listen?

At another place, I see Ehyeh standing on the water waving for people to come on over, saying, "You can do it. I'm right here to help you. Follow me."

And there's Farmer, leaning against the gate of every farm, waiting to have a chat.

Just look for them. Concentrate. I promise they'll show you something cool.

I pushed the button and closed the journal.

The beach full of faces look back at me with a heavenly glow. Guessing they all enjoyed my journal. The silence is soon cut into by some giggling here and there that rolls into laughter as a Monarch butterfly glides in and around them stopping briefly for a visit.

As he gradually worked his way up to me, the crown on his head looked kinda familiar. Soooo, that's what the guys did with the Eater's crown.

He landed on my shoulder and kissed my cheek.

"I love you too, Ebenezer."

"Now let's continue... Reality... It's not what they told you. Any entity or ideology that rejects or compromises with truth is a fantasy. Truth is designed by Farmer, Ehyeh and Ruah. Fantasy is designed by the Eater. Simply put... fantasy is a fabricated prison cell where people exist until they escape though the gate of reality, of which there are two. If they escape in life, they do so only by entering the Book of Life into the reality of godship and blissful eternity. If they escape fantasy in death, their name in the Book of the Dead ushers them into the reality of perdition.

We are light. We are eternal. I'm a god. You are gods. My name is, Ryder. I'm a farmer. Welcome to the god farm" ...